A Lady in Sin

THE FAIRBOURNE SISTERS

BOOK 3

A Steamy Regency Romance Novel

by

Valentina Lovelace

RUBEDIA
PUBLISHING

VALENTINA LOVELACE

Disclaimer & Copyright

This is a work of fiction. Names, characters, places, and incidents are either products of the author's imagination or are used fictitiously. Any resemblance to actual events, locales, or persons, living or dead, is entirely coincidental.

Copyright © 2025 by Valentina Lovelace

All Rights Reserved.

No part of this book may be reproduced, duplicated, transmitted, or recorded in any form—electronic or printed—without the prior written permission of the publisher. Unauthorized storage or distribution of this document is strictly prohibited.

Table of Contents

A Lady's Lessons in Sin 1
   Disclaimer & Copyright 2
   Table of Contents 3
   Letter from Valentina Lovelace 5
Chapter One 6
Chapter Two 15
Chapter Three 23
Chapter Four 33
Chapter Five 42
Chapter Six 51
Chapter Seven 63
Chapter Eight 72
Chapter Nine 79
Chapter Ten 87
Chapter Eleven 96
Chapter Twelve 105
Chapter Thirteen 112
Chapter Fourteen 119
Chapter Fifteen 129
Chapter Sixteen 140
Chapter Seventeen 149
Chapter Eighteen 157
Chapter Nineteen 163
Chapter Twenty 171

Chapter Twenty-One 179
Chapter Twenty-Two 191
Chapter Twenty-Three 200
Chapter Twenty-Four 210
Chapter Twenty-Five 218
Chapter Twenty-Six 226
Chapter Twenty-Seven 234
Chapter Twenty-Eight 245
Epilogue 253
   Also by Valentina Lovelace 262

Letter from Valentina Lovelace

Hello, darling!

I'm Valentina Lovelace, a hopeless romantic with a wicked imagination and a love for all things Regency. If there's a secret rendezvous, a scandal brewing, or a duke about to be undone, I'm there, probably taking notes.

I write steamy love stories where danger lurks behind every fan flutter and heroines never wait politely for permission. My stories are for readers who like their romance with sharp tongues, slow teases, and absolutely no chill.

Off the page, I'm raising two tiny, adorable, future scandal-makers, believing I'm in control of the household (I'm not), pretending tea is a personality trait, and occasionally convincing my husband to "act out" plot research.

If you're into bold women, bad decisions, and ballroom gossip turned foreplay — welcome. I've been expecting you!

Till our next whispered word,

Valentina Lovelace

Chapter One

"Oh, Catharine, you simply *must* tell me about the Duchess of Marlborough's gown," Margaret said, adjusting her pale blue silk skirts as she stood between her sisters at the edge of the glittering ballroom.

The air in the ballroom was thick with the mingled scents of expensive perfumes, beeswax candles, and the faint smokiness from the enormous fireplace that kept the chill at bay.

Margaret could hear the gentle rustle of silk and satin, the soft murmur of general conversation punctuated by bursts of laughter, and beneath it all, the melodic strains of the orchestra, which had been tucked discreetly into the furthest corner.

She leaned closer to her sister, her voice breathless with admiration. "The pearls alone must have cost a fortune."

Catharine, resplendent in deep emerald that complemented her newfound softness since marriage, followed Margaret's gaze across the crowded space. "It's French, I believe. Though I suspect it costs more than what I used to receive from Father for an entire year's wardrobe."

"Trust Catharine to reduce poetry to pounds and shillings," Eliza teased, nudging Margaret's arm affectionately.

Catharine gave her sister a look that was half exasperation, half fondness. "Someone in this family must maintain a sense of practicality."

"Some things never change," Eliza added with a laugh.

Margaret smiled, though something hollow echoed in her chest. Their banter should have comforted her, but tonight, it only emphasised how much had shifted between them.

The Winter Ball had always been their tradition—the three Fairbourne sisters standing together, observing the ton's finest display of wealth and matrimonial scheming. But this year felt different. Catharine wore the quiet confidence of a woman well-settled, whilst Eliza possessed the assured bearing of a duchess who'd found unexpected love.

And Margaret? Margaret remained exactly where she'd always been—the youngest, the one still waiting for her life to truly begin.

"I suppose next year I shall still be attending these events, watching everyone else announce their engagements whilst I remain exactly where I am now," Margaret quipped with forced lightness. "At this rate, I might turn into the bluestocking aunt who spoils everyone else's children."

"You're rather melancholy for someone attending the season's most anticipated event," Catharine observed, her tone gentler than it would have been a year ago.

"I'm perfectly content," Margaret replied, though her fingers worried the pearl bracelet at her wrist. "Simply... taking it all in."

"Which is precisely what concerns me," Catharine said. "You have that look about you tonight—as though you're planning something... inadvisable."

Before Margaret could respond, a ripple of excitement moved through the crowd near the ballroom's entrance. Conversations faltered, fans fluttered more rapidly, and several ladies turned to whisper urgently to their companions.

"Oh my..." breathed Lady Pemberton, appearing beside them with eyes brightened by curiosity. "Ladies, do you know who's just arrived?"

Margaret rose on her toes, craning to see over the sea of elaborate coiffures and gentlemen's shoulders. "Someone important, judging by the reaction."

The whispers grew louder, more urgent. "Impossible," another voice protested. "He never attends these gatherings."

The crowd parted like theatre curtains, revealing a figure that made Margaret's breath catch. Tall and impeccably dressed, the gentleman moved through the ballroom with the sort of effortless confidence that came from knowing every eye was upon him.

There was something almost leonine about him—the way he carried himself, the slight smile that suggested he was perfectly aware of the effect his presence had on the assembled company.

"Lord Nathaniel Strickland," Eliza said quietly, recognition clear in her voice. "The Duke of Ashcombe."

Margaret's interest sharpened immediately. "I've heard the name whispered, but I've never seen him before."

"Small wonder," Lady Ashford interjected with barely concealed glee. "He's been absent from society for months. Some say he was in Paris, others claim he was managing estates in Scotland."

"He rarely appears at social functions," Catharine explained, though her tone carried a note of disapproval. "Prefers more… private entertainments, from what I understand."

"The sort of private entertainments that should not be examined too closely," Eliza added dryly, though even her eyes lingered on the duke.

Margaret studied him as he made his way through the crowd, accepting bows and curtseys with practiced ease. There was something magnetic about him—the way he moved, the slight smile playing at his lips, the manner in which he seemed to command attention without effort.

"He's quite handsome," she said, unable to keep the admiration from her voice.

"Margaret." Catharine's tone sharpened. "You mustn't be taken in by appearances. His reputation—"

"Is hardly worse than Rhys's was," Margaret interrupted, glancing towards her brother-in-law, where he stood in conversation with several gentlemen near the card room. "And look how wonderfully that turned out for Eliza."

"That's entirely different," Eliza protested, though colour rose in her cheeks. "Rhys's reputation was largely gossip and misunderstanding. The Duke of Ashcombe's interests... well, they're rather more deliberately cultivated."

Margaret felt a familiar spark of curiosity. "What sort of interests?"

"The sort that makes any respectable mother lock up her daughters," Lady Pemberton said with delicious scandal in her voice. "Gaming hells, opera singers, duels at dawn. Why, just last year, there was that business with the French comte's wife..."

"Lady Pemberton," Catharine said sharply, "surely such gossip is inappropriate."

"Oh, my dear, where is the harm in a little truth?" She waved her fan dismissively. "The duke makes no secret of his pursuits. Indeed, one might almost say he takes pride in them."

Margaret felt her curiosity sharpen further. "But what sort of—"

"The sort that makes him unsuitable for innocent young ladies," came a new voice, dry with amusement.

Margaret turned to find Julian Ashcroft approaching their group, elegant as always in his perfectly tailored evening wear.

There was something about Julian that had always put Margaret slightly on edge—not unpleasantly, but rather like standing near a fire that gave off heat without showing flame.

"Julian," she said, taking in his familiar figure—tall and lean, with dark hair that always seemed perfectly tousled, and those penetratingly grey eyes that immediately sought out the duke's position. "How convenient that you should appear just when the conversation grows interesting."

"I live to serve," he replied with a dramatic bow that made Catharine roll her eyes. "Though my timing may be less coincidental than convenient. I noticed you watching our newest arrival with rather more interest than might be... wise."

"Wise?" Margaret's chin lifted slightly. "I wasn't aware that looking required wisdom."

"Looking, no. But that particular expression..." Julian's gaze returned to hers, and something flickered there—concern, perhaps, or warning. "That's the look of a woman contemplating conquest."

Heat bloomed on Margaret's cheeks. "Don't be ridiculous!"

Julian moved closer, his voice dropping to a more intimate level. "Tell me, Margaret, what do you see when you look at Strickland?"

Margaret was suddenly aware of Julian's proximity. She forced herself to focus on the duke across the room. "I see a gentleman of obvious breeding and consequence. A duke, no less."

"And what else?"

"Someone who seems quite comfortable in society, despite his alleged preference for privacy. Someone who appears to know precisely the effect he has on people."

Julian's expression grew more serious. "And you believe you might be the one to catch him?"

"I believe I might be the one to try," Margaret said, surprising herself with her boldness. "After all, what's the worst that could happen?"

"From where I stand, dear Margaret, you've lived a remarkably sheltered life. The duke... he's not the sort of man who plays by the rules, you know."

"Neither was Rhys," Margaret pointed out again. "And yet he proved capable of great love and devotion. You speak as though you know him personally," she observed, noting the tension that had crept into Julian's shoulders. "Have you had business dealings with the duke?"

"I know enough." Julian's tone carried a finality that only increased Margaret's curiosity. "Enough to know that he's not a man to be trifled with by innocent young ladies seeking romantic adventures."

"That's the second time tonight you've called me innocent!" Margaret said, the word stinging more than she cared to admit. "I'm five-and-twenty, Julian. Hardly some fresh-faced girl just out of the schoolroom."

"Age and innocence aren't mutually exclusive," he said softly. "And there's nothing wrong with innocence, Margaret. It's simply... incompatible with men like Strickland."

"Perhaps that's exactly what makes him so intriguing," Margaret replied, her chin lifting with a hint of defiance. "I find myself growing tired of being surrounded by stuffy, predictable gentlemen who treat me like I'm made from spun glass."

She glanced once more at the duke, noting the way he leaned slightly towards the lady he was speaking with—close enough to be intimate, not quite close enough to be improper.

"Maybe it's time I discovered what lies beyond the boundaries of propriety."

Julian's jaw tightened almost imperceptibly. "And you believe the Duke of Ashcombe is the man to show you?"

"I believe he's the most intriguing man in this ballroom," Margaret replied, her voice growing stronger with conviction.

"Margaret, listen to me." Julian's hand moved as though he might dare to touch her arm, then stopped. "Some risks aren't worth the potential consequences. And some men are exactly what they appear to be, not what we might hope them to become."

"No, Julian." She turned to face him fully, lowering her voice as she noticed Eliza glancing in their direction with obvious curiosity. "I appreciate your concern, truly I do. But I'm not a child anymore, and I'm not content to remain safely tucked away whilst life passes me by."

Julian studied her face for a long moment, something unreadable flickering in his expression. "And what if I told you that your instincts about people have been sheltered by kindness? That the world contains cruelties you've been fortunate enough to never encounter?"

"Then I'd say you underestimate me entirely!" Margaret felt her pulse quicken—not with fear but with excitement. "Perhaps it's time I trusted my own judgement rather than everyone else's warnings."

The orchestra struck up a new melody, and couples began forming for the next dance. Margaret watched as the duke bowed elegantly to a lady in rose silk, leading her onto the floor with practiced grace.

"He dances well."

"He does many things well," Julian replied grimly. "That's rather the problem."

Something in his tone made her heart skip a beat, though she couldn't quite understand why.

"What if I don't want to be sunshine and laughter forever?" she asked quietly. "What if I want to be something more... complex, more interesting?"

"You're already interesting," Julian said, and for a moment, his voice carried a note of something deeper than mere concern. "You're already enough, Margaret. You don't need to transform yourself to win some man's attention."

"Even if that man is a duke?"

"Especially if that man is a duke like Strickland."

Margaret felt her resolve strengthening. Julian's warnings, her sisters' concerns, the very danger they seemed to perceive—it all only made the Duke of Ashcombe more intriguing.

"Thank you for your concern," she said, her voice carrying new determination. "But I believe I'm quite capable of managing my own affairs."

Julian's expression darkened. "Margaret—"

"The next dance is beginning shortly," she interrupted, watching as new couples took their positions. "I believe I shall position myself where His Grace might notice me when the dance concludes."

She moved away from their group before Julian could respond, her heart racing with excitement and nerves. Behind her, she heard Eliza's concerned whisper and Catharine's sharper response, but she didn't turn back.

Margaret positioned herself where she might catch his eye when the music ended, her pulse thrumming wildly with anticipation.

She was tired of being the protected one. The innocent one. The one who watched on while others lived. Tonight, she would begin to change that.

The dance ended, and the Duke of Ashcombe's eyes met hers across the crowded floor. His smile was slow, knowing, and entirely too confident.

Margaret smiled back, her heart hammering against her ribs.

The Duke of Ashcombe was about to discover that the youngest Fairbourne sister was far more interesting than anyone could ever have imagined.

Chapter Two

"Good God, Julian, you're staring at her like she's a puzzle you can't solve," Rhys said, appearing at his cousin's elbow with the quiet stealth that had once made him so effective on the battlefield.

Julian lifted his brandy glass to his lips—he'd abandoned the champagne in favour of something stronger—not bothering to deny the observation. From his position at the edge of the ballroom, he had an excellent view of Margaret Fairbourne making an absolute spectacle of herself in her attempts to catch Nathaniel Strickland's attention.

"She's... determined," Julian said finally, watching as Margaret positioned herself directly in Strickland's line of sight, her golden curls catching the ballroom's light like spun sunshine, her smile so bright it could have lit the chandeliers.

"She's besotted," Rhys corrected grimly. "With a man who would devour her whole and leave nothing but broken pieces."

Julian's grip tightened on his glass. Margaret was currently attempting what he assumed was meant to be a sultry laugh—the sort he'd observed countless sophisticated women deploy to great effect. From Margaret, it sounded forced, almost desperate. Strickland glanced her way briefly, offered a polite nod, then immediately turned back to Lady Pemberton, whose own laugh was a symphony of feminine wiles.

"She's not very good at it," Julian murmured, unable to keep the note of reluctant affection from his voice.

"At what? Seduction?" Rhys's tone sharpened. "Thank God for that. The very last thing needed is Margaret developing such... skills."

Julian watched as Margaret attempted to fan herself with what she probably thought was elegant grace, nearly dropping the delicate ivory accessory in the process. She caught it just in time, her cheeks flushing pink with embarrassment.

"Rather like watching a kitten attempt to stalk a lion, if you will."

"Which is precisely why you need to put whatever foolish notion you seem to be entertaining out of your mind," Rhys said, his voice dropping to a level that demanded attention. "Margaret is not some sophisticated widow looking for amusement, Julian. She's too romantic, too bloody innocent for a man like you."

Julian turned to face him fully, noting the protective tension in Rhys's stance. "A man like me?"

"You know precisely what I mean." Rhys's grey eyes had turned to steel. "You're brilliant, charming, and utterly without scruples when it comes to getting what you want."

"I confess, I fail to see the particular problem with such refreshing honesty."

"The problem is that Margaret wouldn't believe you if you etched your intentions across your forehead," Rhys said bluntly. "She'd convince herself that she could change you, that her love would be enough to transform you into the romantic hero she's been dreaming about since she was old enough to read novels."

Julian felt something twist in his chest—an uncomfortable recognition of truth. "I'm not entirely without feeling, Rhys."

"No, but you're entirely without a title, without prospects beyond your legal work, and without the sort of romantic nature that would make Margaret truly happy." Rhys's voice gentled slightly. "She needs someone who can love her the way she deserves to be loved—completely, devotedly, without reservation. Can you honestly tell me you're capable of that?"

Julian's gaze drifted back to Margaret, who was now attempting to position herself near the refreshment table where Strickland was accepting a glass of champagne. She moved with the sort of obvious purpose that made Julian wince.

"She's too breakable," he said quietly, the words tasting like ash. "Too good for the likes of me."

"Exactly." Rhys clapped him on the shoulder. "So whatever fascination you're developing, halt it in its tracks now. For both your sakes."

Julian nodded, though his eyes remained fixed on Margaret. As they watched, she approached Strickland with a bright smile, clearly intending to engage him in conversation. The duke turned towards her with the sort of polite attention he might give to any persistent debutante, but Julian could see the calculation in his eyes, the way he assessed her youth, her obvious infatuation, her vulnerability.

"He's going to destroy her," Julian said, his voice harsh with sudden anger.

"Not if she comes to her senses first," Rhys replied.

But Julian could see that Margaret had no intention whatsoever of coming to her senses. She was leaning slightly towards Strickland, her expression animated, her gestures a touch too enthusiastic. Whatever she was saying, it was clearly intended to impress, but Strickland's attention kept drifting to other guests, other conversations.

"She's making a spectacle of herself," Julian muttered.

"She's being young and foolish," Rhys corrected. "It's hardly a crime."

Across the ballroom, Margaret's smile faltered slightly as Strickland excused himself to greet another guest. Julian watched her shoulders drop, saw the way her bright expression dimmed for just a moment before she rallied, turning to engage Lady Cavendish in conversation with determined cheerfulness.

"I should go," Rhys said, glancing towards Eliza, who was holding court with several other young matrons. "My duchess is giving me looks that suggest I'm neglecting my social duties."

"Of course," Julian said absently, his attention still fixed firmly on Margaret.

As Rhys walked away, Julian remained at his post, his brandy growing warm in his hand. He told himself he was merely observing an entertaining social spectacle, but the truth of the matter was far more complicated.

His jaw tightened as he watched Strickland accept the obvious adoration of yet another young lady with the sort of casual arrogance that made Julian's teeth ache. Men like this had never had to work for anything.

The injustice of it all settled in his chest like a boulder.

Later, Julian found Margaret sitting alone in a small alcove near the ballroom's edge, her bright smile finally abandoned in favour of obvious frustration. Her golden curls had lost some of their careful arrangement, and her cheeks were flushed with what looked like a combination of exertion and embarrassment.

"Rough evening?" he asked, settling into the chair beside her without invitation.

Margaret's head snapped up, her blue eyes flashing with irritation. "I'm perfectly fine, thank you."

"Of course you are," Julian said smoothly. "That's why you're hiding in an alcove instead of dancing with your duke."

"I'm not hiding," Margaret said, though her voice lacked conviction. "I'm simply... taking a moment to rest."

Julian studied her face—the stubborn set of her jaw, the way her hands were clenched in her lap, the slight tremor in her voice that suggested she was closer to tears than she wanted to admit.

"You're utterly clumsy at seduction," he said conversationally.

Margaret's eyes widened, colour flooding her cheeks. "I beg your pardon?"

"You heard me." Julian leaned back in his chair, affecting a casual pose that belied the strange tension thrumming through him. "You're about as subtle as a peacock in a chicken coop. Every person in this ballroom can see exactly what you're trying to do."

"I don't know what you mean," Margaret said stiffly.

"Don't you?" Julian's voice carried a note of gentle mockery. "The strategic positioning near the refreshment table? The animated conversations with Lady Cavendish designed to catch his attention? The way you've been trailing after him around the ballroom like a lovesick puppy?"

Margaret shot to her feet, her skirts rustling with indignation. "How dare you—"

"I dare because someone needs to tell you the truth," Julian interrupted, rising to face her.

"And I suppose you consider yourself an expert on such matters?"

"I consider myself a man who understands what draws another man's attention," Julian said, his voice dropping to a more intimate level. "I know what makes a woman unforgettable. What makes her mysterious enough to pursue rather than simply available enough to ignore."

Margaret's angry flush deepened. "You're being deliberately cruel."

"I'm being honest," Julian corrected. "The question is whether you want to continue flailing about, making a fool of yourself, or whether you'd prefer to learn how to succeed."

For a long moment, Margaret stared at him, her expression cycling through hurt, anger, and something that might have been curiosity.

"What exactly are you proposing?" she asked finally, her voice carefully controlled.

Julian felt his pulse quicken. He hadn't planned this conversation, hadn't intended to make such an offer. But watching Margaret's clumsy attempts at flirting, seeing her obvious frustration growing into desperation—all of it had stirred something in him that he couldn't quite name.

"I'm suggesting that if you truly want to win the Duke of Ashcombe's heart, you need to learn the art of *subtle manipulation*," he said quietly. "The difference between being pursued and being the pursuer."

Margaret's eyes narrowed. "And you... Could teach me these things?"

"I would."

"Why?"

It was a fair question, and one Julian wasn't entirely sure he could answer honestly.

"Because," he said finally, "I dislike seeing someone I care about fail when success is entirely within reach."

Margaret studied his face for a long moment, clearly trying to decipher his motives. "You're insane," she said finally.

Julian smiled, recognising the curiosity beneath her scepticism. "Perhaps. But I'm also very good at what I do."

"And what exactly do you do, Julian?"

"I make people want things they didn't know they needed," he said simply.

Margaret's breath caught slightly, and Julian saw the exact moment her resolve wavered. She wanted to say yes—he could see it in her eyes, in the way her lips parted slightly, in the sudden tension in her shoulders.

"I..." she began, then stopped, clearly struggling with herself.

Julian moved closer. "The choice is yours, dear Margaret. You can continue as you are, hoping that persistence will eventually pay off, or you can let me show you how to make the duke desperate to win your attention."

"This is madness," Margaret whispered.

"The best things usually are," Julian replied, his voice soft with promise.

For a moment, he thought she might accept. He could see the war playing out across her expressive face—propriety battling with curiosity, caution wrestling with desire. But then she stepped back, her chin lifting with that familiar stubborn pride.

"You've lost your senses entirely," she said, though her voice lacked conviction.

Julian smiled, recognising defeat as merely a tactical retreat. "Perhaps I have."

He turned to leave, then paused, glancing back at her over his shoulder. "But if you change your mind, you know where to find me."

He walked away without another word, leaving her standing in the alcove with her thoughts and her obvious temptation.

Julian smiled to himself as he made his way back towards the refreshment table. He'd planted the seed. Now he needs only to wait to see if it will take root in Margaret's curious, romantic heart.

The game, he thought with a surge of anticipation, *is about to become infinitely more interesting.*

Chapter Three

"Oh, my dear girl, you simply must come meet the Duke of Ashcombe," Lady Thornton gushed, her ostrich feathers trembling with excitement as she approached the tea table where Margaret sat with studied casualness. "He's just arrived, and he's asking after you specifically!"

The afternoon tea was being held in Lady Thornton's opulent drawing room, where the scent of tea and delicate cucumber sandwiches mingled with the gentle clink of fine bone china around small circular tables draped in pristine white linens.

Margaret's heart leapt with hope until she realised Lady Thornton was addressing Miss Cordelia Hartwell, the stunning brunette who'd been trailing the duke like a devoted spaniel for the past week.

"Another conquest for Miss Hartwell," murmured Lady Cooper, settling beside Margaret with obvious satisfaction at having secured the choicest gossip of the afternoon. "Though I suppose it's hardly surprising. She does have such a way with gentlemen."

Margaret forced her expression to remain pleasantly neutral as she watched Cordelia approach the duke with the sort of confident smile that Margaret had herself been practicing in her mirror all week.

"Indeed," Margaret managed, her voice steady despite the disappointment churning in her stomach. "She's quite... accomplished."

This was becoming a desperately familiar pattern. For the past week, Margaret had attended every social gathering where the Duke of Ashcombe might appear and had employed every conversational gambit she could devise.

And at every event, she found herself relegated to the role of observer whilst other women—more sophisticated, more experienced, more everything—claimed his attention with effortless grace.

"The duke does rather seem to prefer a certain type of lady," Lady Cooper continued, her tone carrying just enough sympathy to make Margaret's cheeks burn with embarrassment. "More... worldly, perhaps."

Margaret's fingers tightened on her teacup. "I'm sure I don't know what you mean."

"Oh, my dear, there's no shame in it," Lady Cooper said, patting Margaret's hand with motherly condescension. "Some women are simply born with an instinct for attracting gentlemen, whilst others must acquire such skill through experience. You're still quite young, after all."

The implication hung in the air like incense—sweet, cloying, and impossible to ignore.

"Perhaps you're right," Margaret said quietly, watching as Cordelia threw her head back in laughter at something the duke had said.

Julian's words from the Winter Ball echoed in her mind:

I know what makes a woman unforgettable, he'd said. *What makes her mysterious enough to pursue rather than simply available enough to ignore.*

Margaret set down her teacup with careful precision. Perhaps it was time to swallow her pride and seek out the one person who might actually be able to help her succeed.

An hour later, Margaret found herself standing outside Julian's London office, her heart hammering against her ribs with nervous anticipation.

The building was respectable but not ostentatious, the sort of discreet establishment that suggested its occupants dealt in influence and information rather than mere commerce.

She'd never visited Julian's professional domain before, and she was surprised by how well it suited him. The outer room was elegantly appointed with dark wood furniture and rich fabrics, whilst maintaining an air of serious purpose that spoke to the importance of the work conducted within these walls.

"Miss Fairbourne," Julian's secretary said, rising from behind his desk with obvious surprise. "What an unexpected pleasure. Mr. Ashcroft is currently with a client, but I'm certain he would wish to be informed of your arrival."

"If you please," Margaret said, grateful that her voice remained steady despite the flutter of nerves in her stomach. "I shall wait."

She settled into one of the leather chairs arranged near the window, trying to calm her racing thoughts. How did one go about asking a gentleman to provide instruction in the art of seduction? The very concept seemed absurd now that she was actually here, surrounded by the trappings of Julian's legitimate professional life.

Twenty minutes later, the inner door opened, and Julian emerged alongside a distinguished gentleman whom Margaret recognised as Lord Pemberton. They spoke in low voices near the doorway, their conversation clearly concluding some matter of business.

"You've been most helpful, Ashcroft," Lord Pemberton was saying. "I shall ensure the documents are prepared according to your specifications."

"My pleasure, my lord," Julian replied, his voice carrying the sort of respectful deference that Margaret had never heard him use in social settings. "Please don't hesitate to contact me if any complications arise."

After Lord Pemberton departed, Julian turned towards Margaret with that familiar teasing smile already tugging at his mouth.

"Well, well," he said, moving towards her with the sort of grace that reminded Margaret uncomfortably of the very techniques she'd come to learn. "Miss Margaret Fairbourne, gracing my humble office with her presence. To what do I owe this unexpected honour?"

Margaret rose from her chair, suddenly acutely aware of how the afternoon light streaming in through the windows caught the gold threads in her green walking dress. Julian's grey eyes swept over her with an assessment that made her pulse quicken for reasons she couldn't quite name.

"I've been thinking about our conversation at the Winter Ball," she said, pleased when her voice came out steady and determined rather than breathless with nerves.

"Come, my dear," he said, gesturing towards the inner door. "We can speak more privately in my office."

Julian moved closer once he had firmly shut the door behind them. "Pray continue, what were you about to say, my dear?"

Margaret lifted her chin, meeting his gaze directly. "You were right. I am utterly inept at seduction, and if I continue as I am, I shall never succeed in winning the duke's attention."

Julian's smile widened instantly, and Margaret caught a glimpse of something that might have been satisfaction in his expression. "A remarkably honest self-assessment. And what, precisely, do you intend to do about this unfortunate situation?"

"You offered to teach me how to make the duke desperate to win my affection. I've come here to accept that offer," Margaret said simply.

For a moment, Julian said nothing, simply studying her face with an intensity that made Margaret's cheeks warm. Then he moved to the sideboard, pouring himself a brandy.

"And what makes you think I was serious?" he asked, not looking at her as he lifted the glass to his lips.

"Because you're many things, Julian Ashcroft, but you're not a man who makes idle offers," Margaret replied. "You saw something at the ball that amused you—my obvious failure, my desperate attempts to gain notice. You offered to help because you knew full well I would eventually come to you."

Julian turned back to her, his expression unreadable. "You give me credit for remarkable foresight."

"I give you credit for understanding human nature," Margaret corrected. "You knew I would exhaust every other option before swallowing my pride and seeking your assistance."

"And have you? Exhausted every other option?"

Margaret reflected back on the past week—the careful conversations that led nowhere, the growing certainty that she was becoming an object of pity rather than desire.

"Completely," she admitted.

Julian set down his glass and moved towards her with the sort of deliberate purpose that suddenly made Margaret's mouth dry. He stopped just close enough that she had to tilt her head back to meet his eyes.

"What precisely are you asking me to do, Margaret?"

"Teach me," she said simply. "Teach me how to intrigue rather than pursue. How to be mysterious. How to make a man want me."

"And you believe such lessons would be... appropriate?"

Margaret felt heat flood her cheeks, but she held his gaze steadily. "I believe that desperate circumstances require unconventional solutions."

Julian was quiet for a long moment, his grey eyes searching her face as though looking for something specific. Finally, he smiled—not his usual charming grin but something smaller, more genuine.

"Very well," he said simply.

Margaret's heart leapt with relief and excitement. "Truly?"

"Oh, yes. But I have conditions."

"Of course you do," Margaret said, though her voice carried more humour than irritation. "Pray tell?"

"First, absolute discretion. What we discuss, what I teach you, remains strictly between us. No confidences to your sisters, no hints to your maid or friends, no journal entries detailing your progress."

Margaret nodded immediately. "Agreed."

"Second, you must trust my methods completely. No questioning my techniques, no suggesting alternative approaches. If you want to learn, you must be willing to be taught."

"I understand." Margaret felt a thrill of excitement mingled with nervous anticipation. "I accept all your conditions."

Julian smiled, extending his hand towards her. "Then we have an agreement. Shall we shake on it?"

Margaret placed her hand in his, noting the warmth of his fingers, the way they lingered just a moment longer than strictly necessary. "We shall."

"Excellent. I suggest we begin tomorrow evening. I shall call upon you at your home at ten o'clock—late enough that your father should have retired, early enough that the household won't be completely settled. Meet me in the library."

"The library? At ten o'clock?" Margaret's eyes widened. "Julian, if we're discovered—"

"We won't be," he said with quiet confidence. "Your father sleeps soundly, and the servants retire early. Besides, should anyone happen upon us, I'm merely a family friend calling to discuss a legal matter with your father. Perfectly innocent."

Margaret felt her pulse quicken at the thought of such clandestine meetings. "I... yes. Very well."

"Excellent. And Margaret?" Julian's voice stopped her as she turned towards the door. "Wear something that makes you feel beautiful. Confidence is the foundation of any effective seduction."

Later, Margaret found herself in her father's study, her mind still reeling from the implications of what she'd agreed to. The space was a sanctuary of masculine authority, heavy with the scent of pipe tobacco and aged brandy. The air was thick and still, broken only by the soft scratch of her father's quill and the occasional creak of settling timber in the old house.

Her father looked up from his correspondence as she entered, his expression settling into the sort of paternal attention that suggested he had something important to discuss.

"Margaret, perfect timing. I was hoping to speak with you."

"Of course, Father." Margaret settled into the chair across from his desk, noting the way his grey eyes studied her with obvious concern.

"I've been watching your behaviour this season," he began, his voice carrying the sort of careful neutrality that made Margaret's stomach twist with apprehension. "You've been... quite focused in your social activities."

"Oh, I've been having the most wonderful time this season!" Margaret replied carefully.

"Indeed. And I believe I understand the... direction of your interests." Lord Fairbourne leaned back in his chair, his expression becoming more serious. "Perhaps it is time we discussed your future more directly."

Margaret's heart began to race. "My future?"

"Your marriage prospects, to be precise. You're five-and-twenty, Margaret. Whilst that's hardly ancient, it is certainly time you began thinking seriously about settling yourself advantageously."

"I have been thinking about it," Margaret said, her voice gaining strength as she remembered her new alliance with Julian. "In fact, I have someone particular in mind."

Lord Fairbourne's eyebrows rose significantly. "Indeed? And who might that be?"

Margaret lifted her chin, meeting her father's gaze directly. "The Duke of Ashcombe."

For a long moment, Lord Fairbourne said nothing, his expression cycling through surprise, calculation, and what might even have been approval. Finally, he nodded slowly.

"An ambitious choice," he said. "And one that would certainly elevate our family's position considerably. The Duke of Ashcombe is wealthy, influential, and well-connected in political circles."

"Oh, yes, those considerations did cross my mind," Margaret admitted.

"I am certain they did." Lord Fairbourne's tone carried a note of paternal pride. "Very well, I shall support your pursuit of the duke, and I shall ensure that any social or financial resources you require are made available."

Relief flooded through Margaret. "Thank you, Father."

"However," he continued, his voice taking on a more authoritative tone, "I must also be practical. If you haven't secured a proposal from His Grace by the end of the season, I shall be forced to consider other options. I've already received several inquiries from gentlemen who would make suitable, if less elevated, matches."

A chill ran down Margaret's spine. "What sort of enquiries?"

"Nothing that needs concern you at present," her father said dismissively. "But I wanted you to understand the stakes. You have until the end of the season to succeed with the duke. If you fail, I shall expect you to accept whatever alternative arrangement I deem most appropriate."

Margaret nodded, her mind reeling. The end of the season was only three months away. She had ninety days to transform herself from the clumsy, obvious girl she'd been into someone capable of capturing a duke's heart.

"I understand, Father," she said quietly.

"Excellent. Then I wish you the very best of luck, my dear."

As Margaret left her father's study, she felt the weight of expectation settling over her shoulders. Success with the Duke of Ashcombe was no longer merely a romantic fantasy—it was a necessity. Failure would mean accepting whatever marriage her father arranged, utterly surrendering her dreams of passion and true love in favour of security and practicality.

But now she had Julian's promise of help, his expertise in the art of seduction, his understanding of what a man like the duke would find irresistible. And tomorrow evening, her education would begin.

The thought should have terrified her. Instead, Margaret found herself tingling with anticipation for the lessons that would either make her dreams come true or destroy her entirely.

Chapter Four

"Are you quite certain about the laudanum? Because in my experience, fathers have an uncanny ability to surface at the most inconvenient moments."

Julian kept his voice low as he slipped through the garden gate, though he couldn't resist adding just enough dramatic concern to make the question sound like the beginning of a particularly scandalous play.

Margaret stood waiting for him in the shadows, still fully dressed in a simple day gown of pale blue muslin, though she had clearly taken great care with her appearance—a detail that sent an unexpected jolt of awareness through him.

"He takes laudanum for his joints," she whispered, leading him towards the servants' entrance. "He shall not wake until dawn."

"How very convenient," Julian murmured, following the subtle sway of her skirts through the shadowed garden. "Though I confess myself rather curious about your sudden expertise in your father's sleeping habits. One might almost think the lady has been planning this particular evening for some time."

Margaret's step faltered almost imperceptibly. "I am merely... thorough in my preparations."

"That is certainly an admirable quality," he agreed, noting the way she avoided his gaze. "But it is wonderfully reassuring," he murmured. "Nothing quite sets a gentleman's mind at ease like the promise of an unconscious patriarch during such clandestine activities."

She shot him a look that could have frozen the Thames. "This is not clandestine, Julian. It is educational."

"My dear Margaret, in my considerable experience, the distinction between education and seduction is rather like the difference between a minuet and a waltz—both involve precise steps, but one is considerably more... intimate in its execution."

The servants' entrance opened with barely a whisper, and Margaret led him further, through corridors he had never seen before—the hidden arteries of a grand house that allowed for discreet movement. She navigated them with surprising confidence, her slippered feet making no sound on the worn stone floors.

"You seem remarkably familiar with these passages," he observed quietly.

"A lady learns many things when she wishes to avoid unwanted conversations with visiting relatives," she replied nonchalantly, but Julian caught the hint of mischief in her tone.

The library, when they reached it, had been transformed into something that belonged more in a Gothic novel than a respectable London townhouse.

Heavy curtains blocked the windows, and a single candelabra cast shadows that danced across the walls like living things. Julian had to admit she had been thorough.

"You have created quite the dramatic setting," he observed, settling his coat carefully on a nearby chair. "I half expect Lord Byron himself to emerge from behind the curtains, quill in hand, composing odes to forbidden knowledge."

"I wanted to ensure we would not be disturbed. And I thought the atmosphere might... help." Margaret's voice carried a tremor she was clearly trying to suppress. "If I am to be mysterious, should I not practice in surroundings that inspire such feelings?"

Julian's lips curved in what he hoped was an encouraging smile rather than the expression of a man fighting a losing battle with his own better judgment. "An excellent point."

"Shall we begin?"

Julian turned to face her properly and felt his carefully maintained composure take a direct hit.

The candlelight caught the gold in her hair, turned her blue eyes luminous, and highlighted the nervous flush on her cheeks in a way that made him acutely aware that this was no longer the sweet girl who had always been on the periphery of his visits to the family.

When precisely had Margaret Fairbourne become so... present? So impossible to ignore?

"Julian?" she said softly, and he realised he had been staring.

"Do you have any comprehension of what you're asking of me?" he said, his voice sharper than he'd intended as he forced himself to focus on the task at hand.

Her chin lifted with characteristic Fairbourne stubbornness. "I'm asking you to honour your word. Unless you were merely boasting about your abilities? Because I should hate to discover that your confidence is nothing more than another ornamental performance."

The challenge in her voice sparked something dangerous in his chest—the same reckless pleasure he felt when facing down a particularly formidable opponent in court. Except this was Margaret, who brought sunshine into every room she entered, and he had no business whatsoever feeling anything resembling desire when he looked at her.

"My dear girl," he said, falling back on his signature showmanship because it was safer than honesty, "I never boast. I simply state facts with considerably more flair than most people find strictly necessary."

"Then prove it."

Julian felt his pulse quicken in a way that had nothing to do with the challenge of the task ahead. This was dangerous territory. But he had given his word, and Julian Ashcroft always kept his promises, no matter how spectacularly they threatened to backfire on him.

"Very well," he said, moving closer because proximity was essential to this particular instruction, not because he wanted to see if her skin was as soft as it looked in the candlelight. "Lesson one: the art of commanding attention without appearing to seek it."

"How does one accomplish such a thing?"

Julian began to circle her slowly, using the movement to regain some measure of control over his wayward thoughts. "By understanding that desperation, my dear Margaret, is the least attractive quality any woman can possess."

He watched her carefully as he spoke, noting the way she held herself, the quick flutter of her hands, the breathless quality of her voice.

"You entered this room like a woman in pursuit," he continued, his voice taking on the measured tone he used in court. "Quick steps. Nervous energy. Fidgeting hands. Every movement you made announced your need."

"But I *do* need something," Margaret protested, and Julian had to resist the urge to ask if she even knew what exactly that something was.

"Yes, but Strickland must never know that." He stopped directly in front of her, close enough to see the way her pupils dilated in the candlelight. "He has women throwing themselves at his feet every night of the week. What he lacks is a woman who appears entirely content with her own company."

"Pray tell, how shall I capture his attention if I do not pursue him?"

Julian's smile was slow and deliberately wicked—the sort of expression that had gotten him into trouble with more than one duke's daughter over the years. "By transforming yourself. Nothing captivates a duke quite like a woman who appears supremely indifferent to his very existence."

"Oh! But that makes no sense at all, Julian. How can one capture someone's attention by ignoring them entirely?"

He gestured towards the far end of the library, trying to focus on the lesson rather than the way the candlelight gilded the delicate skin of her neck in gold. "Walk to the window and back. As you would if you were entering Lady Pemberton's musicale tomorrow evening."

Margaret complied, but Julian winced at her performance. Quick, uncertain steps, slightly hunched shoulders, every line of her body broadcasting anxiety.

"My dear girl, if desperation were an artistic performance, you would just have earned thunderous applause from the cheapest seats. Shall we try for something more... subtle?"

"I am *not* desperate!" The flash of temper in her eyes was infinitely more attractive than her earlier nervousness, and Julian filed that information away swiftly for future reference.

"No? Then enlighten me—what manner of woman crosses a ballroom as though chasing the last carriage to Gretna Green? The effect is rather... urgent."

Her cheeks flamed visibly in the subtle lighting.

"A woman who is... eager? Enthusiastic?" she suggested.

"A woman who is hunting." He moved behind her, telling himself it was necessary for instruction, not because he wanted to be close enough to smell the faint lavender scent of her hair. "Try again. This time, imagine yourself to be the most fascinating person in the room and everyone knows it."

"But I am not—"

"Margaret." Her name slipped out softer than he intended, and he saw her shoulders tense in response. "For the next hour, you are anything I tell you to be. Do you trust me?"

When she nodded, something shifted in his chest—something that felt dangerous and necessary all at once.

"Good. Now walk."

This time she moved differently—slower, more deliberate. Julian watched the way she held her spine, the measured grace of her steps, and suddenly, his mouth went dry. There it was, the hint of the woman she could be: confident, mysterious, and utterly captivating.

"Better," he said, his voice rougher than it should have been. "But you are still performing. Stop thinking about how you look and start thinking about how you feel."

"How I feel?"

Julian moved closer, drawn by something he didn't want to name. "Confident. Mysterious. Like you are in possession of a delicious secret no one else knows." His voice dropped to barely above a whisper. "Like you could have any man in the room, but you have not yet decided if any of them are worthy of your attention."

When she walked this time, there was a natural elegance to her movements that made Julian's pulse quicken in ways that had nothing to do with pedagogy.

"Much better," he said, though the words came out strained. "Now turn and look at me as though you have just noticed I am here."

Margaret turned, and their eyes met across the candlelit space. Julian felt the air leave his lungs in a rush. The look she gave him was exactly what he had been trying to teach her—mysterious, confident, alluring—but it was also something else. Something that made him want to forget entirely about Strickland.

"Like that," he barely managed, his voice considerably huskier than it had been moments before. "Exactly like that."

Margaret's lips parted slightly, and Julian felt his carefully maintained control begin to fray at the edges. This was a mistake.

"When you see His Grace tomorrow evening," he said, stepping back and grasping for his familiar dramatic persona, "you will not seek him out like some lovesick debutante. You will arrive precisely fifteen minutes after the musicale begins—fashionably late. Position yourself where you can be observed and stand there as though you possess the most delicious secret in all of London."

"And then?"

"And then, my dear Margaret, you will let him come to you."

She nodded, though Julian could see the uncertainty flickering in her eyes. "What if he doesn't?"

"He will," Julian spoke with absolute conviction, though part of him hoped desperately Strickland would prove him wrong.

"A man like Nathaniel Strickland cannot resist a puzzle, and you, when properly presented, will be the most intriguing puzzle in the room."

Julian moved towards his coat, needing the physical distance to regain his equilibrium. But as he reached for the garment, he made the mistake of looking back at her.

Margaret stood perfectly still in the centre of the library, blue eyes iridescent with something that might have been either excitement or something altogether more dangerous.

"I believe," he said, his voice barely steady, "that you underestimate your own power, my dear Margaret."

The way she looked at him then—startled, aware, something awakening in her eyes—nearly undid him entirely.

"Julian," she whispered, and his name on her lips, though he had heard it countless times before, now sounded like a prayer and a temptation rolled into one.

Julian felt something crack inside his chest, some carefully constructed wall that had kept him safe from exactly this sort of complication. But Margaret was Lord Fairbourne's daughter, Rhys's sister-in-law, an innocent who deserved a man capable of offering her everything she dreamed of.

"I believe," he said, shrugging into his coat with movements that felt stiff and unnatural, "that concludes tonight's lesson. Tomorrow evening, you shall put theory into practice."

He paused at the threshold, looking back at her one last time. Margaret stood motionless in the candlelight, looking like something from a painting—beautiful, untouchable, and entirely too tempting for any man's peace of mind.

"Margaret?" he said softly. "Wear the blue silk tomorrow. The one with the lower neckline." He allowed himself one last mischievous smile. "Trust me on that."

Julian slipped out through the garden gate and into the London fog, but he couldn't shake the image of Margaret standing in the library, looking at him as though he was the most fascinating man in the world.

Chapter Five

"Oh, but surely you cannot mean to hover by the terrace doors all evening, Miss Fairbourne?"

Margaret forced her most brilliant smile as Lady Pemberton's shrill voice cut through the gentle melody from the musicians' corner. She was fifteen minutes late to the musicale, just as Julian had instructed, and every eye in the salon seemed to be tracking her movements.

"I find the evening air quite refreshing, my lady," Margaret replied, positioning herself precisely where the candlelight would catch the sapphire silk of her gown. "And the view of the gardens is simply divine!"

Lady Pemberton tittered, though her eyes were sharp with curiosity. "How very... unusual. Most young ladies prefer to be nearer to the refreshments. Or the gentlemen."

"Do they?" Margaret tilted her head with what she hoped appeared to be serene indifference. "How fascinating."

She could feel Julian's voice echoing in her mind as she stood there, spine straight, hands folded gracefully. *Command attention without chasing it. Hold still while others shift nervously. Confidence—not effort.*

"Miss Fairbourne."

The voice was smooth as aged whisky, and Margaret's pulse quickened as she turned to find the Duke of Ashcombe approaching. He moved with the fluid confidence of a man accustomed to having doors opened before he reached them, his dark evening coat impeccably tailored, his smile practiced to perfection.

"Your Grace." Margaret dropped into a curtsey that she hoped conveyed both respect and the sort of mysterious allure Julian had attempted to teach her.

"I confess I find myself surprised to find you standing apart from the gathering," the duke said, his keen dark eyes studying her face with an intensity that made her skin prickle.

Here it was—her first real test. Margaret could almost hear Julian's voice whispering in her ear. *Mystery, my dear. Never reveal everything at once.*

"Oh, I find there is often more to be learned from observation than participation," Margaret replied, borrowing shamelessly from Julian's arsenal of exaggerated wisdom. "Do you not agree, Your Grace?"

Something flickered in the duke's eyes—interest, perhaps, or calculation. His smile widened, revealing teeth that were perfectly straight, yet somehow unsettling. "Indeed. And what have you observed this evening?"

Margaret felt her confidence wobble slightly. "That the truly fascinating conversations happen in the margins," she said finally, hoping she sounded mysterious rather than foolish.

"Spoken like a woman of unusual perception." The duke moved closer, close enough that she caught the scent of his cologne—something expensive and vaguely overwhelming that she couldn't identify. "I suspect we shall encounter each other again soon, Miss Fairbourne. London society is remarkably... predictable in its gatherings."

"Indeed, Your Grace," Margaret managed, unsure whether his words held promise or warning. There was something in his tone that made her stomach flutter, but not with the pleasant excitement she had expected.

"Until we meet again, then." His bow was precise, his smile enigmatic, and then he was gone, leaving Margaret standing by the French doors with her heart racing. It had worked—Julian's techniques had worked exactly as he had promised.

The Duke of Ashcombe had indeed approached her, shown clear interest, and even made cryptic promises of future encounters. Margaret's heart soared with triumph, even as a small voice in the back of her mind whispered that something about the interaction had felt slightly... wrong.

She pushed the thought aside. This was what she had wanted, what she was risking her reputation for. The duke was interested, and that was all that mattered.

"Margaret?"

She turned to find her sister, Catharine, approaching, elegant in pearl-grey silk, her expression carefully neutral, as if she were thinking furiously about something.

"Catharine! How lovely to see you here." Margaret kissed her sister's cheek, noting how Catharine's sharp eyes catalogued every detail of her appearance.

"You look radiant this evening," Catharine observed. "That gown is particularly becoming. New, is it not?"

"Oh, this old thing?" Margaret laughed, though it came out higher than usual. "I've had it for ages."

Catharine's eyebrow rose with surgical precision. "Have you? How curious. I could have sworn I saw the exact same silk at Madame Rousseau's shop last week. The shopgirl mentioned it had just arrived from Paris."

Heat flooded Margaret's cheeks. "I... well, perhaps I misremembered when I acquired it."

"That little performance with His Grace showed remarkable polish."

Margaret felt her stomach drop towards her slippers. "I am sure I have no idea what you mean."

"Of course not," Catharine said smoothly.

Margaret opened her mouth to respond, but Catharine had already moved away, gliding towards the refreshment table with the serene confidence of a sister who noticed more than she said.

Margaret's hands trembled as she smoothed her skirts. She had done it—she had successfully deployed Julian's techniques and captured the duke's interest. Now she needed to share her triumph and plan her next move.

Later, she arrived at Julian's office. Inside, Julian sat on the settee, in his shirtsleeves, a woman in deep green silks lounging too close beside him.

Margaret froze entirely, her triumph momentarily forgotten.

With a single glance, he dismissed the woman, who rose with a murmur and swept from the room in a rustle of silk and the lingering scent of jasmine.

Then they were alone.

"Julian!" Margaret almost embraced him in her excitement but caught herself just in time, her hands fluttering uselessly at her sides. "It worked! Everything you taught me worked perfectly!" Her eyes were bright, her voice breathless as she moved closer. "He approached me within minutes! I stood by the French doors, exactly as you instructed, and he came to me like... like a fox to a henhouse!"

Julian leaned back in his chair, a slight smile playing at his lips.

"He said I was a woman of unusual perception, and he spoke of encountering me again at future gatherings. Julian, I cannot thank you enough!"

"Your gratitude is premature, my dear Margaret," Julian said, rising from his seat with a dramatic flourish. "One successful encounter does not guarantee a proposal. You shall need far more sophisticated techniques if you hope to secure a duke's lasting interest."

Margaret's face lit up with renewed excitement. "The second lesson?"

Julian gestured towards the settee. "Tonight. We shall focus on the art of conversation—how to flatter without fawning, how to tease without offending, and how to make a gentleman feel clever whilst guiding the entire exchange to your advantage."

Margaret settled herself on the settee, smoothing her sapphire skirts as Julian moved to pour himself a brandy from the decanter on the side table.

"For this lesson," he continued, returning to lounge in the chair opposite her, "you must practice managing masculine pride whilst maintaining your own dignity."

Julian transformed before her eyes, adopting the bearing and mannerisms of aristocratic entitlement. His voice deepened, became more clipped, and he regarded her with the sort of assessing gaze she had witnessed on countless titled noblemen.

"Miss Fairbourne," he said, perfectly mimicking the duke's smooth tone, "I find myself curious about your thoughts on the recent reforms to the Poor Laws. Surely such matters aren't beyond the scope of a lady's understanding?"

Margaret straightened, recognising the trap. "Oh, Your Grace, I must confess I find myself more interested in the people behind such legislation. Tell me, what observations have you made about the effect on the families in your own estates?"

Julian's approving nod was brief but encouraging. "Good. You deflected whilst flattering his supposed expertise. Again, this time, suppose he asks about your favourite poets."

Julian transformed himself into various approximations of aristocratic entitlement, throwing out questions both banal and pointed, whilst Margaret learned to deflect, redirect, and subtly guide their discourse. He corrected her posture, the tilt of her head, the precise moment to lift her eyes for maximum effect.

"Remember," he said during one exchange about literature, "you must appear interested in his opinions whilst offering just enough of your own thoughts to intrigue him. Like so—'Oh, Your Grace, what a fascinating interpretation! I confess I had not considered Byron's work from that perspective. Might I ask what led you to such insight?'"

Margaret practiced the line, adjusting her tone until it earned her an approving nod from Julian.

"Better. What if he asks about your family's financial situation?"

"He would not dare!" Margaret gasped.

"Dukes dare many things, my dear. If he does, you deflect with grace: 'Surely such practical matters are best left to fathers and solicitors, Your Grace? I confess myself far more interested in matters of the heart.'"

Julian settled back in his chair with well-practiced dramatic artifice. "Now suppose the duke mentions his collection of rare manuscripts. How do you respond?"

Margaret straightened, adopting her most refined posture. "Oh, Your Grace, how utterly fascinating! Your profound intellect and discerning taste in literary treasures surely rival that of... of the great libraries of Alexandria, and your wisdom in acquiring such magnificent works demonstrates a mind so superior that even... even Solomon himself would weep with envy at your scholarly magnificence!"

Julian blinked. Margaret's cheeks flamed as she realised what had tumbled from her lips.

"Good God, Margaret," Julian said slowly, "you sound as though you're composing an ode to his bootblack."

"Oh!" Margaret clapped her hands to her burning cheeks. "That was dreadful, wasn't it?"

Julian's mouth twitched. "Like a vicar's wife praising the church organ with rather too much enthusiasm."

Margaret dissolved into giggles. "Stop! You're making it worse!"

"I'm merely suggesting," Julian said, his own laughter breaking through, "that perhaps we aim for admiration rather than worship. Unless you wish the poor man to think you've taken leave of your senses entirely."

Their laughter filled the office, warm and genuine, until it gradually faded into something softer.

The silence stretched between them, charged with something neither quite dared to name. Margaret became acutely aware of her own breathing, of the way her heart was beating just a little too fast, of the warmth that seemed to radiate from anywhere Julian's gaze lingered. "Perhaps," Julian said quietly, his voice having lost some of its poise, "we could practice something more... subtle."

He rose from his chair and moved to sit beside her on the settee, close enough that she could smell his cologne—something warm and masculine that made her think of leather and tobacco and rain-soaked gardens.

"The art of conversation," he continued, his voice barely above a whisper, "is not merely about words. It is about the spaces *between* them, the glances, the almost-touches that speak louder than any declaration."

Margaret's breath caught as he reached out, his fingers barely grazing her gloved hand.

"Like this?" she asked, mimicking him.

"Precisely so," he said as his thumb traced over her knuckles, and she felt the touch through the thin silk of her gloves like a brand. "A gentleman notices these things, Margaret—the way a lady's breath quickens, the way his touch makes her pupils dilate, the way she leans forward ever so slightly when she is intrigued."

"And what does it mean," Margaret asked, her voice barely audible, "when a lady does *all* those things?"

Julian's grey eyes darkened, and for a moment, she saw something in them that made her pulse race furiously—something that had absolutely nothing to do with lessons or dukes.

"It means," he said, his voice rough, "that she is dangerous in the most delicious ways."

For a moment, something flickered between them—recognition, perhaps, or possibility. Julian cleared his throat and straightened in his chair.

"Remember," he said, his dramatic flair returning, though this time it sounded somewhat forced, "this is merely instruction. You must not confuse practice with reality."

"Of course not," Margaret said quickly, though she felt heat linger in her cheeks. "This is just a lesson."

"Precisely."

Margaret nodded too quickly and rose from the settee. "I should return before my father sends out a search party."

"Indeed."

She moved towards the door, then paused at the threshold. "Thank you, Julian. For all of it."

"Think nothing of it, my dear."

Margaret stepped out into the London fog, pulling her cloak close against the chill. As she walked towards her waiting carriage, her pulse beat in a most irregular rhythm for a reason she couldn't identify.

It was just a lesson, she told herself firmly.

But for a moment there, in the lamplight of Julian's office, it had felt remarkably like flirting.

Chapter Six

"Good God, Julian, you look positively murderous. Surely my birthday celebration cannot be that tedious?"

Julian forced his features into something resembling sociability as Rhys approached, though he suspected the attempt was less than convincing. Around them, the terrace of Ashbourne Hall buzzed with the sort of refined conversation that made Julian want to drink considerably more than was prudent.

"Your celebration is delightful as always," Julian replied, swirling the brandy in his glass with perhaps more violence than necessary. "I am merely contemplating the fascinating complexities of political corruption and how best to expose them without triggering an international incident."

Rhys's eyebrows rose with the sort of practiced scepticism that came from years of friendship. "Ah, yes, the Marlborough affair. I trust your investigation yielded the results you anticipated?"

"Better than anticipated, actually." Julian took a measured sip of his brandy, savouring both the burn and the satisfaction of a job well done. "Lord Marlborough's unfortunate association with that trade bill scandal should be making the rounds of Westminster by tomorrow morning. The evidence was... quite comprehensive."

"And entirely damning, I presume?"

"Utterly. Though I confess myself surprised to discover how many of Strickland's allies seem to have their fingers in similarly questionable pies." Julian's voice carried just enough melodramatic concern to mask the genuine unease he felt.

"One begins to wonder if Strickland's circle of acquaintances might benefit from closer scrutiny."

Rhys was quiet for a moment, his grey eyes studying Julian's face with uncomfortable intensity. "You suspect the man himself?"

"I suspect everyone, dear cousin. It is but one of my more charming qualities." Julian gestured towards the gathering with his glass. "Speaking of which, I see our esteemed duke has seen fit to grace us with his presence this afternoon."

Indeed, Nathaniel Strickland stood near the fountain, holding court amongst a collection of simpering debutantes and their calculating mothers. But Julian's attention was drawn inexorably to the figure approaching the duke's little gathering.

Margaret.

She moved across the lawn with fluid grace and a confidence that made Julian's chest tighten with unwelcome pride. Her posture was perfect, her expression serene, her steps measured with just the right amount of deliberate determination.

"Calmly now," Julian muttered under his breath, catching Margaret's eye across the terrace.

She glided towards the refreshment table with the sort of calculated indifference that would have made Machiavelli weep with admiration. It was, Julian had to admit, a masterful performance.

"She's learning quickly," Rhys observed, following Julian's gaze.

"So it would seem." Julian's voice was carefully neutral, though his fingers tightened around his brandy glass as

Strickland's attention inevitably drifted towards Margaret. "Perhaps too quickly for her own good."

"If you continue glowering like that," Rhys said quietly, "people will talk."

"I am observing." Julian forced himself to look away from Margaret and Strickland's increasingly intimate conversation. "One might even say I am taking a professional interest in... social dynamics."

"One might also say you look like a man watching his rival court the woman he desires."

Julian's brandy glass paused halfway to his lips. "I beg your pardon?"

"You heard me perfectly well." Rhys's voice carried the sort of gentle certainty that Julian found profoundly irritating. "Whatever your newfound connection to my sister-in-law, you're clearly not indifferent to seeing her charmed by Strickland."

"There is no connection beyond the ordinary courtesies of friendship and family ties," Julian said carefully. "Margaret is a delightful young lady, and naturally I wish her well in her... romantic endeavours."

"Do you? Because you look rather as though you wish Strickland would develop a sudden case of plague."

"Your Grace?" A footman appeared at Rhys's elbow, bowing apologetically. "I beg your pardon, but Lord Ventnor has arrived and requests a private word regarding urgent parliamentary matters."

Rhys sighed with obvious reluctance. "Of course he has." He gave Julian a knowing look. "We shall continue this fascinating discussion later, cousin."

As Rhys departed towards the house, Julian was left alone with his brandy and his increasingly dark thoughts.

Later, Margaret appeared at his elbow, her cheeks flushed with triumph and champagne.

"Julian!" Margaret's voice carried the sort of breathless excitement that made Julian's pulse quicken despite his better judgment. "Did you see? It worked perfectly! Just as you said it would!"

"I observed your performance, yes," Julian replied, hoping his tone conveyed appropriate professional satisfaction rather than the complicated tangle of pride and jealousy that was currently wreaking havoc with his composure. "Strickland appeared suitably intrigued by your charms."

"Oh, he was! He asked the most interesting questions about my thoughts on poetry and politics." Margaret's blue eyes sparkled with delight. "He even suggested we might see much more of each other again at Lady Whitmore's soiree tomorrow evening!"

"Did he indeed?" Julian's smile felt like it might crack his face.

"Yes! Oh, Julian, your lessons have been absolutely transformative," she continued in a whisper, glancing around to ensure they weren't overheard. "But might I... that is, would it be possible to schedule another lesson? Tonight, perhaps? I feel as though I am on the verge of success, but I should like to be absolutely certain I am prepared for tomorrow evening's encounter."

Julian glanced towards the house where Rhys had disappeared with Lord Ventnor, then back to Margaret's eager face. "If you feel it necessary."

"Oh, I do! Most emphatically." Her smile was radiant. "Shall we say ten o'clock? At your office?"

"Very well."

Margaret clasped her hands together with delight, then seemed to remember herself and forced her expression into something more appropriately subdued. "I should return to my family before my absence is noted. Until tonight, then."

She swept away in a rustle of blue silk, leaving Julian staring after her with what he suspected was an expression of complete befuddlement.

Ten o'clock arrived with the sort of inexorable certainty that Julian found deeply unwelcome.

Margaret arrived precisely on time, as he had known she would. She knocked once—a soft, almost hesitant sound—and entered without waiting for permission.

"Julian?" Her voice carried a note of uncertainty. "Are you quite certain this is not an imposition? You seemed... distant at the party this afternoon."

"Not distant," Julian replied, gesturing for her to take a seat on the settee. "Merely contemplating the complexities of advanced instruction."

Margaret settled herself gracefully, smoothing her skirts with hands that trembled slightly. "What sort of advanced instruction?"

Julian moved to pour himself a brandy, using the familiar ritual to steady his suddenly unruly nerves. "Physical proximity," he said without turning around. "The art of using closeness to create attraction without appearing forward or improper."

"Oh!" Margaret's voice was small. "And how does one accomplish such a thing?"

Julian turned to face her, brandy in hand, and felt his carefully constructed composure take yet another hit. Margaret sat perched on the edge of the settee, her blue eyes wide with curiosity and something else—something that made his pulse quicken in ways that had absolutely nothing to do with educational responsibility.

"Through dancing," he said, surprised by the huskiness in his own voice. "Specifically, through subtle signals that can be conveyed during a waltz, when executed properly."

"But we have no musicians!"

Julian didn't answer, but he extended his hand in invitation. Margaret placed her hand in his, and Julian felt the contact like a jolt of electricity through his entire body.

"Now," he said, positioning his free hand at her waist with what he hoped appeared to be professional detachment, "the key to using dance as a tool of seduction lies not in the steps themselves but in the spaces between them."

Margaret nodded, though Julian noticed the way her breath hitched slightly when his hand settled against the silk of her gown.

Julian began moving them in a basic waltz pattern, gradually drawing her closer until Margaret's skirts brushed his legs and he could feel the warmth of her body through the layers.

"The idea," he continued, his voice considerably huskier than it had been moments before, "is to create minute moments of connection that feel accidental but are entirely deliberate."

"I see." Margaret's gaze had dropped to where her hand rested against his chest, and Julian noted with fascination the way her lips parted slightly. "What sorts of... connections?"

Julian swallowed hard. "Well, there's the matter of eye contact during the more intimate moments of the dance. And the... the way one might allow one's breath to warm your partner's ear when speaking quietly."

"Show me," Margaret whispered.

Julian's control wavered dangerously. "Margaret..."

"Please." Her blue eyes lifted to meet his, and Julian saw something in them that made his pulse roar, sending hot blood flooding towards his abdomen.

Julian drew her closer still until there was barely an inch between them, until he could feel the rapid rise and fall of her chest and the warmth of her body against the entire length of his. His hand slid from her waist to the small of her back, pulling her more fully against him, and the soft gasp Margaret made sent heat shooting straight into his groin.

"Like this," he murmured, lowering his head until his lips almost brushed her ear. "You lean in, just so, and speak softly enough that your partner must strain to hear you."

Margaret's free hand clutched at his shoulder, her fingers digging into the fabric of his coat. "What... what would one even say?"

"Anything that requires a response," Julian breathed, his lips grazing the shell of her ear. "Perhaps a question about the music or a comment about the other guests. The words themselves are immaterial—it is the intimacy of the act that creates the desired effect."

Margaret turned her head slightly, and suddenly her mouth was mere inches from his own. Julian could see the flecks of darker blue in her eyes, could feel the warmth of her breath against his lips, could smell the champagne she'd consumed earlier, mixed with her own intoxicating scent.

"Julian," she whispered, her voice carrying a note of wonder that undid him wholeheartedly.

"Yes?"

"I think I am beginning to understand why dancing can be considered scandalous."

His laugh came out as more of a groan. "Margaret, we should—"

Her gaze dropped to his mouth, and Julian felt his last vestiges of control slipping away like sand through his fingers.

"Should stop," he managed, though he made no move to release her.

"Should we?" Her hand slid from his shoulder to cup his jaw, her thumb tracing the line of his cheekbone with heartbreaking tenderness. "Because I find myself thinking that perhaps I have been pursuing the wrong sort of gentleman entirely."

Julian stared down at her, reeling with shock at the situation he found himself in and her newfound boldness. "Margaret, you don't understand what you're saying."

"Don't I?" She moved closer still, her body pressed fully against his until Julian could feel every soft curve and gentle line of her. "I am trying to tell you that when I danced with the duke this afternoon, I felt nothing. Less than nothing. But when I am with you—when you look at me as you are now—I feel as if I might spontaneously combust!"

Julian's control snapped in two. He grabbed her, kissing her with a hunger that shocked them both, his mouth claiming hers with nothing short of desperate intensity. Margaret responded with startling passion, her lips parting beneath his, her body melting against him with sweet surrender. Julian's hands tangled in her golden hair, scattering pins to the floor as he deepened the kiss even farther, tasting champagne and innocence and something indefinably precious.

Margaret's arms wound around his neck, pulling him closer still, and Julian lost all sense of time and place. There was nothing beyond the sweet heat of her mouth, the silky feel of her skin beneath his hands, and the soft whimpers she made as he trailed kisses down her throat.

Somewhere in the back of his mind, a voice that sounded suspiciously like his conscience pointed out that this was insanity.

Julian promptly told his conscience to go to hell.

Instead, he lifted Margaret in his arms and carried her to his desk, sweeping aside papers and ledgers with reckless abandon. Margaret laughed breathlessly at the dramatic gesture, her eyes bright with wonder and desire.

"Julian," she gasped as he pressed her back against the solid surface, his mouth finding the pulse point at her throat. "This is... we shouldn't..."

"No," he agreed roughly, his hands already working at the fastenings of her gown. "We absolutely shouldn't."

"I don't understand what is happening to me," Margaret whispered, her fingers fumbling with the buttons of his waistcoat. "I feel so... so strange... like I'm not myself at all."

"You are utterly perfect," Julian murmured against her skin. "Even if a bit scandalous. A veritable catastrophe of propriety that would send the Archbishop of Canterbury into apoplectic fits. Absolutely—"

A sharp knock at the door shattered the passionate moment.

They froze, both breathing hard, staring at each other in the sudden silence. Julian's hair was dishevelled, his cravat askew, his waistcoat gaping where Margaret's eager fingers had worked it. Her gown, in turn, was half-unlaced, and her lips thoroughly swollen from his kisses.

"Mr. Ashcroft?" The voice belonged to the night watchman who made rounds of the building. "Is everything quite all right, sir? I heard a commotion."

Julian closed his eyes, fighting with all his might for composure. "Quite all right," he called back, his voice strained. "I merely... knocked over some papers."

"Very good, sir. Do have a pleasant evening."

The footsteps retreated, leaving them in a silence broken only by their ragged breathing.

Margaret blinked as if waking from a dream, her gaze taking in their dishevelled state, the scattered papers, Julian's undone clothing. The reality of what had just transpired crashed over her like a cold wave.

"Oh..." she breathed, her hands flying to her mouth. "Oh my goodness! What... what did we just..."

Julian stepped back abruptly, running his hands through his hair as the full magnitude of his loss of control hit him squarely in the chest. "Good God..." he whispered. "Margaret, I... what have I done?"

She stood on unsteady legs, her fingers frantically working to restore some order to her appearance. "I don't... I cannot..."

She looked up at him with wide, confused eyes. "Julian, I've never... that is, I didn't know I could feel..."

"This is madness." Julian began pacing, running his hands through his hair. "Complete and utter madness of the most spectacular variety. You are an innocent, and I... I am precisely the sort of charming scoundrel your family would forbid you to associate with."

Margaret's hands trembled as she tried to pin her hair back into some sort of order. "But I... when you kissed me, I thought... I felt..." She trailed off, clearly struggling to articulate emotions she'd never experienced before.

"What you felt was passion," Julian said roughly, finally stopping his pacing to look at her. "Nothing more, my dear. A physical response that means nothing beyond the moment."

The words hit Margaret like a backhand to the cheek. Her face crumpled slightly before she lifted her chin with visible effort. "Is that truly all it was to you?"

Julian felt something crack inside his chest at the hurt in her tone, but he forced himself to maintain his distance. "What else could it be? You came here seeking lessons in seduction, and I... we lost control of the situation. Nothing more."

Margaret simply stared at him for a long moment, tears threatening at the corners of her eyes. "I see," she said quietly, her voice barely steady. "Then I suppose all that remains is to thank you for the... instruction."

"Margaret—"

"No!" She held up a hand, her dignity gathering around her like armour despite her dishevelled appearance. "You are quite right, of course. I don't know what came over me. It was... foolish of me to read more into it than what was there."

Julian wanted to tell her the truth. But the words didn't come.

Instead, he watched as she gathered the last of her composure and moved towards the door.

"For what it's worth," she said without turning around, "I regret nothing about tonight, even if you do."

"Margaret, wait—"

But she was already gone, the door closing behind her with a soft click, leaving Julian alone with his brandy and the scattered papers that bore evidence of his spectacular loss of control.

Outside, the London fog swirled through the empty streets, and Julian couldn't shake the feeling that everything had just changed irrevocably.

Chapter Seven

"Margaret, darling, you look positively radiant this morning," Eliza said, settling herself gracefully beneath the rose-draped pergola with her embroidery basket. "There's a certain... glow about you. Either you've discovered some miraculous new health tonic, or something far more interesting has captured your attention."

Margaret's hand stilled on her teacup, and she felt heat flood her cheeks at the innocent question. Three days had passed since Julian's kiss—three excruciating days during which she felt as though the memory of his lips on her might somehow be written across her face for all the world to see.

"Oh! I am perfectly well," she managed, though her voice came out breathless and higher than usual. "Simply enjoying the morning air. Isn't it divine?"

"Mmm." Eliza's needle paused its work, and those sharp eyes, so much like their father's when he was hunting for secrets, fixed on Margaret's face. "Though I confess myself curious about this sudden... sophistication in your approach to courtship. Wherever did you learn to be so artfully mysterious, little sister? Because I heard that at Lady Pemberton's musicale, you had the Duke of Ashcombe practically mesmerised."

Margaret's mouth went dry. "I'm sure I don't know what you mean."

"Don't you?" Eliza's smile turned positively wicked. "Because if witnesses are to be believed, the way you stood by that window, utterly serene whilst every other young lady in the room was practically throwing herself at his feet—it was quite masterfully done."

"Oh, well, I simply... found myself less eager to chase after gentlemen," Margaret said, her words coming out in that same breathless rush that always betrayed her excitement. "Perhaps I've finally learned the value of... patience? And mystery?"

"Patience and mystery." Eliza's tone was rich with amusement. "How very convenient. Though I wonder if this newfound wisdom came from personal reflection... or perhaps... professional instruction?"

Margaret's teacup rattled against its saucer as she set it down with trembling hands. "Instruction? What sort of instruction could you possibly mean?"

"Well, someone has clearly been teaching you the finer points of attraction," Eliza said, her voice warm with sisterly affection but sharp as a blade with curiosity. "Your transformation has been rather too dramatic and too polished to be entirely natural. So I find myself wondering—wherever did our sweet little Margaret learn to be so artfully devastating?"

"I've been reading," she said finally, her words tumbling out in a nervous rush. "Rather extensively. All sorts of... educational literature."

Eliza's eyebrows rose with surgical precision. "What sort of reading, pray tell?"

"French novels!" Margaret said quickly, feeling her cheeks burn. "Rather... illuminating ones. The sort Catharine would absolutely forbid if she knew I possessed them."

Eliza threw back her head and laughed—a rich, delighted sound. "Margaret Fairbourne! How perfectly scandalous of you. No wonder you've become so accomplished at mysterious allure!"

"Eliza!" Margaret gasped, though she couldn't help the smile that tugged at her lips. "You're absolutely dreadful!"

"I'm realistic," Eliza corrected, though her eyes danced with mirth. "And I'm also rather impressed. It takes considerable skill to capture a duke's attention so completely whilst appearing utterly indifferent to his very existence." The praise should have filled Margaret with a sense of triumph, but instead it left her feeling hollow. Yes, she had captured the Duke of Ashcombe's attention. Yes, Julian's lessons were working exactly as promised. But every moment she spent charming the duke still felt like a betrayal of something precious and fragile that had bloomed between herself and Julian in that shadowed library.

"Mama! Mama!" A small voice interrupted her, and Margaret looked up to see Eliza's son, Edward, toddling towards them with a suspicious smudge on his left cheek.

"Good heavens, Edward!" Eliza laughed, scooping the boy up. "What on earth have you been getting into?"

"Cook gave me cake," Edward announced proudly, displaying sticky fingers as evidence. "Lots of it!"

"I can see that," Eliza said dryly, producing a handkerchief. "And I suspect Cook will be hearing from your father about this later."

Margaret found herself distracted, her thoughts spinning with dangerous possibilities that had nothing to do with dukes and everything to do with grey eyes and stolen kisses.

"Margaret?" Eliza's voice seemed to come from very far away. "Are you quite all right?"

"Oh, I'm fine!" Margaret said quickly, though she felt anything but. "Simply... the heat."

"It's barely past ten o'clock," Eliza observed, but before she could press further, Edward squirmed off her lap and began toddling towards the rose bushes.

"Oh no, you don't, little dove," Eliza said, rising swiftly to chase after her son. "Edward Thomas Ashbourne, you know perfectly well that roses have thorns!"

"There," Eliza said, returning with Edward firmly in hand. "Crisis averted. Though I suspect we should retreat indoors before he discovers something even more dangerous to investigate."

"Yes," Margaret agreed, rising on slightly unsteady legs. "Perhaps we should."

Later that afternoon, Margaret found herself walking the gardens of Ashbourne Hall beside the Duke of Ashcombe, her hand resting lightly on his arm.

"You look particularly lovely today, Miss Fairbourne," the duke said, his voice carrying that smooth charm that had captivated so many ladies before. "That shade of rose becomes you admirably."

"You are too kind, Your Grace," Margaret replied, deploying a gracious smile—warm enough to encourage, mysterious enough to intrigue. "Though I confess I chose this particular gown more for comfort than fashion. These gardens are so wonderfully extensive that I feared I might need the freedom of movement. I could walk here for hours!"

The duke smiled. "How refreshingly honest of you. Most ladies would have credited their modiste or claimed the gown was a family heirloom of particular sentimental value."

"Would they really?" Margaret tilted her head in the way she'd been coached to do, as though this transformation was both surprisingly and faintly amusing. "How very curious! I confess I've never quite understood the appeal of elaborate fabrications when the truth is so much simpler."

"Indeed." His fingers tightened slightly over hers where her hand rested upon his arm, the pressure noticeable even through layers of fabric. "I find your candour most... refreshing, Miss Fairbourne."

"Your Grace..." she began, then paused as a figure approached them along the garden path with urgent purpose.

The man was gaunt as a winter tree with uneven teeth, the colour of old parchment and tobacco, and worn gloves that marked him as decidedly not of their social sphere. He moved with the sort of coiled urgency that suggested business rather than pleasure, his eyes darting about like a cornered animal's.

"Your Grace," the man said, his voice low and rough as gravel. "A word, if you please. Most urgent, it is."

The transformation in the duke was immediate and startling, like watching a mask slip from a face. The warmth vanished from his countenance as though someone had doused a flame with ice water. His posture shifted, becoming somehow more predatory, more calculating. This was not the charming gentleman who had been flattering her moments before—this was something altogether more dangerous.

"Now?" His voice carried an edge sharp enough to cut glass, making Margaret's skin prickle with sudden unease.

"Yes, Your Grace. The matter can't wait. There's been... developments."

The duke's jaw tightened until the muscles stood out like cords. "Miss Fairbourne," he said, turning back to her with considerable effort at maintaining his pleasant demeanour. "I'm afraid I must cut our walk short. A pressing matter requires my immediate attention."

"Oh! Of course, Your Grace," Margaret replied, though confusion swirled through her. "I quite understand."

Without another word, the duke strode away with the stranger, leaving Margaret standing alone and confused amongst the roses.

That evening, Margaret made her way through the shadowed garden paths to Julian's townhouse.

She found Julian in his study, coat discarded and sleeves rolled up as he worked by lamplight. The sight of his forearms, strong and elegant beneath the white linen, made something low in her belly tighten with want.

"You're back," he observed without looking up from his papers, though she caught the slight smile that tugged at his lips.

"I need another lesson," she said, surprised by the breathless quality of her own voice. "Something more... advanced."

That captured his attention entirely. He set down his pen with deliberate care and turned to face her fully, grey eyes sharp with something that might have been concern—or perhaps desire. "Advanced?"

"Touch," she said, the word emerging softer than she'd intended, barely more than a whisper. "You've taught me conversation, taught me how to listen, how to intrigue. But surely there's more to attraction than words alone?"

Julian was quiet for a long moment, studying her face with an intensity that made her pulse quicken. "Touch is dangerous territory, Margaret."

"I'm not some fragile flower that wilts at the first sign of heat," she replied, lifting her chin with determination. "I need to know everything if I'm to succeed with the duke."

"Very well." He rose from his chair with fluid grace, moving towards her until he stood close enough that she could feel the heat radiating from his body. "Give me your hand."

She extended her gloved hand, and he took it gently, his fingers warm. "The first rule of touch," he said, his voice dropping to that low register that made her skin prickle with awareness, "is that less is always more. A woman who touches too freely appears desperate, hunting for attention. But one who withholds... she becomes irresistible as forbidden fruit."

He demonstrated, placing her hand just so upon his arm, showing her how to let her fingers rest with apparent casualness whilst applying the slightest pressure. "Like this. Light enough to seem accidental."

"I see," she whispered, though her voice sounded strange to her own ears, like it belonged to someone else entirely.

"But the real power," Julian continued, his eyes holding hers captive, "lies in skin against skin. The shock of it, the intimacy that cannot be denied."

Before she could respond, his fingers found the tiny pearl buttons of her glove with the precision of a musician tuning an instrument. He unfastened them slowly, deliberately, each small motion sending sparks of electricity racing up her arm. When he peeled the silk away from her fingers, the sensation of cool air against her bare skin made her gasp as though she'd been submerged in cold water.

"There," he murmured, taking her now-naked hand in his. The contrast was overwhelming—his skin warm and slightly rough, entirely masculine in a way that made her knees weak. "Do you feel the difference?"

She did. Oh, how she did. When his thumb traced across her knuckles with reverent care, she bit back a whimper that threatened to escape.

"This," he said, guiding her hand to rest against his waistcoat, "is how you capture a man's complete attention. Not through grand gestures or obvious displays but through moments like this. Small touches that linger just long enough to be memorable, to haunt his dreams."

His voice was doing something to her insides, turning them molten and liquid like honey heated by the sun. She could feel his heartbeat beneath her palm, strong and steady as a drum, and the realisation that she affected him too made her bold as brass.

"Show me more," she whispered, the words slipping out before her rational mind could stop them.

Something flashed in his eyes. His fingers trailed from her wrist to her palm with touches light as butterfly wings, mapping the sensitive skin with the devotion of an explorer charting new territory. When he reached the inside of her elbow, tracing the delicate hollow there with his fingertip, she couldn't suppress the soft sound that escaped her lips.

"Here," he murmured, his breath warm against her ear as he guided her touch along his chest, over the fine wool of his waistcoat. "And here. These are the places that drive a man to distraction."

Margaret's breathing had become shallow, her heart racing like a wild thing trapped in her chest. The air between them had thickened until it felt charged with electricity, dangerous and intoxicating as opium smoke.

His hands guided hers lower, to rest against the solid wall of his chest, and she could feel the heat of him through the layers of fabric that separated them. When he covered her hand with his own, pressing it more firmly against him, she felt his heart racing beneath her palm—proof that this lesson affected him as much as it did her.

"Margaret." Her name on his lips was barely a whisper, rough with something that sounded suspiciously like need, like hunger barely held in check.

She looked up to find his eyes dark with desire, his usual smugness nowhere to be found. This was Julian stripped bare of pretence.

"That's quite enough for tonight," he said, his voice once again cool and controlled, though she caught the slight tremor beneath the words.

Margaret stared at him, dazed and aching with wants she couldn't name, couldn't understand.

"Yes," she managed, though her voice sounded foreign to her own ears. "Quite enough."

But as she turned to leave, pulling her glove back on with trembling fingers, one thought echoed through her mind with crystalline clarity:

This was becoming far too dangerous indeed.

Chapter Eight

"You've made quite the mess of things, haven't you?"

Julian didn't turn from where he stood at the window of his study, though he recognised the familiar tread of boots on Turkish carpet and the particular tone Rhys employed when delivering unwelcome truths. His reflection in the glass looked like a stranger—dishevelled hair, loosened cravat, the unmistakable signs of a man who'd lost a battle with his own restraint.

"Ah, my dear cousin, what a delightfully dramatic entrance," Julian replied, finally turning to face the Duke of Kingswell with what he hoped resembled his usual sardonic composure. "I trust Eliza is well? Young Edward thriving in his domestic bliss? How utterly charming to witness London's most notorious rake transformed into such a devoted paterfamilias. Truly, it warms the very cockles of my cynical heart."

Rhys's grey eyes, so like his own, yet infinitely colder when displeased, fixed upon him with surgical precision. "Don't."

"Don't what, precisely? Marvel at the miraculous transformation of my illustrious cousin from scandalous libertine to respectable family man?" Julian reached for his brandy decanter with movements that suggested perfect equanimity, though his hand trembled slightly as he poured.

"Don't deflect with your stagey nonsense," Rhys said as he stepped further into the room, his presence commanding attention despite his deliberately understated attire. "This is about whatever you have been up to with Margaret."

Julian took a measured sip of brandy, allowing the burn to steady his nerves before replying. "Margaret came to me seeking advice regarding a certain delicate matter of courtship.

Nothing more scandalous than the sort of guidance one might expect, I'm afraid."

"Julian." The single word carried the weight of years of friendship, of shared secrets and mutual understanding. "I've known your ways since we were mere boys stealing apples from the vicar's orchard. You cannot dissemble with me as easily as you do with the rest of the world."

Rhys's accusation hung between them like smoke from a spent pistol. Julian set down his glass with deliberate care, his customary dramatic armour deserting him entirely. In its absence, something far more dangerous emerged—the truth.

"Very well," he said quietly. "She asked me to teach her the delicate arts of attraction. It seems the young lady has developed a rather pronounced attachment for the Duke of Ashcombe and wishes to secure his suit before the season's end."

Rhys's expression darkened considerably. "Nathaniel Strickland? That bastard's been sniffing around half the windows in London, and you thought it wise to—"

"To what, precisely? To assist an innocent young woman in navigating the treacherous waters of courtship? To ensure she possesses the necessary skills to attract the husband she desires?" Julian interrupted, his voice gaining an edge. "Forgive me, but I fail to see the sin in such magnanimous assistance."

"The sin," Rhys said with deadly quiet, "lies in whatever the devil just occurred between you and that girl. Because I've seen that look before, Julian. I wore it myself when I was falling in love with Eliza."

The words hit Julian like a cavalry charge, scattering his defences and leaving him exposed. Love. The most terrifying word in the English language, the one emotion he'd built his entire adult life around avoiding. Yet here he was, caught in its snare like some green boy who'd never learned that hearts were meant to be guarded, not given away to golden-haired innocents with eyes like summer skies.

"You mistake the matter entirely, my dear cousin," Julian said, though the protest sounded hollow even to his own ears. "Margaret is a charming child, nothing more. Any... intensity you observe is merely the natural result of providing instruction in matters requiring a certain degree of... intimate demonstration."

"Christ, Julian, listen to yourself." Rhys moved to the fireplace, his hands clasped behind his back in that familiar gesture that betrayed his growing agitation. "She's not some sophisticated widow playing at seduction. She's Margaret Fairbourne—romantic, trusting, innocent as the day is long. Do you have any conception of what it is you're risking? What you're asking her to risk?"

"She wants Strickland," Julian said, though the words felt like ground glass in his throat. "I'm merely providing the means to achieve her romantic aspirations."

"Are you?" Rhys turned to face him fully, his expression a concoction of concern and barely restrained anger. "Because from where I stand, it appears you're the one doing the desiring. And that, my dear cousin, is a complication neither of you can afford."

Julian laughed, though the sound held no humour. "You speak as though I harbour some sort of... romantic ambitions towards her. I assure you, cousin, I'm perfectly aware of my limitations. Margaret requires a husband of rank, fortune, and impeccable reputation. I possess none of those rather essential qualifications."

The truth of it settled in his stomach like a stone. No title. No estate. No prospects beyond his legal work, however lucrative it might be. The duke could give her everything Julian could not. The fact that Strickland might not be deserving of her was beside the point.

"Don't you dare," Rhys said with quiet fury. "Don't hide behind that self-deprecating charm when we both know—"

"When we both know what, precisely? That I'm a second son with neither title nor estate to my name? That I've built my entire reputation on my God-given ability to navigate other men's scandals whilst carefully avoiding any serious attachments of my own? That I'm precisely the sort of man a father like Lord Fairbourne would never countenance as a suitor for his youngest daughter?"

The silence that followed was deafening. Rhys studied him with an expression that was part sympathy, part exasperation.

"You bloody fool," Rhys said finally. "Do you truly believe title and fortune are all that matter? Eliza chose me when I was nothing but a bitter, broken man with more ghosts than prospects. Love doesn't require—"

"Love is a luxury I cannot afford," Julian interrupted harshly. "And neither can she. Margaret deserves better than a man who can offer her nothing but scandal and heartbreak. She deserves a future worthy of her sweetness, her trust, her... her absolute belief in happy endings."

"And you honestly believe Strickland can provide that?"

Julian's jaw tightened. "He can provide what I cannot. Security. Position. A life free from the sort of compromises that would inevitably arise from an association with a man of my... circumstances."

Rhys was quiet for a long moment, his gaze never leaving Julian's face. When he finally spoke, his voice carried the weight of genuine concern.

"Margaret Fairbourne has more strength than you credit her with. But she's also romantic enough to believe in love conquering all, and that makes her dangerous to a man like you."

"What's that supposed to mean?"

"It means," Rhys said with brutal honesty, "that she'll fall in love with you if you're not careful. Completely, utterly, without reservation. And when she does, she'll expect you to love her back with the same wholehearted devotion. Can you do that, Julian? Can you love her enough to let her choose you over everything her world tells her she should want?"

"The lessons will continue as planned," Julian said finally, his voice steady despite the chaos in his chest. "She will secure her duke, and we shall all continue on with our lives—she happily ever after, and me, well..." He took another sip of his brandy. "Isn't that how these tales are supposed to end?"

Rhys studied him for another moment longer, then shook his head. "Not all of them, cousin. Some of them end with everyone getting exactly what they thought they wanted, only to discover it was never what they needed at all."

With that cryptic observation, Rhys departed, leaving Julian alone with his brandy and his decidedly unwelcome revelations.

An hour later, Julian found himself walking the darkened streets of Mayfair, his thoughts as knotted and tangled as the shadows cast by flickering lamplight. He'd told Rhys the truth: The lessons would continue, Margaret would win over her duke, and he would resume his carefully constructed life of emotional detachment.

The only problem was that somewhere between teaching her the art of conversation and showing her the power of touch, he'd forgotten how to want anyone else.

He was so lost in these disturbing reflections that he almost missed the figure emerging from the shadows near Lady Lyndmere's residence. Almost, but not quite. Years of moving through London's more questionable districts had honed his instincts to a razor's edge, and something about the man's furtive movements set every alarm bell in his head in motion.

Julian pressed himself deeper into the doorway of a neighbouring townhouse, grateful for the concealing darkness as he watched the figure step into the pool of light beneath a streetlamp.

The Duke of Ashcombe, Nathaniel Strickland himself.

Julian's blood turned to ice in his veins. Here was the man Margaret was so determined to marry, skulking through the shadows like a common criminal. Every instinct Julian possessed—legal, personal, protective—screamed that something was very, very wrong with this picture.

He paused at the corner, his head turning left and right in the manner of a man ensuring he hadn't been observed. Even from this distance, Julian could see the tension in his shoulders, the way his gloved hands clenched and unclenched at his sides.

The man's very behaviour screamed of secrets—and dark ones at that, if Julian's experience with London's underbelly was any guide.

After what felt like an eternity, Strickland set off towards his own residence, his pace brisk and purposeful. Julian waited until the duke had disappeared around the corner before emerging from his hiding place, his mind racing with implications.

Lady Lyndmere was a recent widow, young and quite lovely, with a reputation for discretion that made her a favourite among gentlemen seeking uncomplicated companionship. There was nothing particularly scandalous about a duke paying a social call, even at this late hour.

Yet something about Strickland's behaviour troubled Julian deeply. The furtiveness, the obvious anxiety, the way he'd emerged from the servant's entrance rather than the front door—it all suggested something rather more complex than a simple romantic liaison.

As Julian made his way back home through the quiet streets, one thought echoed through his mind with uncomfortable clarity: Margaret Fairbourne deserved to know exactly what sort of man she was so determined to marry.

The stakes, he realised with crystalline clarity, had just been raised beyond anything he could have imagined. This was no longer simply a matter of his own heart or even Margaret's happiness. If Strickland was indeed involved in something sinister, then Margaret wasn't just risking her heart—she might be risking her very life.

And Julian would be damned if he'd stand by and let that happen, no matter what it cost him personally.

Chapter Nine

"We seek discretion, Mr. Ashcroft, and your reputation suggests you understand the value of both silence and justice."

Julian looked up from his morning correspondence to find two figures standing in the doorway of his private study at his Mayfair residence, both cloaked in black silk and wearing veils thick enough to obscure a multitude of sins. The taller of the two spoke with the refined cadence of quality, though her voice carried an undercurrent of desperation that set his legal instincts humming.

"How utterly dramatic of you both—quite the tableau you present," Julian observed, setting down his quill with deliberate care. "Though I confess myself positively fascinated as to how you managed entry to my private sanctuary."

The shorter of the two women stepped forward, her movement betraying a familiar grace. "Your housekeeper was… persuaded that our matter required immediate attention. We apologise for the irregular hour."

"Ladies who require veils and clandestine visits rarely trouble themselves with such conventional courtesies as apologies," Julian replied, rising to gesture towards the chairs before his desk with a flourish. "Though I find myself professionally intrigued by this delightful air of mystery. Pray, be seated and enlighten me as to the nature of your presumably scandalous difficulties."

"We find ourselves at the mercy of a blackmailer," the taller woman said without preamble, her directness cutting through the air like a blade. "By a gentleman with whom we have both… maintained private associations."

"Might I enquire as to the precise nature of these associations? The details, whilst potentially indelicate, are rather crucial to determining the most advantageous course of action."

The women exchanged glances, a conversation conducted entirely in silence before the shorter woman spoke. "We are both widows, Mr. Ashcroft. We have certain... freedoms that unmarried ladies cannot enjoy, and we exercised those freedoms with discretion we believed was mutual."

"Ah." Julian leaned back in his chair, his fingers steepled as understanding began to dawn. "And I assume the gentleman in question has decided that discretion is a commodity to be bought and sold, rather than a courtesy freely given."

"Precisely." The taller woman's voice hardened. "He demands money, property, even family heirlooms. The sums grow ever larger and the threats more explicit. Should we refuse, he promises to make our... indiscretions known to the ton, complete with intimate details that would destroy our reputations entirely."

"You mentioned that others share your predicament?"

"Several," the shorter woman confirmed. "All widows of means, all vulnerable to precisely this sort of manipulation. He chooses his targets with considerable care—women wealthy enough to pay, independent enough to have compromised themselves, and proud enough to prefer financial ruin to public scandal."

"This gentleman—does he perhaps employ others to gather intelligence about his potential victims? Servants, perhaps, or individuals with access to society gossip? Information brokers of the more... unsavoury variety?"

Both women started visibly at the question, their surprise confirming Julian's growing suspicions.

"How could you possibly know that?" the taller woman breathed.

"Because, my dear ladies, I have made it my particular specialty to understand how gentlemen of questionable moral character conduct their affairs," Julian replied smoothly.

"You will help us then?" the shorter woman asked, hope bleeding through her carefully maintained composure.

"I shall consider it most seriously," Julian said carefully. "However, I must insist on considerably more information than you have thus far provided. Names, specific demands, proof of communication—anything you possess that might substantiate your rather grim allegations."

"And if we cannot provide such proof?"

Julian's smile was sharp as winter frost. "Then I suggest you find a way to obtain it with all due haste, because without evidence, you have merely expensive grievances rather than actionable claims. I deal in facts, ladies—not feelings, regardless of how justified those feelings might be."

The women rose to leave, but as they reached the door, Julian's voice stopped them.

"Ladies? This gentleman in question—might he be a person of considerable rank and influence? Someone whose word could carry significant weight against your own in any public dispute?"

The shorter woman's veil trembled with what might have been either fear or rage. "He is, Mr. Ashcroft. Which is precisely why we need your particular... expertise in these matters."

After they departed, Julian stood at his window, watching their carriage disappear into the mist. His mind returned inevitably to the previous evening, to the furtive figure he'd observed exiting Lady Lyndmere's residence under the cover of darkness. The Duke of Ashcombe, moving with the careful precision of a man accustomed to avoiding inconvenient observations.

Julian was still contemplating the implications of this when his study door burst open. Margaret Fairbourne stood in the doorway, her cheeks flushed with exertion and her eyes bright with something that might have been panic.

"Oh! Julian! Thank goodness you're here!" she gasped, pressing one hand to her chest as she struggled to catch her breath, the words tumbling out in a rush. "I require your assistance immediately! There's been the most absolutely dreadful development!"

"Good morning to you as well, my dear Margaret," Julian replied. "Though I confess myself utterly captivated as to what calamity has driven you to such dramatic extremes this morning."

"Oh, this is no time for jests!" Margaret's voice carried an edge of desperation that sobered Julian immediately, her words spilling forth like water through a broken dam. "There's another woman—a debutante—and she's absolutely everything I'm not! She's practically throwing herself at the duke's feet, and he appears to find her absolutely fascinating!"

Julian felt something twist in his chest at the genuine distress in her voice. "Ah. Competition has appeared."

"Oh, it's so much more than competition!" Margaret exclaimed, beginning to pace the length of his study. "She's sophisticated and worldly and utterly confident in her own appeal! Only yesterday, I witnessed her discussing philosophy with him for nearly an hour! Philosophy! Can you imagine? I can barely manage to discuss the weather without stumbling over my own words!"

"Philosophy? How... intellectually stimulating of Strickland. I'm absolutely certain he was positively riveted by her profound thoughts on Aristotelian ethics and the sublime nature of mortal virtue."

"Oh, you're mocking me!" Margaret accused, though there was more hurt than anger in her voice, her words coming in shorter, more emotional bursts. "And I don't understand why! I thought... I thought you wanted to help me!"

"Never would I mock you, my dear girl," Julian replied, though his tone suggested otherwise.

"Oh," she said quietly, her enthusiasm deflating like a punctured balloon. "I see. You think me foolish."

"Forgive me, my dear," he said more gently. "You came seeking assistance. What would you have me do?"

"I need the ultimate lesson!" Margaret exclaimed, her chin lifting with determination, her words tumbling forth once more. "Something that will make me absolutely unforgettable. Oh, Julian, I simply cannot bear the thought of losing him when I've worked so terribly hard."

"The ultimate lesson," he replied carefully. "And what, precisely, do you imagine such comprehensive instruction might entail?"

"Oh, I don't know." Margaret's composure finally cracked entirely, her voice rising in that breathless way that always betrayed her deepest emotions. "But *you* do, and that's precisely why I need you! Oh, Julian, you said yourself that words are only part of attraction! I need to know how to... to use proximity, how to make him feel what I feel when you..." She trailed off, her cheeks now scarlet, gasping softly at her own boldness.

The unfinished sentence hung between them like a loaded pistol, dangerous and impossible to ignore. "Margaret," he said, his voice rougher than he'd intended. "Such lessons venture into territory that—"

"Oh, I don't care about anything but this!" she interrupted him, her words tumbling out in that familiar rush of determination. "Please, Julian, I'm absolutely begging you! Show me how to dance with him so that he'll think of nothing else! Teach me how to move, to touch, to… to make him want me the way…" Again, she faltered, but this time, her meaning was crystal clear.

"Very well, my dear girl," he said quietly. "But understand that such instruction requires considerable…physical proximity. Are you prepared for the rather intimate implications of that?"

Margaret's nod was almost imperceptible, but her eyes held his with steady determination. "Oh, yes! I'm prepared for whatever is necessary."

Julian moved from behind his desk with predatory grace, his usual polished demeanour giving way to something far more dangerous. "Then we shall begin with the fundamental principles of controlled intimacy. Give me your hand."

She extended her gloved hand without hesitation, and Julian took it gently, drawing her towards the centre of the room where a Turkish carpet provided a softer footing.

"The art of seductive dancing, my dear Margaret," he murmured, positioning her before, "lies not in grand gestures but in subtle communications. The brush of fingertips, the alignment of bodies, the whisper of silk against wool."

He placed one hand at her waist, the other keeping hold of her fingers as he guided her into the opening of a waltz. Even through the layers of fabric that separated them, he could feel the warmth of her skin, the rapid flutter of her pulse at her wrist.

"Now the secret lies in the spaces between the steps," he said, his voice dropping to that intimate register that made her breath catch. "The moments when propriety demands distance but desire insists on closeness."

He demonstrated, drawing her incrementally nearer with each turn until her skirts brushed against his legs and he could smell the honeysuckle soap she favoured. Margaret followed his lead with natural grace, her body responding to his guidance as though they'd danced together a thousand times.

"Oh! Like this?" she whispered, allowing her free hand to rest against his chest, her fingers spreading over the fine wool of his coat.

"Precisely, my dear," Julian managed, though his voice sounded strained to even his own ears. "And here—when the music swells, you allow yourself to lean into your partner, just enough to make him acutely aware of your warmth."

Margaret complied, pressing closer until Julian could feel the soft curve of her breasts against his chest. The sensation sent fire racing through his veins, pooling low in his belly with dangerous intensity.

"Oh, Julian," she breathed, looking up at him with eyes dark with dawning awareness. "I can feel... that is... you seem to be..."

"Aroused? Yes, my dear Margaret. That tends to be the inevitable result of holding a beautiful woman in one's arms whilst demonstrating the finer points of seduction."

Instead of pulling away as propriety demanded, Margaret pressed closer... her lips parting in unconscious invitation. "Oh! Good," she whispered. "Then it's working."

Julian's control was shattered completely.

His mouth claimed hers with a hunger that had been building for weeks, all careful restraint abandoned in favour of raw need. Margaret responded with matching passion, her hands fisting in his hair as she kissed him back with an innocent enthusiasm that nearly drove him to his knees.

They stumbled backwards together, Julian's hands roaming over the curves of her body as papers scattered from his desk and ink spilled across forgotten correspondence. Margaret's soft moans filled the air between them, sweet as honey and twice as intoxicating.

When they finally broke apart, both breathing hard, Julian realised they'd crossed a line from which there would be no graceful retreat.

"That, my dear girl," he said with what remained of his composure, "was decidedly not part of the lesson plan."

Margaret's smile was radiant with triumph and something else—something that looked remarkably like love.

"Oh no," she agreed softly. "But it was rather more educational than anything you could have taught me about dancing."

As Julian stared into her luminous eyes, one thought echoed through his mind with perfect, terrifying clarity: He was utterly, completely, and irrevocably lost.

Chapter Ten

"That was..." Margaret whispered, her hands still tangled in Julian's hair as she gazed up at him with wonder. "Oh, Julian! That was absolutely..."

"Utterly inadvisable," Julian finished, though his voice lacked conviction. His grey eyes were dark with lingering desire, and despite his choice of words, his hands remained at her waist as though he couldn't quite bring himself to let go of her.

"But... it felt so right," Margaret breathed, her cheeks flushed, bearing the evidence of their kiss. "Did it not feel... right to you?"

Julian's expression shifted, desire warring with something that looked suspiciously like regret. "Margaret," he said, her name rough on his tongue as his hands finally dropped from her waist. "We cannot... This is not..."

"Oh, but we can," she breathed, pressing closer until she could feel the heat of his body through the layers of fabric that lay between them. "We are, Julian. Right now, we are."

The kiss that followed was desperate, hungry, all careful control abandoned in favour of raw need. Margaret had never imagined that such fire could exist, that her body could respond with such immediate, overwhelming want. When Julian's mouth left hers to trail heated kisses down her throat, she gasped, her head falling back in unconscious invitation.

"You taste like sunshine," he murmured against her skin, his voice carrying that same dramatic quality even in moments of passion. "Like everything innocent and perfect in this utterly mad world."

His hands moved with reverent care, tracing the line of her collarbone through the thin silk of her gown. When his fingers found the small pearl buttons at her neckline, Margaret's breath caught, but she made no move to stop him.

"Tell me to stop, Margaret," Julian said, his fingers hesitating on the first button. "Tell me this is utter madness, that we are courting absolute disaster."

"Oh, but I don't want you to stop! I don't want you to ever stop!" Margaret replied, her voice barely above a whisper. "I've never wanted anything more in my entire life."

With careful deliberation, he unfastened the buttons, his knuckles brushing against her skin as he worked. The silk whispered as it fell away from her shoulders, leaving her chemise as the only barrier between them.

Margaret had never been so exposed before, had never felt so simultaneously vulnerable and powerful. The way Julian looked at her—as though she were something precious and rare—made her feel beautiful.

"You're utterly exquisite, my dear," he breathed, his hands ghosting over the delicate fabric that covered her breasts. "More beautiful than anything my imagination could have ever conjured."

When his mouth found the sensitive hollow at the base of her throat, Margaret gasped, her hands clutching at his shoulders for support against the overwhelming sensations.

"Oh!" she exclaimed as he pressed a kiss to the swell of her breast above the neckline of her chemise. "Julian, I... oh, that feels..."

"What does it feel like?" he asked, his voice low and intimate. "Tell me, Margaret. I want to know absolutely everything."

"Like fire...like the most wonderful fire..." she managed, her words coming in breathless rushes. "Like I'm burning from the inside out. Like I never want this feeling to end. Never ever!"

His response was to lower his head further, pressing reverent kisses to the soft curves revealed by her chemise. When his mouth found the pink peak of her breast through the thin fabric, Margaret cried out, her body arching involuntarily towards him.

"Beautiful," Julian murmured against her skin, his breath warm through the delicate fabric. "So utterly beautiful, so responsive. You undo me completely."

His hands found the ribbons of her chemise, and with gentle care, he loosened them until the fabric fell away from her breasts entirely. Margaret gasped at the sensation of cool air against her heated skin, but before embarrassment could take hold, Julian's mouth was there, warm and reverent and absolutely perfect.

The feeling of his lips against her bare skin was electric, sending sparks of pleasure racing through her entire body. She could hear herself making soft, desperate sounds, but she was beyond caring about propriety or modesty. All that mattered was this moment, this man, this incredible feeling of being alive and desired and completely, utterly lost.

When Julian's tongue traced lazy circles around her nipple, Margaret nearly sobbed with the intensity of it. Her hands tangled in his dark hair, holding him to her as though he might disappear if she loosened her grip.

Julian's mouth lavished attention on her sensitive flesh, alternating between gentle suckling and teasing flicks of his tongue that made her arch helplessly against him. His hands cupped her breasts reverently, his thumbs brushing over her pink nipples in a rhythm that matched the movements of his mouth. When he drew one peak into his mouth, applying gentle suction whilst his tongue swirled around the sensitive tip, Margaret cried out, her entire body trembling with sensation.

"Oh, oh!"

"So perfect," he murmured against her skin, his breath warm and intoxicating. His attention then shifted to her other breast, lavishing the same devoted care whilst his hand continued to caress the dampened peak he'd just abandoned. The dual sensations made Margaret feel as though she might shatter from pure pleasure.

"Ah... Julian!"

Her hands roamed restlessly over his shoulders and back, desperate to feel more of him, to somehow express the overwhelming sensations coursing through her. When he gently grazed her nipple with his teeth before soothing it again with his tongue, she gasped his name like a prayer.

"Please... oh, please!" she whispered, though she wasn't entirely certain what she was asking for. "Please Julian, I need..."

"What do you need, my darling girl?" he asked, lifting his head to look at her with eyes dark as storm clouds. "Tell me precisely what you want."

"I want... oh... I want everything... absolutely everything!" she confessed, her cheeks burning with equal parts desire and embarrassment. "I want you to touch me everywhere! I want to know what it feels like to be completely yours."

His mouth claimed hers with desperate hunger whilst his hands roamed over her exposed skin with growing urgency. Margaret responded with matching passion, her body pressing against his as though she could merge with him entirely.

A LADY'S LESSONS IN SIN

But just as the fire between them began to reach its peak, Julian suddenly pulled away, his breathing harsh and uneven. He stood abruptly, turning his back to her as he struggled to regain his composure.

"No," he said, his voice strained. "This is... We cannot... I cannot do this to you."

Margaret stared at him in confusion, her body still aching with unfulfilled need. She could see the tension in his shoulders, could hear the regret in his voice, and it cut her more deeply than any physical wound could have.

"Oh," she whispered, a soft sound of disappointment that seemed to affect him more powerfully than any argument might have.

"You should go," he said quietly, not turning around. "Before we both do something we'll regret."

Margaret fumbled with her chemise and gown, her fingers shaking as she tried to restore her appearance to some semblance of propriety.

"Julian..." she tried, but he held up a hand to stop her.

"Please," he said, and there was something almost broken in his voice. "Just...please go."

With tears stinging her eyes, Margaret gathered what remained of her dignity and slipped from the room, her heart pounding with a combination of desire, confusion, and something that felt dangerously close to heartbreak.

The walk home through the darkened streets felt interminable, every shadow seeming to mock her for her foolishness. She was well aware of the dangers of walking alone, especially at night, but at that particular moment, she did not care. What had she been thinking? Julian Ashcroft was sophisticated, experienced, and entirely beyond her reach. She was nothing more than a foolish girl playing at games she didn't understand.

But even as she tried to convince herself that what had happened meant nothing, she could still feel the phantom touch of his hands on her skin, could still taste him on her lips. The memory of his reverent whispers, of the way he'd looked at her as though she was something precious, refused to be dismissed so easily.

By the time she reached Fairbourne House, Margaret had come to a decision. She needed to focus on her original goal—securing the Duke of Ashcombe's proposal. Julian had made it clear that whatever was between them could lead nowhere, so she would have to content herself with the life she'd originally planned.

**

The next afternoon found her in the morning room, carefully composing invitations for an intimate gathering. If she were to capture the duke's attention definitively, she needed to create the perfect opportunity—somewhere she could shine without the distraction of dozens of other eligible ladies vying for his notice.

She was deep in thought, her quill poised over cream-coloured parchment, when Catharine appeared in the doorway. Her eldest sister moved with that particular measured grace that had always marked her as the most composed of the Fairbourne daughters, but there was something sharp in her green eyes that suggested she'd noticed more than Margaret might wish.

"How remarkably industrious you appear this afternoon, sister dearest," Catharine observed, settling herself in the chair opposite Margaret's writing desk. "Might I enquire as to the nature of your correspondence?"

"Oh! I'm just planning a small gathering," Margaret replied, trying to keep her voice light and casual. "Nothing elaborate—just a few intimate friends for dinner and perhaps some dancing afterward. Won't it be lovely?"

Catharine's eyebrows rose. "How unexpectedly... enterprising of you. Has something occurred to prompt this sudden interest in domestic entertainment?"

Margaret could feel heat rising in her cheeks, but she forced herself to maintain an expression of innocent purpose. "Oh, well, I simply thought it might be pleasant. The season is progressing so quickly, and I haven't had many opportunities to... to strengthen certain... acquaintances."

"Certain acquaintances," Catharine echoed, her tone suggesting she heard far more in those words than Margaret had intended to convey. "Would these acquaintances perchance include any gentlemen of particular significance?"

"Oh, perhaps!" Margaret admitted, unable to quite meet her sister's penetrating gaze. "I thought I might extend an invitation to the Duke of Ashcombe, if he's available. It would be lovely to become better acquainted with him in a more... intimate setting."

"Indeed." Catharine leaned back in her chair. "And what, pray tell, has brought about this sudden urgency to cultivate His Grace's acquaintance? One might almost suppose you were in some sort of... haste."

Margaret's quill nearly slipped from her fingers, but she managed to maintain her composure. "Oh, I wouldn't say there's any urgency, exactly. I simply think... that is, with the season advancing as it is, it seems prudent to be more decisive about one's... one's romantic preferences."

"Your romantic preferences." Catharine's voice carried that particular note of concern that suggested she suspected there was more to the story than Margaret was revealing. "Margaret, dearest, you seem rather... unsettled lately. Is there something troubling you? Something you perhaps need to discuss with someone who has your best interests at heart?"

For a moment, Margaret was tempted to confess everything—the lessons with Julian, the confusing feelings wreaking havoc inside her, the way her carefully laid plans seemed to be crumbling around her... but how could she possibly explain what she didn't quite understand herself?

"Oh no, Catharine, I'm perfectly well!" she said instead, her words tumbling out in that telltale rush that always betrayed her agitation. "Simply excited about the gathering, that's all. I want everything to be absolutely perfect."

Catharine continued to study her for a long moment, her expression suggesting she wasn't entirely convinced by Margaret's protestations. But finally, she nodded, though concern still lingered in her eyes.

"Very well. But Margaret... should you find yourself in need of guidance, you know you can always come to me. Or Eliza. We're your sisters, after all. Our loyalty to you supersedes all other considerations."

After Catharine departed, Margaret sat alone with her invitations, her heart heavy with the weight of secrets she could not share. She needed to forget Julian Ashcroft and his intoxicating kisses, needed to focus on securing her future with a man who could offer her everything she'd originally wanted.

But as she wrote the Duke of Ashcombe's name on the elegant card, one thought echoed in her mind with uncomfortable persistence:

What if everything she'd thought she wanted was no longer what her heart desired at all?

Chapter Eleven

"Your Grace dances with such remarkable skill," Margaret managed, though the words felt leaden upon her tongue as the Duke of Ashcombe guided her through the familiar steps of a waltz in the drawing room of Fairbourne House.

The gathering had unfolded exactly as she'd envisioned—elegant, intimate, carefully orchestrated to showcase her domestic accomplishments. The other guests moved about the edges of the room, their conversations creating a gentle murmur that should have felt romantic and sophisticated.

Instead, Margaret felt as though she were suffocating.

"And you, Miss Fairbourne, move with such... natural grace," the duke replied, his fingers tightening possessively at her waist. "One might even say you were born to be led."

There was something in his tone that made Margaret's skin crawl, though she couldn't quite identify why. Perhaps it was the way his eyes lingered too long on the modest neckline of her evening gown or how his hand seemed to drift lower on her back—more than propriety should allow. She forced herself to smile, to lean into him the way Julian had taught her, to deploy all the techniques that had seemed so thrilling in the sanctuary of Julian's study.

But where Julian's touch had ignited fire beneath her skin, the duke's contact felt cold, invasive, and utterly wrong. His palm was damp against her glove, and when he drew her closer during a turn, she caught the scent of something sharp and unpleasant beneath his cologne—something that reminded her of the sort of spirits her father consumed when he wished to forget his failures.

"Goodness, you flatter me terribly, Your Grace," she said, employing the sort of modest deflection Julian had coached her to use. "I fear I'm rather clumsy compared to the sophisticated ladies of London."

"Nonsense," the duke murmured, his breath warm against her ear in a way that made her want to pull away rather than melt closer. "Though I confess... watching you move so... rhythmically makes a man wonder what other... natural talents you might possess."

The words hit Margaret like a slap, their implication clear despite the duke's carefully modulated tone. Heat flooded her cheeks—not the pleasant warmth of desire but the burning shame of being spoken to as though she were someone to be purchased rather than courted.

"I beg your pardon, Your Grace?"

"Forgive me," the duke said with a smile that didn't reach his eyes. "I merely meant to compliment your... coordination. Some ladies are so stiff, so resistant to a gentleman's guidance. But you... you yield so submissively. It's remarkable."

Margaret's stomach turned. This was not the romantic triumph she'd dreamed of, not the sophisticated courtship she'd envisioned when she'd planned this evening. The duke's words carried undertones that made her feel soiled, as though he were undressing her with his eyes whilst speaking of things no gentleman should ever reference to an unmarried lady.

She glanced across the room, seeking refuge in familiar faces, and her gaze collided with Julian's. He stood near the fireplace, a glass of brandy in his hand, watching the proceedings with an expression that could have frozen champagne. Something dark and dangerous flickered in his grey eyes—an emotion so raw and powerful that it sent shivers down Margaret's spine.

Jealousy. Pure, undiluted, masculine jealousy.

The realisation hit her like lightning. Julian was jealous! Not amused, not detached, not playing the role of disinterested instructor—he was watching another man touch her, and it was killing him.

"Forgive me, Your Grace," she said suddenly, pulling away from the duke with perhaps more haste than politeness demanded. "I find myself rather overcome by the warmth. The room has grown quite... stifling, don't you think?"

The duke's eyes narrowed slightly, his urbane mask slipping just enough to reveal something calculating beneath. "Of course, Miss Fairbourne. Though I hope you'll allow me to escort you. I should hate for you to feel... unprotected."

"How very considerate, but I wouldn't dream of withholding your presence from our other guests!" Margaret replied, her words tumbling out in that telltale rush that always betrayed her agitation. "Please, do continue enjoying yourself! I shall return momentarily."

Before he could protest, she had fled towards the corridor that led to the powder room, her heart hammering against her ribs like a caged bird desperate for freedom.

The powder room was blissfully cool and quiet, lit only by a single candle that cast dancing shadows on the rose-papered walls. Margaret splashed cool water on her heated cheeks, trying to wash away the memory of the duke's touch, the implication in his words, and the growing uncertainty that everything she'd thought she wanted was turning to ash in her mouth.

The door opened behind her, and Margaret spun around, expecting to see Catharine or perhaps one of the other ladies come to check on her welfare. Instead, Julian filled the doorway, his usually perfect composure nowhere to be found.

"Enjoying your triumph?" he asked, his voice sharp enough to cut glass as he stepped into the small room and closed the door behind him. "The duke seems positively... entranced by your little performance."

"Julian! You mustn't be here..." Margaret gasped, though her treacherous heart performed a complicated series of tumbles at the sight of him. "This is most improper!"

"Improper? My dear, sweet Margaret, I rather think that ship has sailed, don't you? Or have you so easily forgotten our recent... educational sessions?"

"That's entirely different, and you know it perfectly well!" she protested, wrapping her arms around herself as though she could ward off the intensity of his gaze. "Those were lessons! This is... this is real!"

"Real. Yes. I suppose watching you melt into Strickland's embrace was quite tangible indeed. Tell me, did you employ all the techniques I so carefully taught you? Did you lean into his touch to make him feel as though he's conquering you?"

The bitterness in his voice cut through Margaret's worries like a blade. "Stop this, Julian. You're being perfectly horrid."

"Horrid? Forgive me, my dear, but I was under the impression that calculated manipulation was rather the point. After all, what else would you call using a man's deepest feelings for your own social advancement?"

"Feelings? What feelings, Julian?" Margaret demanded, her own temper finally flaring to match his. "You have made it perfectly clear that our... that what had transpired between us meant nothing! You told me to leave! You turned your back on me as though I were some common strumpet!"

"Only because I was trying to protect you, you infuriating little fool!" Julian's control snapped entirely, his voice dropping to a harsh whisper. "Because I knew that if I didn't stop, I'd compromise you beyond all redemption. Because, despite what you might think, Margaret, I do possess some small measure of honour."

"Honour? Is that what you call this?" Margaret's voice rose dangerously. "Because from where I'm standing, it looks remarkably like cowardice!"

The words hung between them like a gauntlet thrown down in challenge. Julian's eyes darkened to the colour of hurricane clouds, and for a moment, Margaret thought he might actually turn around and walk away. Instead, he moved with predatory grace, caging her against the washstand with his arms whilst his body pressed close enough that she could feel the heat radiating from him.

"Cowardice," he repeated, his voice deadly quiet. "How utterly illuminating. Tell me, my dear Margaret, was it cowardice that made me stop before I claimed your innocence on my study floor? Was it cowardice that made me send you away before I could take you and make you mine completely?"

"Perhaps it was!" The words escaped her before Margaret could stop them, driven by frustration and hurt and the terrible ache of wanting something she couldn't name. "Perhaps a braver man would have—"

"Perhaps a braver man would have what, precisely?" Julian's voice now carried a dangerous edge, his eyes flashing with wounded pride. "Ruined you completely? Is that what you think courage looks like?"

The crack of her palm connecting with his cheek echoed in the small room like a gunshot. Julian's head snapped to the side, and Margaret stared at her stinging hand in shock, unable to believe she'd actually struck him.

"Heavens!" she whispered, her eyes wide with horror. "Julian... I didn't mean... I'm so terribly sorry, I—"

But her apology was cut short as Julian's mouth crashed down on hers with desperate hunger. This wasn't the controlled passion of their previous encounters—this was raw, primal, a claiming that spoke of possession rather than instruction. Margaret melted into him instantly, her body recognising its master even as her mind reeled with confusion.

"Is this brave enough for you, my darling?" Julian growled against her lips, his hands fisting in her carefully arranged curls. "Is this what you wanted, Margaret? To drive me beyond reason, beyond honour, beyond any semblance of gentlemanly restraint?"

"Yes!" she gasped, the admission tearing from her very soul. "Yes, Julian, yes!"

His response was to lift her onto the marble washstand, his hands skimming up her silk-stockinged legs beneath her skirts with shocking intimacy. Margaret's breath caught as he positioned himself between her thighs, his mouth finding the sensitive flesh behind her ear that made her entire body tremble.

"You want to know what courage looks like, my dear?" he whispered, his voice rough with desire. "Allow me to demonstrate exactly how brave I can be."

His hands found the ribbons of her pantalets, and Margaret's heart raced wildly as she realised his intent. This was so far beyond anything they'd done before, so scandalous and improper that her mind could barely comprehend it.

"Julian," she breathed, though she wasn't entirely sure if it was a protest or a plea.

"Trust me," he said, his eyes meeting hers with an intensity that stole her breath. "Trust me to show you what you truly desire."

And then his mouth was on her skin, trailing blazing kisses along her throat, down to the modest neckline of her gown. But he didn't stop there. He bent down, and with reverent care, he pushed her skirts higher, his lips finding the sensitive skin of her inner thigh.

Margaret's gasp echoed in the small room as Julian's mouth moved higher, his intentions becoming scandalously clear. The first touch of his warm, wet lips against her most intimate flesh made her cry out, her hands flying to grip his shoulders for support.

"Sweet heavens! Julian, what are you... what are you doing to me?"

"Hush, my darling," he murmured against her heated skin. "Let me taste you, Margaret. Let me show you what pleasures are truly possible."

His tongue traced delicate patterns against her most sensitive flesh, and Margaret thought she might die from the intensity of the sensation. She could feel herself shaking, could hear the soft whimpers that escaped her, though she didn't quite recognise it as her own voice.

Julian's hands held her steady as his mouth worked its magic, alternating between gentle caresses and more insistent pressure that made her arch helplessly against him. She could feel something building within her, a tension that coiled tighter and tighter until she thought she might shatter from the intensity of it.

"I cannot... bear it, Julian... oh!"

"Yes, you can, my darling," he whispered against her slick folds. "Let go for me."

When his lips found the sensitive pearl hidden within her folds and applied gentle suction, Margaret cried out as pleasure exploded through her like lightning. Wave after wave of sensation crashed over her, leaving her shaking and breathless.

Julian held her as she trembled, pressing gentle kisses to her thighs as she slowly returned to earth. When she finally opened her eyes, she found him watching her with an expression of such tender devotion that it made her heart ache.

"What was that extraordinary feeling?" she whispered, her voice still shaky from the intensity of her experience.

"That, my dearest Margaret," Julian said softly, "was what it feels like to be truly, completely worshipped."

She opened her mouth to respond, but before she could even begin to process what had just happened between them, a sharp knock at the door shattered the intimate spell.

"Margaret?" Catharine's voice carried clearly through the thick wooden door. "Are you quite well? You've been absent rather longer than expected."

Margaret's eyes went wide with panic as the reality of their situation crashed over her. Here she was, sitting on a washstand with her skirts around her waist, thoroughly debauched by a man who wasn't her intended husband, whilst her eldest sister waited just beyond the door.

"Dear me," she breathed, scrambling to restore her appearance as Julian stepped back, his own clothing miraculously unruffled.

"One moment, Catharine!" she called out, her voice higher than usual as she struggled with her skirts. "I'm perfectly fine! Just... just making myself presentable!"

Julian caught her hands, stilling their frantic movements. "Margaret," he said quietly, his grey eyes serious. "We must speak of this. This cannot—"

"I know," she whispered, though her heart was breaking even as she said it. "I know it cannot continue. But Julian... what just happened... what does it signify?"

Before he could answer, Catharine's voice came again, this time tinged with concern. "Margaret. I'm coming in."

"The window," Julian said quickly, moving towards the small casement that opened up into the garden. "I'll escape through the garden."

"But—"

"Later," he promised, pausing at the window. "We shall speak of this later, I give you my word."

And then he was gone, leaving Margaret alone to face her sister's questions with the taste of scandal still sweet as honey upon her lips and the echo of her first orgasm still reverberating through her very soul.

Chapter Twelve

"Margaret!" Catharine's voice cut through the powder room's silence like a newly sharpened blade through silk. "What precisely is transpiring in here?"

Margaret's heart stopped beating entirely. In the doorway stood her eldest sister, her countenance a portrait of shock and growing suspicion as her sharp gaze moved between Margaret's flushed face and the still-open window through which Julian had only moments before made his hasty escape.

"Catharine!" Margaret gasped, scrambling to smooth her skirts with trembling hands. "I... that is... I was simply..."

"Simply what, precisely?" Catharine stepped into the room, closing the door behind her with quiet authority. Her green eyes missed nothing—not Margaret's dishevelled curls nor the tell-tale flush that painted her throat. "And pray tell, why is the window standing open on such a cool evening?"

Margaret felt like a butterfly pinned to a board, trapped under Catharine's analytical gaze. "The room grew terribly warm..." Margaret managed, though her voice emerged several octaves higher than intended. "I simply... required fresh air."

"Indeed," Catharine said finally, her tone suggesting she didn't believe a single word. "How very... convenient for you."

But instead of pursuing her interrogation, Catharine moved with characteristic efficiency, producing a small silver comb from her reticule. "Turn around," she commanded, her voice softening marginally. "Your hair is in complete disarray."

Margaret obeyed gratefully, closing her eyes as Catharine's capable hands worked to restore some semblance of propriety to her appearance.

"There," Catharine murmured, making one final adjustment to Margaret's coiffure. "That shall have to suffice. Though I suggest you allow the colour in your cheeks to fade before we return to the drawing room."

"Thank you," Margaret whispered, not daring to meet her sister's eyes in the mirror.

"We shall discuss this later," Catharine said quietly, her tone brooking no argument. "But for now, compose yourself. His Grace has been enquiring after your whereabouts with rather marked persistence."

The mention of the duke sent ice racing through Margaret's veins, chasing away the lingering warmth of Julian's touch. She had entirely forgotten about the duke, about her other guests, about the very purpose of this entire evening.

"Of course," she managed, forcing her voice into some semblance of normalcy. "I should not have abandoned my duties as hostess for so long."

Catharine studied her reflection with penetrating intensity. "Margaret, whatever has occurred this evening... whatever you may be feeling... I trust you understand the importance of discretion?"

Margaret's stomach clenched with anxiety. "Oh! I understand entirely."

"Excellent. Then let us return to the drawing room and attend to your guests."

Back in the drawing room, her father stood near the mantlepiece, his countenance bearing an expression of barely contained satisfaction that made Margaret's pulse quicken with apprehension. Beside him, the Duke of Ashcombe maintained his usual urbane composure, though something predatory flickered in his eyes when they fixed upon her.

"Ah, Margaret!" her father announced, his voice carrying easily across the room. "How fortuitous. His Grace and I have just concluded a most satisfactory discussion."

Margaret's mouth went dry as parchment. "Indeed, Father?"

"Indeed, my dear." Her father's smile was triumphant, the expression of a man who had achieved a long-sought victory. "It appears His Grace has done us the extraordinary honour of requesting your hand in marriage."

The words hit Margaret like a cannon blast, driving the breath from her lungs entirely. Around them, she heard gasps of surprise and murmurs of congratulations, but they all seemed to be coming from a great distance, as though she were hearing them from the bottom of a deep well. This could not be happening...

"How absolutely wonderful!" Eliza's voice rang out with genuine delight as she swept forward to embrace Margaret. "My dearest sister, I am simply over the moon with happiness for you!"

Margaret submitted to her sister's enthusiastic embrace whilst her mind reeled with the impossibility of it all.

"We have arranged to meet next week to discuss the particulars," her father continued, his satisfaction evident in every syllable. "The settlements, the ceremony, all the necessary particulars. His Grace has been most generous in his terms."

Margaret's gaze moved helplessly around the room, seeking... what? Rescue? Understanding? Her eyes found Julian standing slightly apart from the group, his face a careful mask of polite interest. But she could see the tension in his shoulders, the way his knuckles had gone white where he gripped his brandy glass.

"I am... overwhelmed by such generosity," Margaret managed, the words tasting like ash in her mouth.

"As you should be," the duke said smoothly, moving to her side with predatory grace. "I hope you will forgive my presumption in speaking to your father before approaching you directly. But I confess, Miss Fairbourne, that your charms have quite overcome my usual caution."

He lifted her hand to his lips, pressing a kiss to her gloved knuckles that made her want to snatch her hand away. Instead, she forced herself to smile, to play the role of the delighted bride-to-be.

"Your Grace honours me beyond measure," she said instead, the social pleasantries falling from her lips, perfectly spoken but utterly hollow.

"Not at all," the duke replied, his eyes lingering on her face with uncomfortable intensity. "The honour, my dear Miss Fairbourne, is entirely mine."

From the corner of her eye, Margaret saw Julian set down his glass with deliberate care and move towards the door.

He offered a brief bow to the room at large. "If you will excuse me, I fear I have overstayed my welcome this evening. Lord Fairbourne, Miss Fairbourne, Your Grace—my congratulations on your happy news."

His voice was perfectly controlled and his words perfectly proper, betraying nothing of the passion that had burned between them such a short time ago. And then he was gone, leaving Margaret trapped in a nightmare of silk and social expectations.

"Well!" Eliza exclaimed once the door had closed behind Julian. "How perfectly romantic! Though I suppose His Grace will make his formal proposal to you in private, Margaret. How thrilling it must be to finally know his intentions."

Margaret's tongue felt thick and useless in her mouth. "Yes... quite thrilling indeed."

Finally, mercifully, the evening began to wind towards its close. Guests made their farewells, the duke among them, though not before pressing another lingering kiss to Margaret's hand.

"I shall call upon you very soon, Miss Fairbourne," he murmured, his eyes holding hers with uncomfortable intensity. "I believe we have much to discuss in private."

"I look forward to your visit, Your Grace."

When the last of the guests had departed and the servants had cleared away the detritus of the evening's entertainment, Margaret found herself alone in the drawing room with only her sisters.

"Well," Eliza said finally, settling herself onto the sofa. "You certainly do not appear to be a woman who has just received a proposal from one of England's most eligible dukes."

Margaret's carefully maintained composure finally cracked. "I feel rather... uncertain about it all," she admitted, her voice barely above a whisper.

Catharine moved to close the drawing room door before taking her own seat. "Perhaps you might elaborate on the nature of this uncertainty, sister?"

"Oh, Catharine, please do not use that tone with her," Eliza interjected, though not unkindly. "Margaret, dearest, what is troubling you? Any woman in London would be absolutely thrilled to have received such an offer."

"Oh, but that is precisely the problem!" Margaret said, her words beginning to tumble out in that familiar rush. "I should be thrilled! I should be over the moon with happiness! But instead I feel... I feel..."

"Yes?" Catharine prompted gently.

"Trapped," Margaret whispered, the admission raw and heavy in her mouth. "I feel as though I am being asked to imprison myself in a life I no longer want."

Eliza leaned forward, her expression growing serious. "Margaret, what's changed? Only weeks ago, you were determined to secure the duke's suit. You barely spoke of anything else."

"Everything has changed," she said quietly. "Everything. Because I... well, because I have come to realise that my feelings are not what I believed them to be."

"There is someone else, I presume?" Catharine's voice sharpened with sudden understanding.

"Margaret," Eliza said slowly, "what exactly is going on?"

And so, with her heart hammering against her ribs and her cheeks burning with shame and confusion, Margaret found herself unable to speak the full truth. How could she possibly explain what she barely understood herself? Instead, she offered only the barest admission.

"I... I find myself with feelings for someone else," she whispered, her voice barely audible. "Someone who is... who is not the duke."

When she finished this meagre confession, the drawing room fell into a profound silence. Eliza sat frozen, her eyes wide with shock, whilst Catharine's expression had grown increasingly grave.

"Good heavens," Eliza breathed finally. "Margaret, do you understand the gravity of what you've just confessed to us?"

"I understand that I've been foolish," Margaret whispered. "I know that such feelings are... inappropriate. But despite that, the fact of the matter is... I cannot marry the duke. Not when my heart belongs to someone else entirely."

Catharine rose and moved to the window, staring out into the darkened garden where Julian had made his escape. "This is a most concerning complication," she said quietly.

"What am I to do?" Margaret asked desperately. "How can I possibly marry His Grace when every fibre of my being rebels against the very thought?"

"What you should do is think of the family," Catharine said, though her voice lacked its usual conviction. "Consider the scandal that would result from crying off from such an advantageous match."

"But surely," Eliza interjected, "if Margaret's heart is elsewhere—"

"Longings of the heart," Catharine said with gentle finality, "are luxuries that women of our station can rarely afford."

The truth of those words settled over the room like a shroud, extinguishing the last flickering hope in Margaret's chest. She was trapped, caught between duty and desire, between the life she was expected to want and the one her heart craved beyond measure.

And then there was Julian... the man who had shown her Nirvana and who seemed as far beyond her reach as the stars themselves.

Chapter Thirteen

"Perhaps another brandy to drown your sorrows, Mr. Ashcroft?"

Julian glanced up from the scattered papers on his desk to find Hartwell hovering in the doorway. The brandy in his glass sat untouched, growing warm while the contracts before him might as well have been written in ancient Sanskrit.

It had been three days since Margaret's engagement had been announced, and his mind remained stubbornly fixated upon the image of her face as the duke had claimed her hand. The memory burned in his chest like a brand, searing away his ability to concentrate on anything resembling productive work.

"My dear Hartwell, I fear even the finest spirits cannot cure what ails me today," Julian replied, gesturing dramatically at the offending documents. "These contracts appear to be mocking me with their incomprehensible legal jargon."

"Shall I be rescheduling your appointments then, sir?"

Julian waved him away. "Yes, yes. Cancel everything, my good man. I'm clearly in no fit state to advise anyone on matters of law when I cannot even focus on a simple property deed."

Alone again, Julian slumped in his chair and addressed the empty room. "Brilliant work, old man. The great Julian Ashcroft, reduced to a lovesick fool by a pair of cornflower blue eyes."

She was going to marry Nathaniel Strickland. The thought hit him for the hundredth time in three days.

He needed air. Perhaps a visit to Rhys would remind him there were other matters requiring his attention—anything that didn't involve dwelling on Margaret's laugh or the way she'd gasped his name.

"Hartwell!" he called. "Have my horse saddled. I require a change of scenery before I do something dramatically foolish."

When he arrived, the gardens were buzzing with celebration. Eliza's laughter mixed with her son's delighted squeals as the boy chased butterflies between the rose bushes.

"Julian!" Rhys called from the terrace. "Perfect timing. Eliza was just threatening to teach Edward cricket."

"Ah, your windows shall never recover," Julian replied, climbing the steps with forced cheer.

But his wit died when he saw her.

Margaret sat beneath an ancient oak, sunlight filtering through leaves to paint gold in her hair. She was laughing at something Eliza had said, utterly radiant in pale blue silk that made her eyes luminous.

Their gazes met across the garden.

Her laughter faded, replaced by something more complex—awareness, longing, perhaps regret. Julian felt his chest tighten as she quickly looked away, the mask of polite indifference sliding into place.

"Uncle Julian!" Edward raced across the lawn on unsteady legs, curls bouncing. "Come play!"

Julian scooped up the boy, grateful for the distraction. "Good afternoon, young master. I trust you've been terrorising the household appropriately?"

"Butterfly!" Edward exclaimed, pointing excitedly at the garden with chubby fingers. "Pretty!"

"Indeed, they are," Julian agreed. "Though I suspect you've been far more destructive to your poor mama's peace of mind than any mere butterfly could manage."

Edward giggled and clapped his hands, clearly delighted by Julian's attention even though he didn't have the slightest comprehension of the words.

Rhys chuckled. "He's been an absolute terror today. Eliza's convinced he's inherited every ounce of the Fairbourne stubbornness."

"Heaven help us all!" Julian replied, setting Edward down. "I should return to London," he announced. "The great machinery of justice waits for no man, not even one so devastatingly charming as myself."

"Shall we see you at dinner tomorrow?" Rhys asked.

"Perhaps. I may be detained by matters of pressing importance."

Back in his study that evening, a sharp knocking echoed through the house. Julian frowned—past nine o'clock was hardly the hour for social calls. He opened the door to find two heavily veiled figures on his threshold.

"Mr. Ashcroft," the taller woman said, her refined voice carrying an undercurrent of desperation. "We must speak with you. Most urgently, if you would be so gracious."

"Ladies." Julian stepped aside, mind racing. "Pray, come in. I confess myself intrigued by such... spectacular arrivals."

"We are not alone in our... difficulties," the first woman said without preamble, her words carefully chosen yet trembling with suppressed emotion.

Three more figures emerged from the darkness—Lady Hastings, Mrs. Whitmore, and Lady Thornfield. Julian's breath caught as recognition dawned despite their concealing veils.

"Good God," he murmured, understanding flooding through him. "All of you?"

"All of us," Lady Harrow confirmed, lowering her veil with dignified resignation. "And we have reason to believe there are others who dare not yet come forward."

They arranged themselves around his study. Lady Lyndmere finally removed her veil with trembling fingers, revealing cheeks stained with tears and eyes bright with fury and despair. "We have come to you, Mr. Ashcroft, because we believe you possess both the skill and the integrity required for such... delicate matters. The gentleman who has been systematically destroying us, one woman at a time, is the very same man who now seeks to marry Miss Margaret Fairbourne."

"He has been most thorough in his attentions," Lady Hastings added. "Most methodical in his approach to what one might generously call... courtship."

Julian's hands stilled on the brandy decanter. "Lord Strickland."

"The Duke of Ashcombe," Lady Harrow corrected bitterly.

"Tell me everything," Julian said quietly.

What followed was a litany of horrors that grew more damning with each revelation. Lady Harrow spoke first, her voice maintaining its aristocratic composure even as she detailed the most intimate betrayals—Strickland's gradual infiltration following her husband's death, the subtle financial manipulations disguised as gallant assistance, the forty thousand pounds that had vanished.

"When I finally summoned the courage to confront him," she said, her words precise despite the tremor in her hands, "he produced certain correspondence I had written during our... association. Letters that, whilst perfectly innocent in intent, could be interpreted most unfavourably should they reach society's attention."

Lady Lyndmere's account followed. "He maintains detailed records of every lady who has... enjoyed his acquaintance. Their financial circumstances, their family secrets, their deepest vulnerabilities. I glimpsed these ledgers quite by accident during a visit to his estate. The thoroughness was both impressive and utterly chilling."

Mrs. Whitmore's story proved the most insidious. "He never approached me directly, you understand. Instead, he cultivated a network of servants and information brokers—people whose loyalty could be purchased for surprisingly modest sums. My husband's cases, our private arguments, our financial difficulties... nothing remained hidden from his influence."

Lady Thornfield's voice shook with barely controlled rage as she spoke of her young niece. "Eighteen years of age and fresh from the schoolroom when he set his sights upon her. I intervened before any irreparable damage could be done, but not before he had extracted considerable intelligence regarding our family's political connections. He commented, with the most casual cruelty, that he found the younger ones particularly... educational."

"You say you have proof."

Lady Harrow nodded, producing a thick packet. "Letters in his own hand. Financial records showing transfers from my accounts to his. Personal correspondence he used to ensure my silence."

The other women produced similar evidence—bank drafts, receipts for pawned jewellery, servant testimonies, fragments of Strickland's record-keeping system. Julian examined each document with a barrister's precision, his anger growing with every piece of evidence.

"Why come to me?"

"Because you have the Duke of Kingswell's ear," Lady Harrow replied. "Because you understand law and the political machinery protecting men like Strickland. And because we believe you care enough about Miss Fairbourne's welfare to act, regardless of personal cost."

Julian set down the papers, decision crystallising. To expose Strickland meant destroying Margaret's engagement—but also saving her from a marriage that would destroy her.

"What do you want me to do?"

"Destroy him," Lady Lyndmere said simply. "Publicly. Completely. Make it impossible for him to hurt anyone else."

"You understand what this means? If I present this evidence before the House of Lords, there will be no going back. His title will be stripped, his name synonymous with scandal. And Miss Fairbourne..."

"Will be free," Lady Harrow finished firmly. "Yes, there will be gossip. But she'll be alive, whole, with the chance to find genuine happiness. That's worth any temporary embarrassment."

Julian looked around at the five women who had risked everything to sit in his study and expose their deepest shames. They had come not for revenge but to protect others from suffering their fate. Margaret most of all.

"Very well. I'll need time to organise the evidence properly, ensure everything is legally sound and politically devastating. Can you give me a week?"

"The engagement is to be announced publicly at week's end," Lady Hastings said urgently. "After that, extricating Miss Fairbourne will be much more difficult."

"Then we have no time to waste."

The women departed as carefully as they'd arrived, leaving Julian alone with the damning papers spread across his desk. He poured another brandy and contemplated the magnitude of what he was undertaking.

By exposing Strickland, he would save Margaret from a nightmarish marriage. But he would also destroy her dreams of becoming a duchess, her carefully laid plans for social elevation. She would hate him for making the choice without consulting her first.

But she would be safe.

Julian reached for his pen and began to write. He had until week's end to dismantle a duke and save the woman he loved from a marriage that would slowly kill everything bright and beautiful about her.

"Right then, Your Grace," he murmured to the empty room. "Let us see how your charm fares against cold, hard evidence."

Chapter Fourteen

"Margaret, dearest, do sit down," her father said from his position by the window, where he had been standing for the past quarter hour. "Your fidgeting shall make the furniture nervous."

Margaret paused in her circuit of the drawing room, her pale blue silk morning dress rustling against her silk stockings. Every surface gleamed with anticipation—the silver tea service catching the morning light, the crystal sherry decanter positioned just so upon the mahogany sideboard, the carefully arranged hothouse flowers releasing their perfume into the air thick with expectation.

"Oh! But Father, I cannot simply sit still when everything is about to change forever!" she exclaimed, her hands fluttering to smooth skirts that required no smoothing. "This is the most important day of my entire life! How can you expect me to remain calm when His Grace shall arrive at any moment to—"

The words felt like lies coated in honey, but Margaret forced them out with practiced enthusiasm. After her confession to her sisters about Julian, she could hardly reveal her true feelings to her father—not when doing so would expose everything.

"To formalise arrangements that have already been concluded," her father interrupted, turning from the window with that satisfied expression she had come to dread. "The settlements have been agreed upon, signed just yesterday evening, my dear, after His Grace and I concluded our discussions. I thought it a bit out of the ordinary, but the duke was so taken with you that he apparently ordered his solicitor to be ready with the documents before the proposal. Today is merely a matter of... ceremony."

Margaret's breath caught, though she couldn't say why. This was precisely what she had worked toward, schemed for, dreamed of during countless sleepless nights. The Duke of Ashcombe would arrive shortly, tea would be served, and she would become engaged to one of England's most eligible gentlemen.

So why did her stomach feel as though it harboured a nest of agitated sparrows?

"Father," she said, her voice emerging smaller than intended, "might I ask... that is, did His Grace seem... eager when you spoke with him yesterday?"

Lord Fairbourne's grey eyebrows rose slightly, and he adjusted the high collar of his dark coat with precise movements. "Eager? My dear child, the Duke of Ashcombe is a gentleman of considerable sophistication. Such men do not express eagerness like schoolboys pursuing sweetmeats. They express... satisfaction with advantageous arrangements."

The words struck Margaret like drops of ice water against heated skin. "Satisfaction with arrangements," she repeated slowly.

"Precisely. As should you." Her father moved away from the window, his expression growing sharper as he studied her countenance. "Margaret, you appear rather... subdued for a young lady about to achieve her heart's desire. Have you perhaps developed some silly feminine vapours about marriage? Because I assure you, such nonsense shall not be tolerated."

"Oh no, Father! No vapours whatsoever!" Margaret said quickly, forcing brightness into her voice. The performance was becoming more difficult with each passing moment. How could she explain that her heart belonged to Julian when her father expected nothing but gratitude for this advantageous match?

"I am simply... overwhelmed by the magnitude of it all. To think that I, little Margaret Fairbourne, shall soon be a duchess! It is rather like something from a fairy tale, is it not?"

"Indeed," her father replied, though his attention had already returned to the window. "The duke's carriage should arrive shortly. Jenkins has been instructed to—" He frowned, leaning closer to the glass. "How curious."

"What is it, Father?"

"The duke appears to be... late." Lord Fairbourne consulted his pocket watch. "Quarter past the hour. Most unlike him."

Margaret felt something cold unfurl in her chest. "Perhaps his carriage encountered some difficulty. The streets can be so terribly crowded—"

"Carriages of ducal quality do not encounter difficulties, Margaret. They are designed specifically to avoid such... inconveniences."

The silence that followed felt brittle, charged with unspoken anxieties. Margaret moved to the window beside her father, her hands pressed against the cool glass as she peered down at the street below. Everything appeared perfectly normal—a few tradesmen making their rounds, a nursemaid pushing a perambulator, the usual gentle bustle of Mayfair morning activity.

"I am certain there is some perfectly reasonable explanation," she said, though her voice sounded uncertain even to her own ears.

"Reasonable explanations," her father muttered, "are often the most unreasonable thing of all."

Another quarter hour crawled past with agonising slowness.

VALENTINA LOVELACE

"Father," she ventured finally, "perhaps you might send word to His Grace's residence? Simply to enquire—"

"One does not enquire after dukes like lost parcels," Lord Fairbourne snapped, though his own composure showed signs of strain. "If the Duke of Ashcombe is delayed, he shall provide an explanation in due course."

A commotion in the street below interrupted her thoughts. Voices raised in excitement, the clatter of hooves against cobblestones, the creak of carriage wheels moving faster than was considered proper for residential streets.

"Good heavens," Lord Fairbourne breathed, pressing closer to the window. "What the devil—"

Margaret gasped as she saw them—carriages stopped mid-turn, their occupants leaning out windows to call to one another. A messenger on horseback galloped past, his hat flying off as he urged his mount towards the city centre. Another followed, and then another, until the usually sedate street hummed with urgent activity.

"Something has happened," she whispered, her hands growing cold despite the morning warmth. "Father, something terrible has happened."

"Nonsense," Lord Fairbourne said, though his voice lacked conviction. "London is always prone to... dramatic episodes. Some minor political intrigue, no doubt."

But even as he spoke, the sounds from the street grew more pronounced. Shouts echoed between the elegant townhouses, accompanied by the sharp report of carriage doors slamming and the thunder of wheels over stone.

"I must find out what has occurred," Lord Fairbourne declared, moving towards the drawing room door with sudden purpose. "Jenkins! Jenkins, attend me immediately!"

The butler appeared with remarkable speed, his usually immaculate countenance bearing traces of agitation. "My lord?"

"What in God's name is happening in the streets? The noise is unseemly."

Jenkins cleared his throat delicately. "I have just received word from young Thomas, the boot boy, my lord. It appears there has been some sort of... disturbance at the House of Lords."

Margaret felt the blood drain from her face entirely. "The House of Lords?"

"Indeed, miss. Something involving..." Jenkins hesitated, his professional composure wavering. "Something involving His Grace the Duke of Ashcombe."

"What sort of disturbance?"

"I could not say with certainty, miss. But Thomas heard it described as a... scandal of considerable magnitude."

"Scandal?" Lord Fairbourne's voice rose to a pitch Margaret had rarely heard from him. "What manner of scandal? Speak plainly, man!"

"I fear I know no particulars, my lord. Only that the duke's name is being spoken throughout the city, and not... not in terms of admiration."

Margaret's legs suddenly felt as though they had been fashioned from wet ribbon. She sank into the nearest chair, her mind reeling with implications she could not yet bring herself to examine. "But this cannot be possible. His Grace is... he is..."

"He is what, exactly?" her father demanded, turning towards her with eyes sharp as winter frost. "Margaret, is there something you have not told me about the duke? Some reason why such allegations might—"

"No!" she exclaimed, her voice breaking on the word. "Father, I know nothing! Nothing whatsoever! His Grace has been nothing but perfectly proper in all our interactions!"

"We must determine the particulars immediately," Lord Fairbourne declared, striding towards the door. "If our family name becomes associated with scandal through this connection..."

He left the threat unfinished, but Margaret heard it clearly enough.

"Oh Father, surely this is simply some dreadful misunderstanding!" she said, rising to follow him. "Perhaps someone has confused His Grace with another gentleman entirely! It happens all the time in the best families—"

"Dukes," her father said with grim finality, "are not easily confused with other gentlemen."

They made their way to the front of the house, where the sounds of commotion had grown even more pronounced. Through the tall windows flanking the entrance, Margaret could see that their usually quiet street had transformed into something resembling a thoroughfare during market day.

"My lord," Jenkins announced, appearing at Lord Fairbourne's elbow, "young Thomas has returned with additional intelligence, if you wish to hear it."

"Send him in immediately."

The boot boy who appeared in the doorway could not have been more than fourteen, his face flushed with excitement and exertion. He bobbed an awkward bow before launching into his report.

"Beggin' your pardon, my lord, but there's been a right proper to-do at Westminster! Folk sayin' the Duke of Ashcombe..." He paused, glancing nervously at Margaret before continuing in a rush, "...Folk sayin' he's been up to all sorts of wicked business! Takin' advantage of ladies and stealin' their fortunes and such like!"

Margaret's hands flew to her mouth, stifling a gasp that seemed to tear from her very soul. "Oh, good heavens! Surely not!"

"That's what they're sayin', miss," Thomas continued. "And there's been some sort of formal accusation made right there in the House of Lords! With witnesses and documents and everything!"

"Witnesses?" Lord Fairbourne's voice had gone dangerously quiet. "What manner of witnesses?"

"Ladies, my lord. Several of 'em, all veiled and mysterious-like. They're sayin' the duke's been blackmailin' widows and such, threatening to ruin their reputations if they don't pay him money!"

The room seemed to spin around Margaret like a child's top set in motion. She gripped the doorframe for support, her mind struggling to reconcile this horrific account with the charming gentleman who had danced with her just days earlier.

"This cannot be true," she whispered. "Father, this simply cannot be true!"

But Lord Fairbourne's expression had gone from concerned to calculating, his mind clearly racing through the implications for their family's situation. "Thomas, is the duke still at Westminster?"

"Oh no, my lord! Word is he fled the scene entirely when the accusations were read out! Ran off like a common criminal, he did!"

Margaret felt as though she might faint entirely. The duke—the man she had worked so desperately to win—had fled Parliament like a hunted animal. Everything she had dreamed of, planned for, sacrificed for, was crumbling to ash before her eyes.

"We must go there immediately," she said suddenly, surprising herself with the firmness in her voice. "Father, we must go to Westminster and learn the truth of this matter!"

"Margaret, absolutely not. Ladies do not—"

"Ladies do not what, Father? Seek truth when their entire futures hang in the balance?" She could hear her voice rising, feel her careful composure finally beginning to crack. "I have a right to know what has happened! If my name is to be destroyed by association with scandal, I shall at least understand why!"

For a moment, father and daughter stared at each other across the entrance hall, the air between them charged with years of unspoken frustrations and carefully suppressed rebellions.

"Very well," Lord Fairbourne said at last. "We shall go. But Margaret—whatever we discover there, you will comport yourself with dignity befitting our name. Is that understood?"

"Yes, Father," she said softly. "Oh!" Margaret exclaimed suddenly, a new horror occurring to her. "Father, what if Julian knew? What if he suspected something and tried to warn me, but I was too foolish to listen?"

Lord Fairbourne's eyes sharpened dangerously. "Julian? Julian Ashcroft? What does he have to do with any of this?"

"I... that is..." Margaret felt heat flood her cheeks as she realised her slip. "He simply made some comments about His Grace's character that I perhaps dismissed too readily."

"When did Julian Ashcroft make comments to you about the duke's character?"

Margaret's mind raced, seeking some explanation that would not expose the truth of her recent interactions with Julian.

"At... at various social gatherings, Father. Nothing specific, merely... general observations about gentlemen of the duke's reputation."

Lord Fairbourne studied her with the penetrating gaze that had made her squirm since childhood. "Margaret, I have the distinct impression that there are aspects of this situation which you have not shared with me."

"Father, I—"

"But we shall address those concerns later," he continued, effectively cutting off her protest. "For now, we must focus on determining the extent of the damage to our family's position."

"Father," she said as the carriage lurched into motion, "what shall become of us if these allegations prove true?"

Lord Fairbourne was silent for a long moment, his grey eyes fixed on the passing street scene.

"That, my dear daughter," he said finally, "depends entirely upon how thoroughly our name has been entangled with his."

As their carriage joined the stream of vehicles flowing towards Westminster, Margaret pressed her face to the cool glass and tried not to think about Julian's warnings, about the look in his eyes when he'd spoken of the duke's true nature, about the growing certainty that she had been played for the greatest fool in all of London.

The city rushed past in a blur of smoke-blackened buildings and urgent faces, carrying her towards answers she was no longer certain she wished to hear.

Chapter Fifteen

"My lords, though it gives me little pleasure to be the bearer of such grim news, I hereby present evidence before this chamber of a conspiracy so vile, so systematic in its cruelty, that it shall no doubt shock every civilised man amongst us to his core."

Julian stood with the easy confidence of a man born to command attention, though the irony was not lost on him that he had spent most of his life avoiding precisely this sort of scrutiny.

"Good heavens, Mr. Ashcroft," Lord Pembroke called from his seat, "what manner of conspiracy could possibly warrant such dramatic preamble?"

Julian's mouth curved in that slow, sardonic smile that served him so well. "The sort, my lord, which transforms a duke into little more than a common predator. Though I suppose one might argue about how uncommon such behaviour truly is amongst your elevated peers."

"By Jove, that's a serious accusation!" Lord Hastings exclaimed.

"Indeed, it is, my lord," Julian replied. "Which is precisely why I have taken such considerable care to ensure my evidence is irrefutable as the morning sun.

"The Duke of Ashcombe," Julian continued, his voice carrying its signature dramatic flourish, "has been conducting what one might generously call... an enterprising business venture. Though 'extortion and systematic corruption' seems a rather more accurate characterisation."

Lord Ventnor leaned forward sharply. "That is an extraordinarily serious accusation to bring against a noble gentleman, Mr. Ashcroft."

"Quite so, my lord. And I should never dare make such claims without evidence substantial enough to convince even the most sceptical amongst you." Julian gestured to his secretary, who stepped forward with a leather portfolio.

"Seven ladies of good standing have been systematically targeted, manipulated, and drained of their resources. But the duke's method was far more ingenious than simple opportunism."

"Pray continue, Mr. Ashcroft," Lord Pembroke urged, his voice tight with concern.

"His Grace deployed... associates, information brokers, if you will," Julian explained. "Using servants strategically placed in households, tradesmen with access to financial records, and even seemingly innocent social acquaintances whose sole purpose was to identify women who met the needed criteria—wealth and vulnerability."

"Preposterous!" Lord Hastings's voice cracked slightly. "You cannot seriously suggest that—"

"That a peer of this great establishment would orchestrate such systematic corruption?" Julian's eyebrows rose in mock surprise. "My dear Lord Hastings, I assure you, I am doing considerably more than merely suggesting it. I am providing irrefutable proof."

"What manner of proof?" Lord Ventnor demanded sharply.

"We have sworn testimonies from no less than twelve servants who were approached by men acting on the duke's behalf," Julian replied with obvious satisfaction. "Seven different information brokers are also willing to testify, placing

His Grace at meetings where such intelligence was purchased. Bank sheets showing payments that align precisely with the dates when such damaging information was acquired."

The murmurs grew louder around him, and Julian's voice rose to carry over the din. "This was no happenstance, my lords. This was a business enterprise, as calculated and organised as any merchant worth his salt's ledger. The duke identified wealthy widows and unmarried women, deployed his henchmen to discover their secrets, seduced them, and then used that information to systematically drain their fortunes through threats of public exposure and scandal."

"The sheer audacity!" Lord Pembroke exclaimed.

"Indeed, my lord. But the most damning evidence," Julian continued, his voice dropping, "comes from the victims themselves. I have in my possession letters, in which the duke details in his own hand exactly what befalls ladies who refuse to cooperate with his requests."

Julian unfolded a sheet of expensive parchment. "I shall spare this assembly His Grace's... colourful vocabulary, but the essential message is clear: compliance ensures discretion, whilst refusal guarantees that certain... intimate details shall become the subject of drawing room gossip throughout London."

"Monstrous!" Lord Hartwell declared.

Lord Ventnor's voice cut through the quiet like a judge's gavel. "Your Grace, do you wish to respond to these allegations?"

Julian turned his attention to Strickland with the lazy interest of a cat watching a particularly entertaining mouse. The man who had charmed his way through London's most exclusive circles now resembled a peacock caught in a downpour—all his magnificent plumage reduced to soggy feathers clinging pathetically to a rather ordinary bird.

"These... these accusations... are..." Strickland's voice cracked like an adolescent boy's. "Vindictive women seeking to destroy—"

"Destroy what, precisely, Your Grace?" Julian's voice was honey dripping on steel. "Their own reputations? Their social standing? Their chances of ever marrying respectably? Forgive me, but that seems rather an elaborate form of self-incrimination."

"This is a conspiracy! These women have coordinated their fabricated lies to—"

"To what end?" Julian tilted his head with genuine fascination. "These ladies gain nothing from exposing their own compromising correspondence. Quite the opposite. They risk social ruin by admitting to the very indiscretions you threatened to reveal."

Strickland's face cycled through a kaleidoscope of colours. "I... you cannot possibly expect this assembly to swallow these preposterous—"

"I expect this assembly to examine the facts," Julian replied pleasantly. "For instance, this receipt from White's gambling house, signed by Your Grace, settling a debt of three thousand pounds on the very same day that one victim's bank records show a mysterious withdrawal of an identical amount. Quite the coincidence."

"How dare you!" Strickland's composure finally cracked entirely. "I am a peer of this realm! I shall not be subjected to this humiliating inquisition run by some jumped-up solicitor with delusions of—"

"Jumped-up solicitor?" Julian's charm returned in full force. "My dear duke, I would prefer to think of myself as a legal advocate, specialising in the dramatic revelation of inconvenient truths. Though I suppose Your Grace *would* be the expert on delusions of grandeur."

"Your Grace"—Lord Pembroke's voice carried the weight of absolute authority—"these accusations demand a substantive response. The evidence appears quite overwhelming."

"I... excuse me..." Strickland muttered, rising abruptly.

And what happened next would be discussed in clubs and drawing rooms and parlours alike for decades.

The Duke of Ashcombe simply ran.

He pushed past startled peers with all the grace of a fleeing pickpocket, his breathing audible even from Julian's position—harsh, panicked gasps that spoke of absolute defeat. A clerk attempted to step aside but wasn't quick enough. Strickland collided with the poor man, sending papers scattering like autumn leaves, and then he stumbled towards the exit without pause or apology.

The massive oak doors slammed shut with finality. Then Lord Ventnor's voice cut through the stunned silence. "Well. That was certainly illuminating."

Julian inclined his head gracefully, though something hollow was already gnawing at his chest. "Justice has a rather dramatic flair, my lord. It rarely subscribes to conventional notions of subtlety."

"Mr. Ashcroft, this has been most extraordinary," Lord Pembroke agreed. "The Crown owes you a debt of gratitude."

"The ladies who came forward were the ones who displayed true courage," Julian replied automatically. "I was merely their advocate, my lord."

"Nevertheless," Lord Ventnor said, pausing meaningfully. "Such exemplary service deserves recognition."

Julian's gaze drifted to the gallery where members of the public and family traditionally observed proceedings.

His heart stopped. She was there. Naturally, her engagement to the duke had secured her one of the few places reserved for family in the gallery.

Margaret Fairbourne stood pale and rigid beside her father, her face a mask of shock and devastation that hit Julian like a physical blow. Even from this distance, he could see tears threatening to spill from her eyes, could read the complete betrayal written in every line of her body like a book opened to its most painful chapter.

Their eyes met across the chamber, and Julian felt something crack inside his chest. The look she gave him wasn't anger—not exactly. It was pure, bewildered hurt, the expression of someone discovering that their most trusted ally had been their secret enemy all along.

Margaret shook her head sharply at something her father whispered, then turned and began making her way towards the exit.

Julian found himself moving before conscious thought intervened, pushing through the crowd of excited nobility.

"Margaret!" he called as he emerged into the corridor.

She stopped but didn't turn around, her shoulders rigid with the effort of maintaining composure.

"Please, allow me to explain."

She turned to face him, the devastation in her eyes nearly bringing him to his knees. Tears streaked silver tracks down her cheeks, but her voice was steady when she spoke.

"You knew."

"Margaret, I—"

"You knew..." she repeated, her voice growing stronger with each word. "All this time, through every lesson, every moment we spent together... you knew exactly what he was... and you said nothing. Nothing!"

Julian stepped closer, desperate to bridge the distance between them. "I was trying to protect you. If you had known, if you had changed your behaviour towards him, the investigation would have been compromised, and those women—"

"Those women?" Margaret's voice cracked slightly, and Julian heard the familiar rushing quality that marked her deepest emotions. She spoke in a whisper, loud enough for only him to hear. "Oh! But what of Lady Lyndmere, Julian? What about Mrs. Fairfax? They're my friends! I *introduced* Mrs. Fairfax to him at Lady Pemberton's musicale because I thought... because I believed he was charming and honourable!"

"How did you—"

"I recognised their handwriting from your evidence. I would know it anywhere, Julian!"

Julian's blood turned to ice. "Margaret... you couldn't have known—"

"Couldn't I?" Her laugh was sharp and bitter.

"You're not responsible for—"

Margaret's voice rose frantically. "I noticed that strange man who approached the duke during our walk in the gardens—the way the duke's entire demeanour changed—and I simply dismissed it as nothing because I was so focused on winning a monster's affections!"

"He was likely one of the information brokers. You had no way of understanding the significance—"

"Only because you didn't tell me! Because you chose to keep me in ignorance!" The words exploded from her with such force that several passing clerks turned to stare. Margaret bit her lip, dropping her voice slightly. "You allowed me to pursue him still, let me plan a future with him, all while my friends suffered at his hands!"

"If I had warned you, you likely wouldn't have believed me anyway, especially not without evidence. And Strickland... he would have simply found other victims, Margaret," Julian said desperately. "This way–"

"This way, Julian Ashcroft could be the hero and the puppet master both." Margaret finished with devastating accuracy. "This way, you could save me from my own poor judgment whilst ensuring I had plenty to be saved from. Meanwhile, people I care for paid the price for my ignorance."

The accuracy of her assessment was breathtaking and devastating. Julian felt every carefully constructed defence crumble under the weight of her insight.

"That's not—"

"No? Pray tell, Julian, when you offered to help me win his heart, was it because you genuinely wished to see me happy? Or because you already suspected what he was and saw an opportunity to gather intelligence while maintaining the perfect excuse for proximity?"

The colour drained from Julian's face. The question hung between them like a gauntlet thrown in battle, and he realised with startling clarity that any answer he gave would damn him entirely.

"I see," Margaret said softly, reading his expression with devastating accuracy. "And when did you first know? Before you offered to help me?"

"I had my suspicions long before, but I knew the second week," he admitted quietly, the truth falling from his lips like stones in still water. "But Margaret, I couldn't—"

"The second week." She nodded as though confirming something she had already known. "So, you spent six weeks instructing me to be alluring whilst you gathered evidence behind the scenes against the very man I hoped to marry."

"I was building a case. The evidence had to be irrefutable, or he would have simply denied everything and continued—"

"No. You were building your reputation," Margaret corrected, her voice steady as granite. "Today, you stood before the most powerful men in England and commanded their absolute attention. You are the saviour of the hour, the brilliant investigator who exposed corruption at the highest levels. Pray tell me that didn't feel intoxicating."

Each word she uttered was a dagger thrust between his ribs with surgical precision.

"I truly thought you were different," she continued, the disappointment in her voice worse than any anger could have been. "I thought you saw me as more than just another pawn in whatever game you were playing. But I was wrong, wasn't I?"

"Margaret, no. What I feel for you—"

"What you feel for me?" Her laugh was as hollow as an empty promise. "When you kissed me, when you looked at me as though I was the most precious thing in the world... Was any of it real? Or was it simply another of Julian Ashcroft's great performances?"

Julian opened his mouth to answer, to explain that every moment they had shared had been more real to him than anything he had ever experienced—but how could he possibly explain that his feelings had bloomed in soil fertilised by deception?

"Do you know what the most devastating part is? I might have helped you, Julian. If you had only dared to trust me with the truth, I might have been your ally instead of your unwitting accomplice."

"I was trying to protect you," he said weakly.

"No," Margaret replied with quiet certainty. "You were protecting your investigation. There's a difference, and we both know it."

She turned to go, and Julian felt panic rise in his throat. "Margaret, wait. Please."

She paused without turning around. "Do you have anything to say that shall make this incredible hurt you've caused me bearable?"

Julian opened his mouth to answer, but the words wouldn't come.

"I thought as much," Margaret said softly.

And with that, she walked away.

Julian remained where he was, surrounded by the echoes of his greatest professional triumph, feeling no satisfaction whatsoever. Behind him, he could hear the continuing buzz of conversation from the chamber. Ahead of him, Margaret's figure grew smaller until she disappeared around a corner.

He had achieved everything he had set out to accomplish. Strickland was thoroughly ruined, his victims would see justice, and Julian's own reputation was considerably enhanced.

But all he could think of was the devastation in Margaret's eyes and the knowledge that in saving her from one form of ruin, he had delivered her into another—and this time, *he* was the one responsible for her tears.

Chapter Sixteen

"Margaret, dearest, you simply must eat something," Eliza said, settling onto the edge of the bed with the careful grace of someone approaching a wounded animal. "You cannot sustain yourself on tears alone."

Margaret sat curled against her pillows like a broken doll, her golden curls tangled and her blue eyes swollen from days of weeping. The breakfast tray beside her remained untouched, the sight of food making her stomach rebel as violently as her heart had when witnessing the aftermath of Julian's performance in the House of Lords.

"Oh! I cannot," she whispered, her voice hoarse from crying. "Every time I attempt to take a bite, I remember the look in his eyes when he saw me in that gallery! As though I were some unfortunate obstacle in his grand triumph."

Catharine entered without ceremony. She surveyed the scene with clinical efficiency—Margaret's untouched meals, the drawn curtains, the general air of romantic devastation that hung over the room like morning fog.

"This exhibition of despair has continued long enough," Catharine announced, settling herself in the chair beside the bed. "You have sequestered yourself in this chamber for four days, Margaret. Four entire days of wallowing whilst the rest of London gossips about your supposed involvement with that dreadful man."

"Let them gossip," Margaret replied with bitter resignation. "What does it matter now? I am ruined either way!"

"You are not ruined," Eliza said with her characteristic directness, reaching for Margaret's hand. "Inconvenienced, perhaps. Embarrassed, certainly. But hardly ruined beyond repair."

Margaret pulled her hand away, wrapping her arms around her knees in a gesture of self-protection that made her look younger than her years. "Oh, but you did not see the way Lady Pemberton looked at me! As though I were some fascinating specimen of foolishness on display for her amusement!"

"Lady Pemberton is a vicious creature," Catharine replied with characteristic bluntness. "Her opinion should carry as much weight as a feather in a breeze."

"But it is not merely her opinion, is it?" Margaret's voice cracked, the words tumbling out in a rush. "I have heard the whispers, seen the scandal sheets! 'The Duke's Discarded Darling.' And 'Miss Fairbourne's Mortifying Miscalculation.' They're making sport of my humiliation, and I simply cannot bear it!"

"The papers print whatever nonsense will sell copies," Eliza said with dry practicality. "Next week, some other poor soul will provide fresh entertainment, and you will be yesterday's news."

"That is hardly comforting," Margaret muttered.

"Perhaps not," Catharine agreed, "but it is truthful. And truth, however unpalatable, is infinitely preferable to the romantic delusions that landed you in this predicament."

Margaret flinched as though Catharine had struck her. "My romantic delusions? You speak as though I deliberately courted scandal!"

"Did you not?" Catharine's eyebrow arched with surgical precision. "You pursued a man of questionable character with remarkable persistence, despite having no real knowledge of his nature or intentions."

Margaret's voice rose, the words rushing together in her distress. "Was I so terribly wrong to hope for affection? For genuine regard? For something beautiful and real?"

"Not wrong, perhaps, but certainly naïve," Catharine replied without mercy. "You allowed yourself to be guided by romantic fancy rather than practical sense."

"Pray tell, Catharine," Margaret snapped, her composure finally cracking entirely, "when has practical sense ever brought anyone happiness? When has careful calculation led to love? Never, that is when!"

Catharine's mouth tightened almost imperceptibly, but she said nothing.

"Both of you found love," Margaret continued, her words rushing out like water through a broken dam. "Yet you counsel me to abandon hope entirely? To settle for something cold and practical?"

"We advise you to protect yourself," Eliza said, though not unkindly. "To learn from this experience and move forward with greater wisdom."

"Move forward to what?" Margaret laughed, but the sound held no humour whatsoever. "To spinsterhood? To a marriage of convenience with some dreadful man who will overlook my tainted reputation in exchange for a hefty dowry?"

"To a respectable life," Catharine said with firm conviction. "To security and comfort and the gradual restoration of your good name."

Margaret stared at her eldest sister, feeling as though she were looking at a stranger. "Oh... is that truly what you believe I should want? Security over passion? Comfort over connection? How terribly sad that sounds!"

"I believe you should want to survive," Catharine replied with stark honesty. "Romance is a luxury, Margaret. A pretty ornament few of us can truly afford."

"How can you even say such things?" Margaret's voice broke entirely. "You who found a love match? You who defied every expectation to follow your heart? How can you be so cruel, Catharine?"

"Because I was fortunate," Catharine said quietly, something vulnerable flickering in her eyes. "Because Alaric saw past my sharp tongue and difficult nature to find something worth cherishing. But luck is not something one can depend upon, dearest. And you… you have already spent your portion of good fortune, I'm afraid."

Margaret wrapped her arms tighter around herself, trying to hold together the fragments of her breaking heart.

"You think I'm foolish…" she whispered. "You think my feelings are nothing more than girlish infatuation."

"We think you are hurting," Eliza said, her voice gentling. "And when we hurt, we sometimes mistake intensity for truth. It is only natural."

"But what if it is true?" Margaret looked up at her sisters with desperate hope shining in her eyes. "What if what I felt… what I still feel is real? What if his feelings, despite everything that's happened, were genuine?"

The silence that followed was contemplative, though heavy with concern as the sisters recalled Margaret's confession about being in love with another man on the evening of her engagement.

"Margaret," Catharine said finally, her voice gentler, "even if this gentleman's feelings were sincere, what does that change?

You have been caught in the aftermath of a scandal. Any association with you now would be... complicated."

Margaret felt tears threatening again, hot and bitter against her swollen eyelids. "So what would you have me do? Forget him entirely? Pretend that what we shared meant nothing at all?"

"We would have you think clearly," Eliza said with typical directness. "Think about what you truly want from life. Think about whether pursuing someone under such circumstances is wise."

"But what if my heart has already chosen regardless of wisdom or practicality?" Margaret's voice was barely above a whisper.

"Then we will support you," Catharine said finally, though her tone suggested she found the prospect troubling. "Whatever you choose, we will stand beside you. That is what sisters do."

Margaret felt something crack open in her chest—not breaking but expanding. Despite their concerns, her sisters would not abandon her. "Oh... I need to tell you something," she said quietly, gathering her courage. "Something I perhaps should have confessed days ago. About whom it is that I..."

Both sisters leaned forward slightly, their attention sharpening with familial concern.

"You see... it was not just the duke's attention I was seeking..." Margaret's voice grew steadier as she spoke, as though the confession were bringing her strength. "Someone offered to help me to learn to be more... sophisticated, more alluring."

"Margaret–" Eliza began, but Margaret held up a hand.

"What started as instruction became... intimate. Not merely physical, though there was that as well, but emotional. I felt like myself for the first time in my life. Not the youngest Fairbourne sister, not the sweet one, but Margaret. Simply Margaret."

Her sisters exchanged a look loaded with meaning and shared concern.

"And despite everything that's happened," Margaret continued, her voice growing stronger with each word, "despite the deception and the humiliation and the scandal, I cannot simply stop feeling what I feel. I cannot pretend that what we shared was meaningless."

"Margaret, please get to the point," Catharine said gently.

Margaret took a deep breath, feeling as though she were stepping off a cliff. "I am in love with Julian Ashcroft."

Eliza's face went completely white. "Julian?" she whispered as though she'd misheard.

Catharine shot to her feet so abruptly that her chair scraped against the floor. "Rhys's cousin?"

"Yes," Margaret said weakly, suddenly realising the enormity of her confession.

"Good God," Eliza breathed, sinking back against the bed as though her legs had given out. "Margaret, what have you done?"

"I have not done anything wrong!" Margaret protested, though her voice shook with uncertainty. "We... he was—"

"Providing you with scandalous lessons. And somewhere along the way, you managed to fall in love with him while he was using you to investigate the duke!" Catharine's voice rose with every word, her usual composure completely shattered.

"Margaret, do you have any comprehension of what this means?"

Tears spilled down Margaret's cheeks. "Oh, Catharine, don't start. I know how it looks, but I cannot believe it was all just a performance. You should have seen the way he looked at me, the tenderness in his voice…"

"All performance?" Eliza repeated, her voice climbing towards hysteria. "Margaret, what exactly happened during these 'lessons'?"

Margaret's cheeks flamed. "Nothing improper! Well… nothing entirely improper. He was teaching me to command a man's attention—"

"By compromising you?" Catharine demanded.

"No!" Margaret cried, though even as she said it, she knew it was not entirely untrue. "He was… we were…"

Catharine began pacing. "This is catastrophic. If one word of this gets out…"

"It won't," Margaret said desperately. "No one knows except—"

"Except the very man who has just exposed a duke and become the toast of London society. Who now holds every detail of your most private moments in his hands."

Margaret felt the blood drain from her face. "He would never!"

"No?" Catharine whirled to face her. "He has already proven he will sacrifice your well-being for his advancement."

Margaret shot to her feet, desperation making her voice crack. "I know his heart! When we were together, when he touched me, it was real! He would never betray me like that."

The two older sisters exchanged a look of pure horror.

"Touched you?" Catharine's voice was deadly quiet.

"Margaret," Eliza interjected carefully, "exactly how far did these lessons... progress?"

Margaret wrapped her arms around herself, suddenly feeling exposed. "I... We..."

Catharine sank into the chair as though her strings had been cut. "We are ruined. Utterly, completely ruined."

"We are not ruined!" Margaret objected. "No one knows, and Julian would never—"

"Julian has already demonstrated what he is capable of," Eliza said with devastating clarity.

Margaret felt her world crumbling. "You are wrong about him."

Catharine looked up at her with something like pity. "Oh, my dear, foolish sister. Do you honestly believe that?"

"Yes," Margaret whispered, though her voice barely held any conviction. "It has to be."

The three sisters sat in stunned silence for a while, the weight of Margaret's confession settling around them.

Finally, Catharine spoke, her voice heavy with resignation. "Then we must hope—for all our sakes—that your faith in Julian Ashcroft is not misplaced."

Fresh tears spilled down Margaret's cheeks, but for the first time in days, they were tears of gratitude rather than despair. Whatever happened next, whatever society might say, she would face it with her sisters beside her.

And perhaps, just perhaps, she would also face it with her heart intact.

Chapter Seventeen

"Brilliant stratagem this was, even for me," Julian muttered, lifting his brandy glass in a mockery of a toast to no one in particular. "Absolutely magnificent in its thoroughness."

He sat slouched in a worn leather chair in Rhys's office like a man who had just witnessed his own execution, the amber liquid in his glass tasting like victory laced with arsenic. Across from him, Rhys occupied his chair with characteristic restraint, while Alaric had claimed the window seat, his scarred profile sharp against the afternoon light streaming in through the tall windows.

The victory of exposing Strickland meant nothing. Less than nothing, if such a thing were possible.

Yes, the scandal had broken precisely as Julian had orchestrated. Yes, the House of Lords had moved with unprecedented swiftness—Strickland's title suspended pending formal inquiry, his social ruin spreading through London's drawing rooms like wildfire. And yes, Julian had emerged as the conquering hero, the brilliant legal mind who had exposed corruption at the highest levels.

But all he could think about was the devastation in Margaret's eyes as she turned from him in that corridor.

"You're brooding," Rhys observed with typical directness. "It's rather unlike you."

"My dear cousin, I prefer to think of it as contemplating the delicious irony of achieving everything I set out to accomplish whilst simultaneously destroying the very thing that actually mattered." Julian's smile held no humour whatsoever. "There's something almost poetic about such spectacular failure disguised as triumph."

"You protected her from a worse fate," Alaric said quietly. "That has to count for something."

Julian laughed bitterly. "Protected her? I used her as unwitting bait in my investigation whilst teaching her to seduce the very man I was planning to destroy. I'm not entirely certain the word 'protection' applies to such methodology."

"You couldn't have known—" Rhys began.

"Couldn't I?" Julian interrupted, setting down his glass with more force than necessary. "I might have found a way to warn her without making her the unwitting centrepiece of a public scandal. I might have trusted her with the truth. Instead, I used her pursuit of him as perfect cover for my investigation whilst I gathered evidence."

The weight of his self-recrimination settled between them. Julian rose from his chair and began pacing, his movements restless as a caged animal.

"She introduced victims to their tormentor, Rhys. Can you imagine how thoroughly she must despise me?"

"You're being rather hard on yourself," Alaric said finally. "You handled it poorly, perhaps, but that doesn't negate the necessity of what you accomplished."

"I wonder what the other ladies would say if they had known that their salvation would come at the cost of an innocent girl's reputation. Would they have considered it fair trade?"

Before either man could respond, the study door opened with quiet authority. Lord Ventnor stepped into the room like a man accustomed to command, his presence immediately shifting the atmosphere. He possessed the sort of aura that could sway decisions in the House of Lords, each word he uttered polished to diamond-like perfection.

"Your Grace." Lord Ventnor nodded to Rhys, then turned his attention to Alaric. "Lord Ravensedge." His eyes finally settled on Julian with something approaching approval. "Mr. Ashcroft. How fortunate to find you all together."

Julian straightened instinctively. "Lord Ventnor."

"To what do we owe the pleasure?" Rhys asked with smooth courtesy.

"To Mr. Ashcroft's rather spectacular dismantling of the Duke of Ashcombe," Lord Ventnor replied, settling himself with practiced ease. "What you accomplished—exposing nobility wrapped in corruption, unravelling a network of deceit, liberating those poor women—has not gone unnoticed in the highest circles."

Julian felt his pulse quicken despite himself. "I simply followed the facts where they led me, my lord."

"Indeed, you did. And with remarkable thoroughness, I might add." Lord Ventnor's eyes never left Julian's face. "The documentation you provided was so comprehensive that Strickland's legal counsel advised him to flee rather than attempt a defence. That level of preparation speaks to considerable foresight and strategic thinking."

"I simply pursued justice, my lord," Julian said carefully. "Nothing more dramatic than that."

"Ah, but there you underestimate yourself." Lord Ventnor's smile was razor-sharp. "It was bold. It was brilliantly executed. Showcasing the sort of moral fibre and courage that attracts... supporters."

The room fell silent except for the gentle ticking of the mantle clock. Julian studied Lord Ventnor's expression, searching for the trap that surely lay beneath such flattery.

"Supporters?" he echoed.

"Indeed. Questions have been raised about whether a man of your... capabilities might be better utilised in service to the Crown, Mr. Ashford." Lord Ventnor paused meaningfully, pressing his palms together. "A dormant ducal title has become available—the late Duke of Ashwick passed away last month without an heir."

Julian's mind reeled as the implications of Lord Ventnor's words crashed over him.

"You're not seriously suggesting—"

"I am stating that the governance of this great country recognises exceptional service when it encounters it," Lord Ventnor replied smoothly. "Your actions have done more to restore faith in British justice than a dozen parliamentary reforms. The public sees you as incorruptible, Mr. Ashcroft—a man who places principle above all else."

Julian nearly choked on the irony. If only they knew how thoroughly his personal feelings had influenced his every decision.

"The title would come with estates in Yorkshire and Devon. Respectable holdings, including several profitable coal mines. The annual income would be... substantial. Certainly sufficient to support a ducal lifestyle without compromising one's independence."

Julian blinked at him, feeling as though he were witnessing someone else's life unfold. "Such generosity is quite overwhelming, my lord."

"The offer naturally comes with certain expectations," Lord Ventnor continued. "The Crown would expect you to take your seat in the House of Lords, to speak on matters of justice and legal reform. Your voice would carry considerable weight, given your recent triumph."

Julian practically felt the room spinning slightly, as though he had consumed far more brandy than he had. "And if I were to consider such... what would the timeline attached thereto be, my lord?"

"The formal ceremony could be arranged within a fortnight," Lord Ventnor replied. "His Majesty is most eager to demonstrate royal support for those who uphold justice. Consider it carefully, Mr. Ashcroft. The formal offer will be presented to you within the week."

With that pronouncement, he rose and swept from the room as efficiently as he had entered it, leaving the three men in stunned silence.

"Good God," Alaric breathed. "A dukedom."

"Everything you once claimed you didn't want," Rhys observed quietly, studying Julian's face with shrewd eyes.

"A mere fortnight..." Julian said wonderingly. "From ordinary solicitor to duke in the span of two weeks. It's almost absurd enough to be one of my own fabrications."

He stood abruptly, suddenly desperate for air that didn't taste of brandy and shattered dreams. "I need to walk. I need to think. I need to... God knows what I need."

"Julian," Rhys called as he reached the door.

"What?"

"If my wife is to be believed, Margaret has dreamt of marrying a duke since she was a child."

Julian's hand froze on the door handle. "After betraying her so thoroughly?"

"After proving you're worthy of her trust," Rhys corrected. "Your exposure of Strickland protected her just as much as anyone else. She'll see that in time."

"Will she?" Julian's voice carried a note of desperate hope. "Or will she see it as the ultimate manipulation? Imagine how this appears—the man who taught her to seduce a duke, orchestrating that duke's downfall, to claim both title and bride for himself."

"You are being dramatic, even for you," Alaric pointed out. "She fell in love with you before any of that. Before you had this title."

Julian stepped out without responding, his mind spinning like a compass needle seeking north.

The corridor outside Rhys's office felt like a different world entirely—one where the impossible had become inevitable, where a man's entire future could shift in the space of a single conversation. Julian walked slowly, his footsteps echoing against the polished floors as he tried to process what had just occurred.

A duke. Everything he had judged and proclaimed he didn't want, offered to him now like some cosmic jest. God, it seemed, possessed a twisted sense of humour—offering a man everything precisely when he had destroyed any hope of happiness.

Or perhaps, his treacherous heart whispered, it was offering him the means to win her back. To make things right.

He turned the corner and stopped dead.

She was there, across the street with Eliza, her golden hair catching the light from the tall windows. Margaret looked pale and fragile, like porcelain that had been cracked but not yet shattered. When she noticed him, she froze entirely, her blue eyes growing wide with something that might have been panic.

For a heartbeat that stretched into eternity, they simply stared at each other across the space that might as well have been an ocean. Julian felt his heart hammering against his ribs like a caged animal desperate for freedom.

Eliza murmured something to Margaret, her expression sharp with protective warning. Margaret shook her head slightly, but her gaze never left Julian's face.

He had to speak with her. Had to explain. Had to somehow bridge the chasm that his choices had created between them.

Julian began walking towards them, each step feeling like a leap into an abyss. Margaret's chin lifted with familiar stubbornness, though he could see the tears threatening to spill from her eyes.

"Margaret," he said softly when he reached them. "Might I have a word?"

Eliza stepped forward, her voice cold. "Mr. Ashcroft, in light of recent events, I hardly think it appropriate for you to approach my sister so directly. There are curious eyes everywhere."

Julian inclined his head, recognising the wisdom in her words. Several peers lingered nearby, watching with barely concealed interest. "Of course, Your Grace. Perhaps it would be more appropriate for me to call upon Lord Fairbourne instead."

As he walked away, Julian's mind was already calculating. Lord Fairbourne was a practical man who understood advantageous matches. Perhaps the promise of another dukedom would be enough to secure Margaret's hand—even if the formal ceremony was still a fortnight away.

The one thing he didn't particularly want to contemplate was whether Margaret would accept his proposal or chase him away entirely.

Chapter Eighteen

"Oh, Margaret, surely you cannot mean to remain hidden away like this forever."

Catharine's voice drifted through the locked door, carrying that particular note of exasperation she reserved for behaviour she deemed unreasonable. Margaret pulled the silk counterpane over her head, blocking out both her sister's reproach and the afternoon sunlight that insisted on streaming through her curtains despite her preference for eternal darkness.

"I am not hidden away," Margaret called back, her voice muffled by fabric and misery. "I am merely... strategically retreating from society until they find someone else to entertain themselves with."

"Dearest—" Eliza's gentle tone replaced Catharine's brisk impatience. "It has been a full week. People are beginning to worry."

A week. Had it truly only been seven days since Julian had destroyed the Duke of Ashcombe so spectacularly in front of half the House of Lords? It felt like months had passed since she herself had become the ton's most spectacular scandal, her name bandied about in drawing rooms and scandal sheets with gleeful creativity.

The Duke's Discarded Darling.

Miss Fairbourne's Foolish Fancy.

The Lady Who Loved a Liar.

Each headline had been more inventive than the last, the columnists apparently competing to craft the most humiliating moniker for her romantic downfall. This morning's edition had dubbed her 'The Almost-Duchess Who Almost Knew Better'—a title that stung with particular accuracy.

"Margaret?" Catharine tried again. "Will you not at least take some tea? Cook has prepared those lemon cakes you are so fond of."

Lemon cakes. As though sugar and citrus could somehow sweeten the bitter taste of being London's premier cautionary tale.

"I'm not particularly hungry!" Margaret mumbled into her pillow.

The truth was far more complicated than loss of appetite. The scandal sheets hadn't merely reported her association with the disgraced duke. Oh no, that would have been far too tame for London's grapevine. According to the rumours now circulating through every tearoom and ballroom in Mayfair, she hadn't simply been pursuing that horrid man's hand in marriage.

She had been his *mistress.*

The accusation was so vile, so utterly shocking that Margaret felt sick whenever she thought of it. They claimed she had shared his bed willingly, repeatedly, enthusiastically. That her pursuit of his hand had been merely a desperate attempt to legitimise what had already been scandalously consummated.

"Have you not heard?" Margaret said. "The morning papers suggested I had been conducting 'intimate correspondence' with him. Apparently, my romantic optimism was evidence of... previous experience with the duke's particular talents."

A soft gasp came from beyond the door—Eliza, no doubt.

Margaret rolled onto her back, staring at the ceiling where afternoon shadows danced like accusations. The irony was almost laughable. She hadn't been Nathaniel Strickland's mistress, but she had allowed Julian to teach her things no unmarried lady should know. She had let him touch her in ways that still made her breath catch in the dark hours before dawn.

And now? Julian was gone, vanished as thoroughly as morning mist after exposing the duke's crimes. He'd saved her from a marriage to a monster, but in doing so, he'd left her reputation in tatters and her heart in pieces she couldn't seem to gather back together.

"Margaret." Catharine's voice had softened considerably. "I know this feels insurmountable, but scandals do pass. Society moves to fresh gossip with remarkable speed."

"Do they?" Margaret laughed, but the sound held no humour. "Tell me, Catharine, when was the last time you heard Lady Woodbury's name mentioned without reference to her affair? Or Mrs. Crompton's without mention of her gambling debts?"

Silence greeted this observation, which was answer enough.

"Just go away, both of you!" Margaret grumbled. She closed her eyes, remembering the single occasion she'd ventured downstairs since the scandal broke. Even the household staff had looked at her differently, their usual warm smiles replaced by curious speculation. If her own servants stared, what hope did she have with society at large?

A former friend had cut her directly outside Hatchard's bookshop. Lady Pemberton, with whom she'd shared countless afternoon teas and morning calls, had looked right through her as though Margaret had suddenly turned invisible, the deliberate snub more devastatingly cutting than any headline could have been.

And the worst part—the part that made her stomach churn with something deeper than shame—was knowing Julian had been right about the disgraced duke all along. Every warning, every raised eyebrow, every moment of disapproval had been justified. Julian had seen the danger whilst she'd been blinded by coronets and calculations.

And she had dismissed his concerns like some infatuated girl who believed titles and love could transform monsters into princes.

Her thoughts scattered like startled birds every time she tried to untangle the mess of feelings Julian had left behind. Anger at his high-handed decision to expose Nathaniel Strickland without consulting her. Gratitude for saving her from a marriage that would have been her destruction. Confusion about the way he'd looked at her during their last encounter—as though she mattered more than mere lessons or convenience.

And underneath it all, a hollow ache that seemed to intensify rather than fade with each passing day.

"Miss Margaret," came the butler's formal voice through the door, interrupting her spiralling thoughts, "your father requests your immediate presence in his study."

Margaret's blood turned to ice. Her father's 'requests' were never optional, and his study was where pronouncements of consequence were delivered with absolute, irrevocable authority. Perhaps he had received word from the disgraced duke's family? Had he somehow managed to arrange some form of exile for her to the countryside, where she could hide her shame from society's judging eyes?

Or perhaps—and this thought made her stomach lurch—he had found her a husband willing to overlook her tainted reputation in exchange for her dowry.

"Tell him I shall be down directly," she managed.

Margaret caught sight of herself in the mirror as she rose—pale as winter moonlight, eyes swollen from days of crying, golden curls hanging limp around her shoulders. She looked exactly like what she was: a ruined woman whose dreams had been crumbled to ash.

The journey downstairs felt like walking towards her own execution. Each step echoed through the quiet house, marking time towards whatever fresh humiliation awaited. She paused outside the study door, her hand hovering over the brass handle as she took a deep breath, summoning what little remained of her courage.

Whatever lay beyond this threshold would determine the rest of her life, and she was no longer the naïve girl who had once believed in fairy-tale endings.

Margaret straightened her shoulders, lifted her chin with the ghost of her former confidence, and opened the door.

What she found on the other side stopped her short like a carriage hitting a brick wall.

Julian Ashcroft stood beside her father's desk, his familiar form both shocking and somehow inevitable. He looked exactly as she remembered—charming, well-dressed, carrying himself with that same charming presence that had once made her pulse race.

But now his grey eyes held something else, something she'd never seen there before: uncertainty.

"Oh!" she breathed, despite herself. "What are *you* doing here?"

Her father answered her instead, his tone that of a man who had just concluded a pleasing business arrangement, his words falling like stones dropped into still water.

"Margaret, Mr. Ashcroft has come to ask for your hand in marriage."

Chapter Nineteen

"I beg your pardon?"

The words slipped from Margaret's lips like breath from a drowning woman. Surely she had misheard. Surely her father couldn't have said what she'd thought he'd said.

But Lord Fairbourne's expression remained impassive as granite, his voice carrying the same tone he might use to discuss the morning's correspondence. "Mr. Ashcroft has accepted a dukedom as reward for his service to the Crown in exposing the Duke of Ashcombe's criminal enterprise. In light of this elevation, he has come to request your hand in marriage."

Margaret's gaze snapped to Julian, searching his face for some sign of jest, some indication that this was merely another one of his performances. But his grey eyes held steady, watching her with an expression she couldn't decipher.

"A dukedom," she repeated slowly, the word tasting strange on her tongue.

"The Duke of Ashwick," Julian said quietly. "The title became available recently."

"How... convenient." Margaret's voice sharpened like a blade finding its edge. "And this proposal of marriage—another convenient solution to clean up the mess you've made?"

"Margaret." Her father's voice carried a note of warning. "Perhaps you might listen to the full explanation before passing judgment."

But Margaret barely heard him. Fury was building in her chest like steam in a kettle, threatening to boil over in ways that would shock them both. "No discussion? No choice?

Simply another arrangement made without consulting the very woman whose life you are reshaping?"

"It is the only viable solution," Lord Fairbourne said firmly. "Your reputation has been thoroughly compromised by the association with Nathaniel Strickland. No other reputable gentleman shall ever offer for you now. But a marriage to a newly elevated duke—a man publicly lauded for his moral courage—would restore both your standing and our family's honour."

The room felt suddenly airless, as though the walls were closing in around her. Margaret looked between the two men who had apparently decided her future over brandy and legal documents, and something dangerous sparked in her chest.

"How perfectly efficient," she said, her tone bright as shattered glass. "Tell me, Your Grace, did you plan this entire debacle? Supported my pursuit of the disgraced duke, knowing you would destroy him, leaving me so thoroughly ruined that I'd have no other choice but to accept your magnanimous offer?"

Julian's face went pale. "Margaret, you cannot possibly believe—"

"No? You disapproved of the duke since the Winter Ball. You warned me against him repeatedly. Yet," Margaret continued, choosing her words carefully in the presence of her father, "you continued to aid me, advising me in my pursuit of him, gathered evidence of his crimes whilst allowing me to dig my own social grave deeper and deeper with each encounter." Her voice rose with each accusation. "How very thoroughly you've managed all of it, Your Grace!"

"Margaret! That is quite enough," Lord Fairbourne interjected sharply. "Such wild accusations are beneath you."

But Margaret's control had finally snapped like an overstretched violin string. "Beneath me? According to the scandal sheets, nothing is beneath me anymore! They claim I was his mistress, Father! That I shared his bed willingly, that I pursued a marriage to legitimise what had already been consummated. My reputation is in tatters, and you present me with a convenient duke as though he were a consolation prize!"

Julian stepped forward, his expression tortured. "Margaret, please. Allow me to explain privately—"

"Oh! How generous! Another private lesson? What shall you teach me this time—how to be grateful for my own rescue?"

Her father's voice cut through the tension like a whip crack. "You shall speak to His Grace with appropriate respect."

The title hung in the air between them, foreign and somehow obscene. Margaret stared at Julian—truly looked at him—and saw a stranger wearing a familiar face. When had he become this person who orchestrated scandals and accepted titles as payment for destroying others?

"Very well," she said, her voice suddenly calm as a winter lake. "I believe I shall speak with His Grace. Privately."

She walked towards the French doors leading to the garden without waiting for permission, her spine straight as a sword blade. Behind her, she heard Julian's footsteps following, measured and careful as a man walking towards his own execution.

The morning air bit at her cheeks as she stepped onto the terrace, but she welcomed the cold. It helped clear her head, helped her think beyond the white-hot fury that threatened to consume what remained of her rational thoughts.

"Margaret." Julian's voice was gentle, reasonable—the same one he'd used during their lessons when correcting her posture or her conversation. "This isn't what you believe it to be."

She whirled to face him, her skirts swirling around her ankles like storm clouds. "Isn't it? Then pray, enlighten me. How exactly should I interpret this rather perfectly timed proposal of yours?"

"As an attempt to make amends for the damage my actions caused you." He ran a hand through his dark hair, disturbing its careful arrangement. "I knew exposing Strickland would create a scandal, but I couldn't allow you to marry him. Not when I knew what manner of man he truly was and what that would mean for you."

"So you decided for me." The words dropped between them like stones. "Without consultation, without warning, without giving me the chance to make my own choice."

"What choice would you have made?" Julian's composure cracked slightly. "If I had told you Strickland was a blackmailer and a predator, would you have believed me? Or would you have thought I was simply jealous of a rival?"

The question hit its mark with uncomfortable accuracy. Margaret had dismissed his warnings, had attributed his disapproval to possessiveness or wounded pride. But that didn't excuse what had come after.

"Perhaps I would have been foolish enough to question you," she admitted, wrapping her arms around herself against the morning chill. "But that was my foolishness to make. My mistake to learn from. Instead, you orchestrated my salvation whilst ensuring I had no other choice but to accept it."

Julian stepped closer, close enough that she could see the exhaustion etched around his eyes, the way his carefully maintained charm had worn thin over the past week.

A LADY'S LESSONS IN SIN

"Margaret, I never intended for the scandal to touch you so severely. I thought… I hoped the evidence would speak for itself without implicating innocent parties."

"Innocent parties?" Margaret laughed, but it held no warmth. "How naïve you must think me. Did you truly believe I could pursue a duke publicly for weeks without becoming associated with his downfall?"

"I thought I could protect you from the worst of it."

"By what means? By arranging to marry me yourself?" She shook her head, golden curls catching the morning light like spun gold. "This isn't protection, Julian. It's acquisition. You've simply replaced one titled husband with another—yourself!"

His face went white as though she'd struck him. "You think this has all been about…acquiring you?"

"Isn't it? You've gained a title, exposed a criminal, enhanced your reputation, and secured a wife whose family connections could benefit your new political position. A rather comprehensive victory, wouldn't you say?"

For a moment, Julian simply stared at her, something raw and wounded flickering behind his grey eyes. Then his expression shuttered, returning to that careful neutrality he'd worn in her father's study.

"Perhaps you're right," he said quietly. "Perhaps this is simply another transaction disguised as romantic salvation."

The easy agreement stung worse than any protest could have. Margaret felt something vital crack inside her chest, a fault line she hadn't known existed until this moment of impact.

But her father was right. There were truly no other options and none likely to come. That had been made brutally clear.

Marriage to Julian or spinsterhood shadowed by a sandal. Her family's reputation or her own stubborn pride. Those were her choices.

"Very well," she said, her voice steady as the ground beneath her feet. "I accept your proposal."

Relief flickered across Julian's features, but Margaret held up her hand before he could speak.

"However, there shall be terms. This marriage shall be one of convenience only. You require a duchess. I require respectability. Beyond what is necessary for public appearances, there shall be no expectation of... intimacy or affection. We shall maintain separate lives within the bounds of social propriety."

Each word felt like a small death, but Margaret forced herself to continue. "You shall have your political alliance, and I shall have my name restored. Nothing more."

Julian's jaw tightened almost imperceptibly. "If those are your terms."

"They are."

"Then I accept them."

His easy surrender lodged in her throat like a thorn. Of all the wounds he'd inflicted, his willingness to agree to a loveless marriage stung most deeply. But what had she expected? Passionate protests? Declarations of feeling? Julian was always theatrical, except when he needed to be, and she was being utterly ridiculous with her expectations.

"Margaret! Julian!"

Eliza's voice carried across the garden like salvation, though whether from heaven or hell remained to be seen. Margaret turned to see her sister approaching with Rhys, their faces creased with concern and unmistakable curiosity.

"We heard..." Eliza began carefully, her intelligent eyes darting between them as though trying to read the charged atmosphere. "Is it true? About the engagement?"

Margaret felt her face transform, muscles rearranging themselves into an expression of radiant joy so bright it could have outshone the morning sun. The mask slipped into place with practiced ease, every lesson in deportment she'd ever received suddenly serving this moment of perfect deception.

"Oh, Eliza! Yes, it's perfectly true!" She clasped her hands together as though overwhelmed by happiness, her voice rising with musical excitement. "Julian has done me the extraordinary honour of proposing, and I have accepted! Can you imagine? A duchess! Who would have dreamed such a wonderful thing could come from such a dreadful week?"

The words sparkled and danced in the air like champagne bubbles—effervescent, celebratory, and utterly hollow.

Eliza's face brightened with genuine pleasure, but her eyes remained sharp with sisterly intuition. "How perfectly wonderful! And how unexpected... though I suppose love rarely follows conventional timing."

"Love," Margaret repeated, the word feeling strange and bitter in her mouth. "Yes, quite unexpected indeed!"

Rhys stepped forward to clasp Julian's hand with warm congratulations. "Well done, cousin. About time you settled yourself advantageously."

"About time indeed," Julian replied, his charm sliding back into place like armour. "Though I'll confess myself simply stunned by my good fortune in securing dear Margaret's acceptance."

Margaret watched this exchange of masculine satisfaction with growing nausea. They spoke of her as though she were a particularly fine horse they'd successfully bid upon at Tattersalls.

"We must celebrate properly," Eliza declared, already planning in that decisive way that made her such an effective duchess. "A dinner party, perhaps? Of course, we should post an announcement in the papers."

"How delightful," Margaret said, her smile never wavering even as something died quietly inside her chest. "I'm certain everyone shall be utterly captivated and fascinated to read about my sudden elevation from ruined woman to future duchess. What remarkable transformation a little bit of scandal can achieve when properly managed."

The garden fell silent except for the distant sound of carriages passing by and the soft rustle of autumn leaves overhead. Margaret could feel Julian's eyes on her, could sense his growing alarm at her little performance, but she refused to meet his gaze.

"Well then," she announced brightly. "I believe I shall return inside to... to plan my wedding. Such exciting preparations await!"

Without waiting for anyone to respond, Margaret turned on her heels and walked back into the house, her steps measured and graceful despite the fact that her entire world had just narrowed to the width of a coffin.

Behind her, she could hear the murmur of concerned voices, but she didn't pause. She had played her part perfectly—the grateful, glowing bride-to-be whose reputation had been magically restored by a rather convenient proposal.

Now she simply had to survive the performance for the rest of her life.

Chapter Twenty

"Another clean shot," Rhys observed dryly, his arms crossed against the early morning chill. "Your aim remains impeccable, even when your temperament resembles that of a wounded bear."

Julian reloaded the pistol in his hands without comment, the familiar weight steady in his grip. The shot that followed echoed across the empty field—a stretch of frost-bitten grass bordered by bare oak trees, their skeletal branches clawing at the grey morning sky—sharp and final as a judge's gavel. Pieces of straw scattered from the hay bale like his thoughts—fragments that refused to arrange themselves into anything resembling coherent reflection.

"It's my wedding day," he said by way of explanation, though the words felt strange in his mouth. "A gentleman should celebrate such occasions with precision shooting, shouldn't he?"

"Hmm. Most gentlemen celebrate with champagne and nervous laughter." Rhys watched another bale disintegrate under Julian's aim. "Though I suppose your approach is rather more honest about the violence involved in matrimony."

Julian lowered the pistol, finally meeting his cousin's shrewd gaze. "She detests me."

"She's angry with you. There's a distinction."

"Is there?" Julian set the weapon aside, his hands surprisingly steady despite the chaos in his chest. "Because from where I stood last week, watching her announce our engagement with that exaggerated, glittering joy that could have cut glass, the difference seemed rather academic."

The morning air nipped at his exposed skin where his collar lay open, but Julian welcomed the discomfort. Physical sensation helped to ground him when his thoughts threatened to spiral into territories that he couldn't afford to explore, like the way Margaret's eyes had flickered with something that might have been hurt when he'd simply accepted her cold terms so readily.

"She's protecting herself," Rhys said matter-of-factly. "You shattered her trust, orchestrated her salvation without consulting her, and then presented her with a convenient solution that benefits your own interests remarkably well. Can you truly blame her for maintaining distance?"

Julian's laugh was sharp as winter wind. "When you phrase it like that, you make me sound positively mercenary, dear cousin."

"Aren't you?"

The question hit its mark with uncomfortable precision. Julian had spent years perfecting the art of manipulation disguised as assistance, of achieving goals whilst convincing others he was merely being helpful. He had years of experience twisting and spinning scandals for benefit... It was what had made him so effective in legal circles, what had allowed him to build influence without title or inheritance.

But with Margaret, the lines had all blurred together until he could no longer properly distinguish between protecting her and claiming her for himself.

"Perhaps I am," he admitted quietly.

They walked back towards the waiting carriage in silence, their footsteps muffled by the frost-hardened grass beneath their feet. The morning sky hung low and grey, threatening rain that would perfectly match Julian's mood.

"You know," Rhys said as they reached the vehicle, "there was a time when you scorned gentlemen as pompous peacocks who'd inherited privilege they'd never earned."

"I still do."

"And yet here you are, Duke of Ashwick now, about to marry a woman who dreamed of nothing more than a coronet and respectability." Rhys paused meaningfully. "The irony is rather delicious, even for you, don't you think?"

Julian accepted the brandy flask that Rhys offered, letting the liquor burn away some of the cold that had settled in his bones. "The universe does possess a rather twisted sense of humour. Offer a man everything he once claimed to despise, precisely when he's destroyed any hope of happiness—it's like handing someone the crown jewels whilst they're standing on the gallows."

"Or perhaps it's offering you the means to win her back."

"Win her back?" Julian's voice cracked slightly. "Rhys, the woman has agreed to marry me on condition that we never share anything more intimate than a dinner table. She's made it abundantly clear that this union is purely transactional—my title and her respectability, nothing more."

"Then prove her wrong," Rhys said simply. "Show her this marriage could be more than mere convenience."

Julian stared at him as though he'd suggested flying to the moon. "How precisely does one prove affection to a woman who's made it clear she wants nothing to do with such sentiment? Margaret has built walls around herself that would make fortress architects weep with envy."

The carriage wheels' steady rhythm over cobblestones carried them towards the church where Julian would pledge his life to a woman who considered him little more than a necessary evil. Through the window, he watched the city awaken—shopkeepers opening their doors, vendors setting up their stalls, ordinary people beginning ordinary tasks that wouldn't end with marriage to someone who hated them.

"The Prime Minister wishes to meet next week," Julian said abruptly, pulling his own attention away from self-pity. "Lord Ventnor mentioned parliamentary committees, legal reform initiatives, speeches to be written and delivered... Apparently, the Duke of Ashwick's title comes with a collection of rather extensive responsibilities."

"Nervous about your new role?"

"Terrified," Julian admitted honestly. "I've spent years mocking the very institution I'm now expected to serve with distinction. What if I'm completely unsuited to this life? What if accepting this title was the most elaborate mistake I've ever made?"

Rhys's expression softened with something approaching sympathy. "Then you'll learn, cousin. Besides, your irreverence might be exactly what Parliament needs—someone who questions privilege from the inside rather than simply accepting it as divine right."

The church loomed ahead, its ancient stones weathered by centuries of ceremonies both joyful and dutiful. Julian's stomach clenched as the carriage stopped, knowing that Margaret was somewhere inside, probably sitting stiff as a marble statue whilst her family prepared her for a marriage that would save her reputation and destroy any remaining hope of happiness.

"One last drink?" Rhys offered the flask again.

Julian accepted it gratefully, savouring the burn that served as a temporary distraction from the hollow ache expanding in his chest. "To marital bliss and political ambition."

"To not making a complete hash of either."

Julian nodded before fixing his cravat and stepping out, his boots clicking against the floor as he made his way inside St. George's Chapel.

The church had filled respectably. It was not the grand affair that Margaret deserved, but sufficient to make their union official in society's eyes. Julian took his position at the altar, his hands clasped behind his back to hide their trembling, and waited for his bride to appear.

And when she did, the sight of her nearly stopped his heart entirely.

Margaret moved down the aisle like a woman walking to her own doom, her face pale but composed, her arm tucked through her father's with dutiful precision. She wore a dress of ivory silk that caught the light streaming in through the stained-glass windows, transforming her into something ethereal and untouchable.

She didn't look at him. Not once.

Julian felt the space between them like a physical barrier, an invisible wall she'd erected to keep him at a safe distance. When she reached his side, the scent of her perfume—something delicate with notes of jasmine—hit him like a blow to the stomach.

"Dearly beloved…" the minister began, his voice echoing through the stone arches that had witnessed countless unions over the centuries, "we have gathered here today to celebrate the union…"

The ceremony proceeded with nothing less than mechanical efficiency. Julian spoke his vows with the same precision he used to present legal arguments, whilst Margaret's responses came in carefully modulated tones that showed no sign of the woman who had once laughed with uninhibited joy in his arms.

When the minister instructed him to kiss his bride, Julian hesitated. Margaret's blue eyes met his for the first time all day, and what he saw there—resignation mingling with something that might have been a plea of some kind—nearly undid him completely.

His lips brushed against hers with the reverence reserved for handling something precious and fragile. The contact lasted mere seconds, but the warmth of her mouth, the faint tremor he felt in her lips, would be seared into his memory until his dying day.

"I now pronounce you man and wife."

The words echoed like a death knell in the hushed church. Margaret stepped away before Julian could offer his arm, creating that careful distance she'd maintained during the brief courtship between their engagement and wedding. He followed her down the aisle, acutely aware of the curious stares from their guests.

Outside, their carriage waited like a hearse, black and imposing against the grey morning sky. Margaret climbed inside without assistance, settling herself as far from him as the confines would allow. Julian took the opposite seat, noting how she fixed her gaze on the window as though the passing London streets were far more fascinating than her new husband.

The silence stretched between them like a chasm neither seemed willing to bridge. Julian studied her profile—the stubborn set of her jaw, the way her fingers worried the fabric of her gloves, the careful control she maintained over her every expression.

"We needn't maintain this arctic silence for the entire journey," he said finally, his voice carrying just enough charm to mask the uncertainty beneath.

"No?" Margaret's response came without her turning from the window. "I rather thought cold civility was precisely what this arrangement demanded, Your Grace."

"Perhaps we might aim slightly higher than mere civility. Cordial neutrality, perhaps?"

Now she did turn to look at him, and Julian felt the full force of her blue eyes like a bucket of ice water poured over his head. "Very well, Your Grace. Shall we discuss the weather? Or perhaps you'd prefer to outline your expectations for our new domestic arrangements?"

The cold formality in her address hit him like a physical blow. She'd called him by his name for weeks during their lessons, the word falling from her lips with increasing intimacy until it had become music to his ears. Now she spoke to him like a stranger, and the distance felt wider than the Atlantic.

"I expect nothing beyond what you're willing to give," he said carefully.

"How remarkably progressive of you." Her tone could have frosted the carriage windows. "What an interesting choice of phrasing for a marriage, Your Grace."

They rode the rest of the way in a strained silence that felt heavier than lead, each lost in thoughts that could not bridge the careful distance they'd constructed between them. When the carriage finally stopped before his—now their—London townhouse, Julian climbed down first and offered his hand to assist her.

Margaret accepted his help with the same impersonal politeness she might show any gentleman, her fingers barely grazing his before she stepped away. She studied the elegant façade of her new home with the detached interest of someone viewing a painting in a gallery.

"It's quite lovely," she said.

"It is perfectly adequate," Julian noted, leading her towards the front door where his housekeeper waited with barely concealed curiosity. "The dukedom comes with estates that require attention. Yorkshire primarily, though there are holdings in Devon as well."

"Of course. Dukes must have multiple estates. How could I have forgotten such essential details?"

Despite her sarcasm, Julian bit back a response, recognising that anything he said would likely make matters worse. So instead, he focused on the practical realities of their new life: introductions to be made, responsibilities to be explained, the careful choreography of a marriage that must appear genuine to the outside world whilst remaining hollow to its core.

But as he watched Margaret accept his housekeeper's congratulations with perfect grace and fabricated joy, Julian couldn't shake the feeling that he'd won everything he'd never wanted whilst losing the only thing that truly mattered in the process.

Chapter Twenty-One

"So much for the romantic marriage I once dreamed of."

Margaret stood in the entrance hall of their London townhouse, staring at the marble floors that gleamed like mirrors. Everything was elegant, perfectly appointed, and utterly foreign.

"Mrs. Hopkins," Julian addressed the elderly housekeeper who waited with barely concealed curiosity, "perhaps you might show Her Grace through the house?"

"Of course, Your Grace. It would be my pleasure."

Margaret followed the woman through rooms that whispered of wealth—a drawing room decorated in shades of blue and gold, its silk wallpaper adorned with hand-painted birds; a large library lined with leather-bound volumes that looked more ornamental than read; and a dining room with a mahogany table that could easily seat twenty guests.

"The previous owner was fond of entertaining," Mrs. Hopkins explained as they moved through yet another perfectly coordinated sitting room. "Though I understand His Grace prefers... quieter pursuits."

"Indeed," Margaret murmured, though she wondered how they were supposed to fill these vast, silent rooms with anything resembling a life together.

"The breakfast room overlooks the gardens," Mrs. Hopkins continued, leading her to windows that revealed a small but exquisite space filled with winter roses and carefully trimmed hedges. "His Grace had it redesigned when he acquired the property."

Margaret studied the garden, noting how everything was beautiful, controlled, and utterly lacking the messy vitality of actual living.

"And upstairs," Mrs. Hopkins said, gesturing towards an elegant staircase, "the master suite, guest rooms, His Grace's study. All quite spacious and comfortable."

Margaret's stomach clenched at the thought of that shared space, of expectations she didn't quite understand.

"Perhaps I might rest a bit before dinner," she said quickly. "The day has been rather... eventful."

"Of course, Your Grace. I've prepared the rose room for you—it has the loveliest view of the square."

The room proved to be a sanctuary of cream silks and pale pink roses with windows that caught the afternoon light and a sitting area arranged around an elegant writing desk. For the first time since getting up that morning, Margaret felt as though she could breathe properly.

"Dinner will be served at eight," Mrs. Hopkins said with a curtsey.

"Thank you, Mrs. Hopkins."

Alone at last, Margaret sank onto the edge of the bed and finally allowed herself to absorb the full weight of what had occurred. She was married. Duchess of Ashwick. Living in this beautiful, sterile house with a man who'd agreed to marry her out of duty, convenience, and conscience.

But as she sat there watching shadows lengthen across the square below, something shifted in her chest. Not hope—she wasn't ready for that quite yet—but something closer to determination. They certainly couldn't have the kind of love her sisters had found. Julian had made that clear when he'd accepted her cold terms so readily. But perhaps...they could have something else. Something that made her feel less like she was drowning in emptiness.

Margaret rose and moved to the mirror, studying her reflection with new eyes, realising that she was utterly ignorant of the most fundamental aspect of matrimony. Both her sisters had spoken of it in careful euphemisms, of the joy to be found in marital intimacy. Catharine had blushed and mentioned 'surprising pleasures', whilst Eliza had become positively dreamy, only hinting at aspects of married life.

But they were vague, and Margaret deserved to understand. She deserved to experience what they'd experienced, even if the emotional connection wasn't there.

The thought was shocking and somehow liberating all at once.

When she finally arrived for dinner, Julian was waiting in the smaller dining room, having changed into evening attire that made him look devastatingly handsome and completely untouchable. The space felt more intimate than the grand dining room—a round table set for two with candles casting golden light.

"I trust your room is satisfactory?" he asked as he seated her.

"Quite lovely, thank you."

They ate in relative silence, perfectly prepared courses served by silent footmen, polite conversation about the house and new estates, careful avoidance of any topic that might lead to awkwardness. It was civilised, proper, and utterly lifeless.

"We needn't stay here long," Julian said as the plates were cleared. "The main estate is in Yorkshire, and it requires considerable attention. There are tenants to meet and—"

"Julian."

His name fell from her lips like a prayer or a challenge. He looked up, bewildered, as it was the first time she'd used his given name since their engagement.

"Yes?"

Margaret rose from her chair, heart hammering against her ribs. "I don't know how to do this…"

"Do what?"

"Be married. Live in this house. Pretend we're content with polite conversation and separate lives." She moved around the table towards him, each step requiring more courage than she'd known she possessed. "I don't know how to exist in a marriage neither of us truly wanted."

Julian stood as she approached, wariness flickering across his features. "Margaret—"

"But I know what I do want…" She was close enough now to see the pulse beating at his throat, close enough to catch his scent, something warm and masculine that made her head spin. "I want to know what it feels like to be claimed, desired, to matter to someone in ways that have nothing to do with duty."

His eyes went dark, hands clenching at his sides. "You don't understand what you're asking."

"Perhaps not." Margaret stepped closer, her skirts brushing his legs. "But I want my wedding night, Julian."

He opened his mouth to respond, but before she could lose her nerve, she reached up and pressed her lips to his.

The kiss caught him off guard. She felt his sharp intake of breath, the way his hands rose, then settled carefully on her waist. For a heartbeat, he remained frozen, and Margaret feared she had made a catastrophic miscalculation.

Then Julian's mouth moved against hers with sudden hunger, and the world tilted off its axis.

Her fingers found the buttons of his waistcoat, working at them with determined clumsiness while his hands tangled in her hair. The kiss deepened, becoming something wild and urgent that bore no resemblance whatsoever to the kiss they'd shared in the church.

"Margaret," Julian gasped, pulling back just enough to speak. "What are you doing?"

Her fingers moved to his shirt buttons, surprising herself with boldness. "I want to understand what this feels like."

Julian caught her hands. "You're confused. Frustrated. You don't know what you're truly asking for."

The patronising words ignited a fury that burned away her remaining hesitation. "I am tired of men telling me I don't know my own mind!"

Before Julian could respond, Margaret turned her back on him, presenting the long row of tiny pearl buttons that secured her wedding gown. "Please," she whispered, her voice steady despite the tremor in her hands. "Help me."

Julian's fingers worked at the buttons with excruciating care, each one revealing another inch of creamy skin beneath. The ivory silk whispered to the floor as he eased it from her shoulders, pooling around her feet, leaving her clad in nothing but the finest satin chemise and her stays.

Julian went utterly still, his eyes drinking in the sight of her with an intensity that made her skin burn everywhere at once.

"You're torturing me," he said hoarsely.

"Then perhaps you understand how I've felt through every lesson." Margaret lifted her chin with newfound courage. "Now stop being noble and claim your wife."

For a long moment, they simply stared at each other. Then Julian moved, closing the last fraction of distance between them, his mouth finding hers with desperate hunger.

This kiss was nothing like any that had come before. Julian kissed her as though she were the air and he'd been drowning, his hands roaming over her curves with reverent urgency.

"Are you certain?" he murmured against her lips. "Because once we cross this line—"

"I've never been more certain of anything."

Julian searched her eyes, then nodded with something like surrender. "Then let us do this properly. Let me show you how it should be."

He took her hand, their fingers intertwining as he led her towards the staircase. Margaret's heart pounded so loudly she was certain he could hear it, but she followed without hesitation.

His chambers were filled with candles flickering from silver sconces and decorated in deep blues and gold, dominated by a massive four-poster bed draped in midnight silk.

"Margaret," Julian said softly, turning to face her fully. "Are you truly certain? We needn't—"

She silenced him by pressing her fingers to his lips, feeling the warmth of his breath against her skin. "I want *you*, Julian."

Something shifted in his expression—surprise, relief, and something deeper that made her breath catch. Slowly, reverently, he lifted his hands to frame her face, his thumbs tracing the line of her cheekbones.

"Then let me worship you properly," he whispered, pressing gentle kisses to her forehead, her cheeks, the tip of her nose. "Let me show you how precious you are to me."

His mouth found hers again, but this kiss was different—slower, deeper, a thorough exploration that made her knees weak and her core ache with unfamiliar need. Margaret melted against him, her hands fisting in his shirt as liquid heat pooled between her thighs.

"My wife…" Julian murmured, his voice rough with wonder as he traced the line of her collarbone. "… My beautiful wife."

The words sent unexpected tremors of warmth flooding through her. His hands moved to the ribbons of her chemise, not with the urgent hunger she remembered from their lessons but with the careful reverence of a man unwrapping something infinitely precious. When she arched closer, pressing her body against the hard length of him, he slowly eased the satin from her shoulders until it whispered to the floor.

Margaret gasped at the sensation of cool air against her heated skin, at the way Julian's eyes darkened to stormy grey as he drank in the sight of her bare breasts, her nipples already perked and aching for his touch.

"God above," he breathed, his voice husky with desire. "You're exquisite."

Then his mouth was on her breast, and Margaret cried out at the shock of wet heat that shot straight to her core. Julian's tongue circled her nipple with maddening precision before drawing the sensitive peak between his lips, suckling gently until she was making sounds she didn't recognise as her own voice.

"Julian!" she gasped, her hands tangling in his dark hair, holding him against her as pleasure coursed through her. "Oh! I… ah… I…"

"I know, love," he soothed, his breath warm against her damp skin as he lavished the same attention to her other breast. "Will you let me take care of you?"

She nodded, and with infinite gentleness, he lifted her and carried her to the bed, laying her down on midnight silk sheets that felt cool and luxurious against her bare skin. Margaret watched through heavy-lidded eyes as he shed his clothing with urgent efficiency, revealing a carved masculine body that made her mouth go dry and something deep within her clench with want.

His chest was broad and muscled, tapering to a lean waist and narrow hips. But it was the sight of his arousal—thick and hard and ready for her—that made overwhelming heat flood her cheeks and something needy pulse between her legs.

"You're magnificent..." she breathed, reaching out to trace the definition of his chest, marvelling at the way his muscles jumped beneath her tentative touch.

"As are you, my darling wife," Julian said, his voice strained as he settled beside her on the bed, his hands beginning a leisurely exploration of every curve and hollow.

When his fingers finally found the slick heat between her thighs, Margaret arched off the bed with a cry of surprise and overwhelming pleasure. "I... I remember this," she whispered as his fingers began their intimate dance. "From before."

"This is different," Julian said softly, his thumb finding the sensitive pearl hidden between her folds while one finger slipped inside her welcoming heat. "This is our beginning, not a stolen moment in shadows." Margaret writhed against his hand, clutching at his shoulders as waves of pleasure threatened to drown her entirely.

"Julian... please!" she gasped, not even certain what she was begging for, only knowing she needed more of whatever he was doing to her. "I feel so... oh!"

"I know, love. You are so responsive." His voice was strained with his own need as he added another finger, stretching her carefully while his thumb continued its maddening circles. "Come apart for me, Margaret. Let me see you fall."

The coil of tension inside her snapped without warning, pleasure crashing over her in waves so intense she saw stars behind her closed eyelids. Her body clenched rhythmically around his fingers as she cried out his name, lost to everything but the overwhelming sensation.

"You come undone beautifully," he murmured, pressing gentle kisses to her face as the tremors gradually subsided.

When she could breathe again, Margaret found him watching her with an expression of such tender hunger it made her heart race anew.

"I want more..." she whispered.

Julian's control visibly snapped. He positioned himself above her, the tip of his engorged manhood hovering against her core as his eyes locked with hers.

"This may hurt at first," he warned, his voice thick with restraint. "But I'll be as gentle as I can."

Margaret nodded, trusting him completely as he slowly, carefully began to push inside her. The stretch was intense and uncomfortable, but not unbearable. When he encountered the barrier of her innocence, he paused.

"Breathe, darling," he whispered, pressing gentle kisses to her face. "The worst will be over quickly."

With one smooth thrust, he buried himself fully inside her. Margaret gasped at the sharp pain, tears pricking her eyes, but Julian held perfectly still, his forehead pressed to hers as they both adjusted to the intimate joining.

"You are so tight," he groaned, his body trembling with the effort of remaining motionless. "Are you all right?"

Gradually, the pain faded, replaced by a feeling of fullness that wasn't entirely unpleasant. Margaret experimentally shifted her hips, surprised by the answering flutter of pleasure that raced through her.

"Better," she whispered.

Julian began to move—slow, careful thrusts that gradually built into an exquisite friction, each measured stroke hitting places deep within her. His mouth found hers, swallowing her soft cries of pleasure as their bodies moved together in an ancient rhythm.

"Look at me," he commanded softly, waiting until her dazed eyes focused on his. "I want to see you when you come apart again."

The intimacy of his gaze, combined with the exquisite friction of their joined bodies, pushed Margaret towards another peak. When Julian shifted his weight, spreading her legs wide open, he plunged even deeper into her, and she shattered completely, her entire body clenching around him as pleasure cascaded through her in endless waves.

He followed her over the edge with a hoarse cry, his hips jerking as he pulsed deep within her, filling her with the seed of his love. He collapsed against her, both of them breathing hard as their hearts hammered together in perfect synchronisation.

For a long moment, they lay entwined, skin damp with perspiration, still intimately connected. Margaret felt fundamentally changed, not just by the physical act but by the tenderness Julian had shown her, the way he'd made her feel both treasured and desired.

"How do you feel?" he asked finally, pressing a gentle kiss to her temple as he carefully withdrew from her body.

"Transformed," Margaret whispered, surprised by the truth of it as she curled against his side. The word felt inadequate for the storm of sensations still coursing through her—the lingering echoes of pleasure, the unfamiliar ache between her thighs, the way her entire body seemed to thrum with newfound awareness.

Julian's arms tightened around her, drawing the silk covers over their cooling bodies. "You were magnificent," he murmured against her hair. "Absolutely magnificent, my dear."

The reverence in his voice made her heart flutter, but as the euphoric haze began to clear, darker thoughts crept in like shadows at twilight.

Had he spoken those same words to other women? Had he touched them with the same tender care, whispered the same endearments into their hair as they lay sated in his arms?

Margaret closed her eyes, trying to banish such torturous speculation, but the questions multiplied like weeds in fertile soil.

Was the tenderness she'd witnessed genuine affection or merely the well-practiced performance of a man devastatingly skilled in the art of seduction? Had he been thinking of her—truly her—in those moments of passion, or had she simply been a convenient vessel for desires that belonged elsewhere?

The rational part of her mind understood the cruelty of such thoughts. Julian had been nothing but gentle, patient, even worshipful in his attentions. But the wounded, weary part of her—the part that remembered his easy agreement to her cold terms in this marriage of convenience—couldn't quite silence the whisper that perhaps she was simply another obligation he'd discharged with efficiency.

"Margaret?" Julian's voice carried a note of concern as he felt her body tense against his. "What troubles you?"

She forced herself to relax, schooling her features into an expression of drowsy contentment. "Nothing at all. I'm simply... overwhelmed by everything that's happened today."

It wasn't entirely a lie. She was overwhelmed—by sensation, by emotion, by the terrible vulnerability of lying naked in the arms of a man who'd married her out of duty rather than desire. Physical intimacy, she was discovering, was far more complex than her sisters' euphemistic hints had suggested. The body might find satisfaction, but the heart... the heart remained perilously exposed to wounds that had nothing to do with the breaking of maidenhood.

As Julian's breathing gradually deepened into the steady rhythm of approaching sleep, Margaret lay awake in his arms, caught between gratitude for his gentleness and the aching fear that she had just given her body—and perhaps her heart too—to a man who would never truly be hers. The physical joining had been everything she'd dreamed of and more, but it had also opened a chasm of longing she hadn't known existed.

She was his wife now, in every way society recognised, but as she listened to his heart beating against her ear, Margaret couldn't shake the devastating, heartbreaking suspicion that she was still, in all the ways that truly mattered, utterly alone.

Chapter Twenty-Two

"The Yorkshire estate alone produces nearly three thousand pounds annually from coal mining," Mr. Harrison, the senior steward, explained whilst spreading ledgers across Julian's desk. "Though the Devon holdings are more pastoral in income—excellent for sheep and grain."

Julian nodded, forcing his attention to the figures that swam before his eyes like hieroglyphics. Three days had passed since their wedding, and he could barely focus on anything more complex than buttoning his waistcoat without his thoughts spiralling back to Margaret's soft gasps as she trembled beneath him.

"Your Grace?" Mr. Harrison's voice cut through his distraction. "Shall I arrange meetings with the tenant representatives for next week?"

"Yes, of course." Julian dragged his attention back to the present, where Rhys lounged in a chair by the window, observing the proceedings with barely concealed amusement.

"The Ashwick title also comes with hereditary obligations to the Crown," Rhys interjected. "Parliamentary committees, charitable patronages... ceremonial duties that cannot be delegated or ignored."

Julian's stomach clenched at the reminder. Tomorrow, he would take his seat in the House of Lords, where he would be expected to champion legal reform initiatives with the same moral authority he'd demonstrated in exposing Strickland's crimes.

"The Prime Minister wishes to discuss prison reform legislation," Mr. Harrison continued, consulting his notes with bureaucratic efficiency. "Your expertise in criminal law makes you an ideal advocate."

"Naturally," Julian murmured, though privately he wondered how he was supposed to advocate for justice when he'd orchestrated his own wife's circumstances with all the subtlety of a chess master arranging pieces for checkmate.

"I believe that covers the most pressing concerns," Mr. Harrison said, gathering his papers with satisfaction. "Shall I arrange for the Yorkshire estate manager to visit? He's been most eager to meet the new duke."

"Yes, by all means," Julian agreed, rising as the steward prepared to depart. "I'm certain we'll have much to discuss."

After the man's departure, Rhys sprawled in his chair, studying Julian with the shrewd attention of someone who'd known him since childhood.

"You know, most people would consider a dukedom and a beautiful wife rather enviable," Rhys observed, swirling the brandy in his glass.

Julian moved to the window, staring out at the London street below. "Most people haven't married a woman who considers them little more than a necessary evil, dear cousin."

"Ah. And how is married life treating you otherwise?"

The question hit its mark with uncomfortable precision. Julian's mind immediately conjured titillating images of Margaret's shy boldness, the way she'd responded to his touch with such innocent passion, how she'd fallen asleep in his arms as though she belonged there, as though she wanted to be there.

But since then, she'd been politely distant, treating him with the same courteous detachment she might show any houseguest. Pleasant conversations at meals, careful avoidance of meaningful contact, and absolutely no reference to the intimacy they'd shared.

"Splendidly," Julian lied smoothly. "Margaret is the perfect duchess—gracious and well-mannered."

"How romantic of you both."

Julian's laugh held no humour. "Romance was never part of our arrangement. We're both perfectly content with the practicality of our alliance."

"Are you? Because you've been utterly distracted, cousin. Even now, you're staring out that window as though searching for something that's missing from your supposedly perfectly arranged life."

Before Julian could formulate a response that wouldn't reveal too much, rapid footsteps echoed in the corridor outside. Both men turned as the study door opened without ceremony.

Margaret stood on the threshold, her golden hair hanging loose around her shoulders instead of pinned in its usual careful arrangement. She wore a simple morning dress of soft blue silk that complemented her eyes, but it was her expression that made Julian's breath catch—determined, almost fierce, with an undercurrent of something that looked dangerously close to hunger.

"Rhys," she said without preamble, her gaze fixed on Julian with startling intensity. "I require a word with my husband in private. Immediately, if you wouldn't mind."

Rhys's eyebrows rose towards his hairline, but he stood with obliging grace. "Of course. I was just leaving anyway." He paused beside Margaret on his way out, lowering his voice just enough to be heard by all three of them. "Try not to destroy any furniture. Some of those pieces are rather valuable."

The door closed with a decisive click, leaving the married couple alone in the sudden quiet. She remained by the entrance for a moment, studying Julian with an expression he couldn't decipher, then strutted across the room purposefully.

"Margaret," Julian began, but she silenced him by placing both hands flat against his chest, pushing him backwards until his legs hit the desk edge.

"Don't make this complicated with words or explanations or that maddening reasonableness that you've perfected."

Before he could respond, with movements that were both shocking and somehow inevitable, she whirled them around, gathering her skirts as she settled herself onto the desk, her legs parting just enough to accommodate his body between them.

Julian's breath left his lungs in a rush. "What are you doing?"

"Something I should have done yesterday," she replied, her voice steady despite the flush climbing up her neck. "And the day before."

Her hands moved to his waistcoat, working at the buttons with determined efficiency whilst Julian stood frozen between shock and rapidly building arousal.

"We shouldn't—not here, not like this—"

"Why not?" She met his gaze with startling directness. "We're married. This is our house. And I want my husband."

The words hit Julian squarely in the chest. Any pretence of rational thought abandoned him as Margaret's hands found the evidence of his building arousal, her fingers warm against him as she fondled him through the fabric of his trousers.

"You're going to be the death of me," he groaned, his hands finally finding her face.

"Then at least you'll die a satisfied man," Margaret replied with a boldness that made his head spin.

Julian's control snapped like an overstretched wire. His mouth crashed against hers with ravenous hunger, months of restraint and days of longing pouring into the kiss like water through a broken dam. Margaret met his passion with equal fervour, her arms winding around his neck as she pulled him closer.

"I've dreamt of you," she confessed against his lips, her breath warm and sweet and utterly intoxicating. "About the way you touched me... how you made me feel..."

Julian chuckled against her lips. "Have you now? And what, pray tell, did you dream, my darling wife?"

"You," she demanded breathlessly, "filling every inch of me."

"Ah, greedy little duchess," Julian murmured approvingly, his hands pushing her skirts higher until he could see the creamy expanse of her thighs above her silk stockings. "Tell me what you want, my dear."

Margaret's cheeks flamed, but her eyes held steady. "I want what you did before. With your mouth. I want to feel that again."

Her bold request nearly stopped his heart entirely. Without hesitation, he dropped to his knees before her, his hands caressing the smooth skin of her legs as he settled between her parted thighs.

"My pleasure, Your Grace," he said, his breath warm against her intimate flesh.

The first touch of his tongue against her intimate folds made Margaret cry out, her hands gripping the edge of the desk for support. Julian devoured her with slow, deliberate, thorough strokes, alternating between gentle teasing and focused suckling until she was writhing against him, soft whimpers of pleasure escaping her lips.

"Julian..." she gasped, her voice breaking, "I need..."

"I know precisely what you need," he said against her slick core, his tongue finding that sensitive bundle of nerves that made her entire body arch tight as a bowstring. "Let me have you. Let go for me, Margaret."

Her breath became almost ragged, each soft gasp turning into a moan that climbed higher and higher until she exploded with a cry that would have scandalised half of London, her body pulsing against his mouth as a squirt of pure pleasure erupted from her. Julian held her through the storm, his hands steady on her trembling thighs as she came back to herself.

"You are so beautiful when you surrender to my pleasure," he murmured, pressing gentle kisses to her inner thigh.

But Margaret wasn't finished. As Julian rose to his feet, she groped the fastenings of his breeches, tugging on them with trembling hands.

"Now I want all of you," she demanded, her eyes dark with renewed desire. "Here. Now. Don't make me wait."

Julian's remaining restraint evaporated, and he freed his aching arousal with urgent movements, his breath hissing through clenched teeth as the cool air hit his wet, fevered, intimate skin. He was painfully hard, his entire body throbbing with a need that had been left unsatisfied for days while he watched her move through their home like a ghost he couldn't touch.

"God above," he groaned as he positioned the swollen length of him at her slick entrance, his eyes locking with hers. "You are so wet for me."

Margaret's pupils dilated as she felt him pressing against her, teasing her with soft, circular movements. "I want you inside me, Julian."

He pressed forward with care, biting back a groan as her tight heat slowly enveloped him, inch by torturous inch. The sensation was overwhelming, velvet fire that gripped him like a silken fist, drawing him deeper into her welcoming body until he was buried to the hilt.

"Sweet Christ..." Julian breathed, his forehead dropping to rest against hers as they both held perfectly still, their bodies pulsating at the intimate joining.

"Yes," Margaret breathed as he filled her completely, her legs wrapping around his waist to draw him even deeper. "This is what I wanted... what I needed."

Julian set a rhythm that was nothing like their tender wedding night. It was raw and desperate, edged with something that felt dangerously close to claiming and plundering. The desk shook beneath them as their bodies moved together, papers drifting to the floor like forgotten responsibilities.

"Mine," Julian growled against her neck, his control shredding as Margaret met each thrust with equal fervour. "My wife. My duchess. Mine."

"Yours," she agreed breathlessly, her nails raking across his shoulders. "Always yours, Julian."

The admission pushed him over the edge he'd been approaching. With a hoarse cry, Julian buried himself as deeply within her as humanly possible, his body pulsing as release claimed him. Margaret followed seconds later, her inner walls clenching possessively around him as she found her own sweet release.

For a few moments, they simply remained joined, breathing hard, sweat dripping from their skin. Julian pressed gentle kisses to Margaret's temple, tasting the salt of perspiration and something sweeter that was uniquely her.

"Did I hurt you?" he asked, noting the slight tremor in her limbs.

"No," Margaret whispered, though she didn't quite meet his eyes.

But even as she spoke, Julian could sense her beginning to withdraw—not physically but emotionally, rebuilding the careful walls that kept their arrangement safe and impersonal. For the first time in his life, Julian felt slightly used by a woman—but in the best way possible.

She slipped from the desk with fluid grace, straightening her clothing with practiced efficiency whilst Julian watched helplessly. Within moments, she looked every inch the proper duchess once again, save for the tell-tale flush on her cheeks and the slight swelling of her lips.

"Thank you," she said quietly, her tone polite as though thanking him for holding a door. "I shall leave you to your work now, Your Grace."

And then she was gone, the study door closing behind her with a decisive click.

Julian remained where she'd left him, surrounded by scattered papers and the lingering scent of her perfume, feeling simultaneously satisfied and utterly bereft. She'd given him her body with such generous passion, but her heart remained as guarded as ever.

He wanted more than stolen moments and convenient pleasures. He wanted her trust, her laughter, her dreams whispered in the dark hours before dawn. He wanted a real marriage, not this careful dance of desire and distance.

But Margaret seemed perfectly content with their arrangement.

The realisation that he was in love with his wife and wanted more of her than he could even begin to explain hit him with startling clarity.

Julian sank into his chair, staring at the chaos Margaret had left in her wake, and wondered how the hell he was supposed to survive a lifetime of having everything and nothing all at once.

Chapter Twenty-Three

"The tenancy agreements require your signature, Your Grace," his newly appointed clerk, a thin man with pale skin and expensive spectacles by the name of Henderson, said, spreading yet another collection of documents across Julian's already overflowing desk. "And the Yorkshire steward has confirmed the meeting regarding the coal mine expansion proposal."

Julian nodded absently, his attention focused solely on the intricate legal language that governed his new ducal responsibilities. In reality, his mind was entirely occupied by memories of his wife's passionate gasps from the night before, the way she'd trembled in the aftermath of their shared passion before vanishing one more, like smoke dissipating in the morning air.

Seven days. Seven nights of the same maddening pattern since their wedding—Margaret would appear in his study during the most infuriatingly untimely hours, her hair loose around her shoulders and her eyes dark with desire. They would make love with desperate intensity, sometimes on the Turkish carpet before the fireplace, sometimes against the tall windows that overlooked the gardens, and once—memorably—on the dining table after she'd swept aside the remnants of an expertly cooked meal with casual disregard.

And then, invariably, she would leave.

The irony wasn't lost on him that whilst he prepared to advocate for legal justice in the House of Lords, his own marriage had become a beautiful kind of prison, one where he was granted free access to his wife's body but never her heart.

"Your Grace?" Henderson's voice cut through Julian's distracted thoughts. "The papers?"

"Yes, of course." Julian forced himself to focus on the contracts before him, though the words seemed to blur together like watercolours in rain. "These appear to be in order."

The clerk gathered his papers with efficient satisfaction. "Excellent. I shall make the appropriate arrangements, then. Would there be anything else, Your Grace?"

Julian shook his head, and the man departed. Julian rose from behind his desk and began the restless pacing that had become his evening ritual. The study felt simultaneously too large and suffocatingly small—too large for the loneliness that echoed in every corner and too small for the frustrated energy that thrummed through his veins like electricity seeking ground.

They would move to the Yorkshire estate eventually, once his parliamentary duties were properly established and the season's social obligations fulfilled. Ashwick Manor awaited them, a sprawling ducal estate with grand reception rooms suitable for entertaining nobility, a library that rivalled those of even the most ancient universities in England, and bedchambers appointed with silk hangings and furniture that belonged in palaces. The estate's income put him in a position to afford a life of extravagance and unimaginable luxury.

But Julian would have traded it all for one honest conversation with his wife.

Margaret had adapted to her new role with the same graceful efficiency she applied to everything else. She charmed the household staff, corresponded with local ladies about charitable endeavours, and played the part of the Duchess of Ashwick with such convincing performance that even Julian sometimes forgot she was acting.

Most of the time, she treated him with polite courtesy—pleasant yet meaningless conversation at meals, gracious assistance when estate matters required a duchess's attention, careful maintenance of the appropriate distance between a titled gentleman and his properly bred wife.

But when the mood struck, she transformed into someone else entirely.

"Your Grace," came the butler's voice from the doorway, "dinner will be served at your convenience."

"Thank you, Henderson. Please inform Her Grace that I shall join her shortly."

Julian straightened his waistcoat and prepared to endure another meal of careful conversation and meaningful glances that led absolutely nowhere. Margaret had perfected the art of being present without truly being there, of sharing space without sharing anything of substance, anything that mattered.

The dining room glowed with candlelight that caught the crystal and silver, creating an atmosphere of intimacy that was utterly false. Margaret sat at the opposite end of the table, beautiful as a portrait and just as unreachable.

"How were your meetings today?" she asked, cutting her salmon with precise moments.

"Productive. We've finalised the arrangements for expanding the mining operations in the north Yorkshire holdings." Julian watched her face for any flicker of genuine interest. "The income should increase considerably within the year."

"How wonderful. Financial security is always such a comfort."

The polite response hung between them like a wall of good manners. Julian set down his fork, suddenly unable to stomach the charade.

"Margaret."

She looked up, surprise flickering across her features.

"Is this truly how you desire to live? Do you intend for us to have polite, meaningless conversations and have separate lives, connected only by legal documents and... physical encounters?"

Colour rose to her cheeks, but her voice remained steady. "I believe we agreed upon the terms of our arrangement quite clearly."

"Well, perhaps if you cared to take a closer look, you would find your husband no longer satisfied with those terms."

Margaret's fork clinked against her plate as she set it down with deliberate care. "I see. And what would you prefer instead, Your Grace?"

The formal address stung, as she'd undoubtedly intended. Julian leaned back in his chair, studying his wife's composed expression whilst frustration built in his chest like steam in a kettle.

"I'd prefer honesty. Connection. Something resembling an actual marriage rather than this... elaborate performance we've constructed."

"Performance?" Margaret's eyes flashed with something that might have been either anger or indignation. "I fulfil my duties as your duchess with perfect propriety. What more could you possibly require of me?"

"You. I require *you*, Margaret. Not the role you're playing, not the careful mask you wear. I want the woman who comes to me in the darkness, who kisses me like she might burn alive from wanting."

The words hung between them like a gauntlet thrown at dawn. Margaret's breathing had quickened, though whether from anger or something else entirely, Julian couldn't determine.

"Those encounters serve a practical purpose, do they not?" she asked carefully. "After all, physical compatibility makes our arrangement more... manageable."

"Manageable." Julian tasted the word like poison. "Is that what you call it when you desperately call out my name? When you cling to me as though I'm the only solid thing in your world?"

Margaret's composure cracked just enough to reveal something vulnerable underneath. "Oh, you're being ridiculous!"

"Am I? Because from where I sit, it seems I'm the only one being honest about something you seem determined to ignore entirely."

She rose from her chair in one swift motion, her silk skirts rustling as she moved towards the door. "I believe this conversation has reached its natural conclusion."

"We're not finished discussing this."

"Oh, yes, we are!" Margaret paused with her hand on the door handle, not turning around. "You received exactly what you bargained for, Julian—a duchess who fulfils her obligations without troubling you with inconvenient emotions. Don't complicate our arrangement with sentiment neither of us can afford."

The door closed behind her with controlled precision, leaving Julian alone with his cooling dinner and the growing certainty that he was in love with a woman who'd built walls around her heart that would challenge royal fortress architects.

An hour later, he heard her familiar footsteps in the corridor outside his study. Right on schedule, as predictable as sunrise, Margaret appeared in the doorway wearing nothing but a silk robe that outlined every tempting curve of her body.

She didn't speak. She rarely did during these encounters. Instead, she moved across the room with purpose, her intentions clearly written in every line of her posture.

But tonight, Julian was ready for her.

Their lovemaking was explosive from the first touch—desperate, almost angry in its intensity. Margaret's hands roamed over his body with possessive hunger whilst Julian worshipped her with everything he had until she was gasping his name like a prayer.

When they finally came together, it was with the sort of raw passion that left them both shaking, their bodies moving in perfect synchronisation, as though they had been created specifically for this joining, this purpose.

Afterward, as Margaret began her familiar ritual of withdrawal, Julian caught her wrist in a gentle but implacable grip.

"Stay," he said quietly.

Margaret froze, her blue eyes growing wide with something that looked like panic. "Julian–"

"Stay with me tonight. Sleep in my arms. Let me wake up beside you like a proper husband should. Would you deny me that?"

"That wasn't part of our agreement."

"Then perhaps our agreement needs revision." Julian sat up, still holding her gaze. "How long will you punish me, Margaret? I'm tired of pretending this is merely convenient. What we share—it is more than just mere physical release, and we both know it."

Margaret's expression shuttered completely. "You're confusing intimacy with sentiment. They're not the same thing."

"Aren't they? Because when you look at me during those moments of ecstasy, when you whimper my name as though it's something sacred—I can see something in you that goes far beyond physical satisfaction."

"You're seeing what you want to see."

Julian's patience finally snapped. "For God's sake, Margaret! Stop running from this! Stop pretending you don't feel anything for me beyond desire when we're together!"

"I'm not pretending anything!" Margaret's voice rose to match his, her careful composure also finally cracking. "I'm just being practical about the realities of our situation!"

"And what realities would those be?"

"That this is a marriage born of necessity, not affection! That you married me to solve a problem of your own creation, not because you care about me! That whatever connection we share physically means nothing more, nothing beyond convenience!"

The words were designed to wound, and they did. Julian rose from the bed, reaching for his discarded shirt with movements sharp enough to betray his agitation.

"Is that truly what you believe? That everything between us—every touch, every kiss, every moment of pleasure we've shared—means nothing more than mutual satisfaction?"

Margaret's chin lifted with stubborn defiance, but Julian caught the slight tremor in her hands as she pulled her robe more tightly around herself. "What else could it possibly mean?"

"Love, you impossible, infuriating, stubborn woman!" The confession exploded from him with the force of something long suppressed. "Do you not realise that every time you leave me feeling hollowed out and desperate for more? You leave me yearning for more than just stolen moments and physical release!"

Margaret's face went pale as winter moonlight. "Julian—"

"No, let me finish! You want honesty? You want to know what our arrangement truly means to me? It means being wretched and lying awake after you're gone, wondering how long my heart can survive wanting someone, aching for someone who is deliberately, wilfully keeping her heart locked away like the bloody crown jewels in the Tower of London!"

"Stop." Margaret's voice was barely a whisper. "Please... just stop."

"Why? Because hearing the truth makes you uncomfortable? Because acknowledging that what we share might be real would complicate your perfectly ordered emotional distance? You are being cruel, Margaret!"

Margaret's eyes filled with tears, but she refused to let them fall. "Because it changes nothing! Because even if what you say is true... even if you do... care for me... it doesn't alter the fundamental nature of what this marriage is and how it came to be!"

"And what is it, in your estimation?"

"A transaction! A convenient solution that serves both our purposes without the complication of feelings that could destroy us both!"

Julian stared at her, recognising the fear beneath her anger, the way she wielded practical reasoning like armour against vulnerability. "You're terrified to trust me again."

She scoffed. "I'm being sensible!"

"You're being a coward."

The accusation hung between them like a blade, sharp enough to cut. Margaret's face flushed with fury, her hands clenching into fists at her sides.

"How dare you—"

The acrid smell of smoke suddenly filled the air between them, cutting off Margaret's indignant response. Julian's head snapped towards the corner of the room where thin, grey whisps were curling upwards from behind the bookshelves.

"God!" he breathed, his mind immediately shifting into crisis mode. "The house is on fire."

Thick smoke began pouring into the room with alarming speed, accompanied by the ominous crackle of flames taking hold somewhere in the walls. Julian grabbed Margaret's arm, pulling her towards the door as panic surged through his veins.

"We need to get out. Now."

But even as they stumbled towards the corridor, Julian could see that escape wouldn't be simple. Smoke was already billowing in the hallway, and the sound of splintering wood suggested that the fire had spread far more quickly than should have been possible.

Margaret stumbled beside him, her bare feet sliding on the polished marble as she struggled to keep pace. Her foot caught on the edge of an expensive carpet, sending her crashing against a heavy oak table with enough force to knock the breath from her lungs.

"Margaret!" Julian's heart stopped entirely as she disappeared into the thickening smoke, her white robe swallowed by grey fumes that seemed to rise from the very floors like ghostly hands reaching towards them both.

The smoke turned to fire in his throat as he dropped to his knees, searching desperately through the choking haze for any sign of his wife. Behind him, the study erupted in flames that licked hungrily at the ceiling, whilst ahead lay smoke so thick he could barely see his own hands.

"Margaret!" he called again, his voice raw with smoke and terror.

But there was no response, only the growing roar of the fire consuming everything they had tried to build together.

Chapter Twenty-Four

"I can't breathe..."

The words escaped Margaret's lips in a desperate whisper as smoke filled her lungs like liquid poison. Each breath felt like swallowing glowing embers, her vision blurring at the edges, whilst invisible hands seemed to constrict her throat tighter and tighter. Panic clawed at her chest like a living thing, threatening to consume what little air remained in her burning lungs.

The fallen table had trapped her ankle beneath its weight, sending sharp bolts of pain up her leg every time she tried to free herself. Around her, the study had transformed into something from Dante's imagination—flames licking hungrily at the walls whilst smoke poured through every crack and crevice like malevolent spirits actively seeking destruction.

"Julian!" she tried to call, but her voice emerged as barely more than a strangled rasp.

Through the thickening haze, she thought she heard his voice somewhere beyond the doorway, shouting her name with increasing desperation. But the smoke between them might just as well have been an ocean for all the good it did either of them.

Just when darkness began creeping in from the edges of her consciousness, strong arms wrapped around her waist, lifting her body from the floor. The world tilted sideways as her rescuer swept her into his embrace, carrying her through the choking air towards what she desperately hoped was safety.

"Hold on," he commanded roughly, his voice barely audible above the roar of the flames. "Just hold on, Margaret, love. We're almost there."

Fresh air hit her face like a benediction, cool and sweet as spring water after the hellish heat from the burning house. Margaret gasped great lungfuls of it, her body shivering and shuddering as oxygen flooded her starved system. The chaotic sounds of emergency filled her ears—servants shouting instructions, horses stomping nervously in their traces, the splash of water being thrown uselessly against an inferno that had already claimed the better part of their new home.

"Margaret?" Julian's face appeared before her, his grey eyes wide with terror and relief in equal measure. "God... when I couldn't find you I... I thought..."

His hands trembled slightly as he cradled her against his chest, and Margaret realised with a shock that the unflappable Julian Ashcroft was utterly undone by fear—fear for her, specifically.

"I'm all right," she managed, though her voice sounded foreign to her own ears.

"Like hell you are." Julian's arms tightened around her as though he could somehow shield her from what had already happened. "When that table fell and you disappeared into the smoke, I nearly... Christ, Margaret, I couldn't lose you. Not like that. Not ever."

The raw vulnerability in his voice hit her harder than any declaration of love could have. This was Julian, stripped of his theatrical charm, his careful masks, his practiced composure. This was a man confronting the possibility of losing something infinitely precious to him.

"Your Grace!" Henderson appeared at Julian's elbow, his usually immaculate appearance dishevelled by smoke and urgency. "We've managed to contain the fire to the upper floors, but the damage is considerable. The fire brigade is on its way."

"Yes, yes, do whatever is necessary," Julian replied without taking his eyes from Margaret's face. "Spare no expense in ensuring everyone's safety."

"Forgive me, Your Grace... but there's something else." Henderson's voice carried a note of barely contained alarm. "The footmen caught someone lurking in the mews behind the house. A gentleman who was... watching the flames spread. When they confronted him, he had lamp oil on his hands and clothing."

Margaret felt Julian's entire body go rigid with lethal focus.

"He... he claims to be Lord Nathaniel Strickland, former Duke of Ashcombe, Your Grace. He claims he was merely passing by when he saw the fire, but Your Grace..." Henderson's voice dropped to an urgent whisper. "He was smiling. Watching your home burn like it was a performance for his entertainment..."

Julian's laugh was sharp and predatory. "Bring him to me. Now."

Within moments, two groundskeepers emerged from the smoky darkness swirling around them, flanking a figure Margaret recognised with sickening certainty. The man who stood before her bore no resemblance to the polished gentleman who had once charmed his way through London's ballrooms. His usually immaculate clothing was dishevelled, his face streaked with soot, and his eyes burned with a hatred so pure it seemed to radiate a heat all its own.

"Julian Ashcroft!" Strickland spat, struggling against his captors' grip. "Or should I say, Your Grace? How perfectly fitting that you should inherit a title through the destruction of your betters!"

"Better men don't blackmail widows and terrorise innocent women," Julian replied with dangerous calm, settling Margaret more securely in his arms. "Neither do they perform acts of arson."

Strickland's gaze slid to Margaret with unconcealed malice. "Still playing the role of gallant protector, I see. Tell me, does it sting to know you were nothing more than a convenient excuse for his moral crusade?"

"That's enough." Julian's voice cut through the air like a blade. "State your business or be gone."

"My business?" Strickland's smile was all edges. "My business was enjoying the most delightful evening's entertainment. First, the charming tableau through your study windows—such passion you showed, Ashcroft. And your bride, quite... spirited in her affections. But that was merely the opening act." His eyes glittered with vicious satisfaction. "The real performance began when I lit the stage ablaze. Nothing quite compares to watching one's enemies' world burn down to the ground with them in it, quite literally."

Margaret's blood turned to ice as the implication hit her. "You started the fire."

"Prove it," Strickland challenged. "I dare you to prove that a disgraced former duke would stoop to common arson to inconvenience the man who destroyed his reputation."

"Actually," came a new voice from the darkness, "we might be of some assistance."

Lady Harrow stepped into the circle of torchlight, her elegant travelling dress marked with soot, but her dignity intact. Behind her stood two other women Margaret recognised—Lady Lyndmere and Mrs. Whitmore, both former victims of Strickland's blackmail schemes.

"We followed him here, Your Grace," Lady Harrow said, "When we learned he'd returned to London despite fleeing after your exposure of his crimes, we feared he might attempt something desperate. We've been taking turns watching for any sign of him. He's been living like a hunted animal, but we knew his pride wouldn't let him simply disappear."

"Three bitter old women playing at being investigators?" Strickland snarled.

"Three ladies who refuse to let you destroy any more lives," Lady Harrow corrected with steel in her voice. "We saw you circling this property for hours before the fire started. We watched you pour lamp oil beneath the study windows. And we have witnesses."

Margaret felt the final pieces of understanding click into place like tumblers in a lock. "You've been helping them..." she said to Julian, sudden comprehension flooding through her. "The blackmail victims... my friends—you've been coordinating their efforts to stop him."

"Among other things," Julian admitted, his attention still fixed on Strickland with predatory focus. "It seemed an appropriate use of my particular skills."

"How touching." Strickland sneered with vicious amusement. "The great reformer and his charitable works. Tell me, Ashcroft, have you informed your bride about all the women who grace your study for private consultations? About all the intimate details you've gathered regarding their compromising situations?"

"Enough." Julian's voice carried the full authority of his new rank, and Margaret felt rather than saw the way the assembled staff straightened in response. "Henderson, have him secured in the wine cellar until morning. Post two footmen as guards. At first light, we'll send for the magistrate and have Lord Strickland formally charged with arson and attempted murder."

"This isn't finished!" Strickland warned as the groundskeepers began leading him away. "You think a shiny title makes you untouchable? You think your marriage will last when she learns exactly who you really are, Ashcroft?"

"I know exactly who he is," Margaret said quietly, surprising herself with the steadiness of her own voice.

Strickland's laugh was menacing and ugly. "Do you? Do you know about the hordes of women who've shared his bed? About the secrets he's gathered like trophies? About the fact that you were never anything more than another case to be managed?"

Margaret felt Julian's arms tense around her, felt the way his breathing stopped entirely as the poison found its mark. For a moment, she wavered, old doubts and fresh fears threatening to overwhelm her rational thought.

Then she remembered the terror in Julian's eyes when he'd thought he might lose her. The way he'd torn through a burning building to reach her. The tremor in his hands as he held her, and the heartbreaking concoction of love and hurt in his grey eyes when they had fought before the fire broke out.

"Take him away," she said firmly, her gaze cold as it settled on Strickland's face. "His Grace and I have more important matters to attend to than listening to the mad ravings of a criminal seeking revenge."

Strickland's expression twisted with fury at her dismissal, but he had no choice but to allow himself to be led into the darkness beyond the torchlight.

"Well," Julian said once they were alone again, his voice carefully neutral, "that was certainly illuminating."

Margaret tilted her head back to study his face in the flickering light. "Was it? I found it rather predictable, actually.

Desperate men often resort to desperate measures when their carefully constructed worlds collapse."

"Margaret, I—"

"No," she said softly, pressing her fingers to his lips. "Whatever explanations or justifications you're prepared to offer, I don't require them. Not tonight."

Julian's eyes searched her face, clearly trying to read her thoughts. "You don't?"

"Tonight, I nearly lost my life. You risked yours to save me. Everything else seems rather insignificant by comparison, don't you think?"

She felt something shift in the way he held her—less like a man protecting something fragile, more like a man being proud to claim something as his own.

"Rather," he agreed roughly. "Though I should mention, for the sake of honesty and transparency, that helping the victims was never truly about charity or justice. It was always only about protecting you from a marriage that would have destroyed you."

Margaret considered this, surprised by how little it mattered anymore. "So my welfare was always your primary concern, even when you were pretending it wasn't?"

"Always," Julian admitted. "From the very first moment you asked for my help, everything I did was designed to keep you safe. Even when it meant becoming the villain in your story."

The confession settled something restless in Margaret's chest. Not forgiveness, precisely—that would require more time and conversation than a single night could provide. But understanding, perhaps. Acceptance that their story had been complicated from the beginning, and that complicated stories rarely had simple resolutions.

"Then perhaps," she said, settling more comfortably against his chest, "we might finally stop pretending this marriage is merely convenient and acknowledge that we've both been rather thoroughly compromised by feelings that were always there, deep and true, despite what our actions have shown."

Julian's sharp intake of breath was answer enough. "You mean—"

"I mean," Margaret said, pressing a gentle kiss to his cheekbone, "that nearly dying has a remarkable way of clarifying one's priorities. And my priority, it seems, is ensuring that my husband understands just how precious he is to me."

Julian's arms tightened around her until she could barely breathe, but Margaret had never felt safer in her entire life.

"Margaret," he whispered against her hair, and she heard a lifetime of promises in the way he spoke her name.

Chapter Twenty-Five

"You look like hell."

Rhys's blunt observation carried none of his usual diplomatic polish, though Julian supposed that was fitting given the circumstances. The fire had left its mark on more than just the townhouse—it had stripped away the last of his defences.

"I feel considerably worse than I look, which is saying something given my current resemblance to a chimney sweep," Julian replied, accepting the brandy with hands that still trembled slightly. The acrid scent of smoke clung to everything, a constant reminder of how close he'd come to losing everything that mattered.

Through the broken study windows, Margaret's voice carried clear and authoritative as she directed the restoration efforts.

"She's been writing letters all morning," Julian said, following Rhys's gaze. "Lady Harrow arrived with three maids, and Mrs. Whitmore brought enough provisions to feed the staff. Even Lady Lyndmere sent over a set of china."

"The blackmail victims?"

Julian nodded, his heart swelling with pride. "Margaret's been helping them, too, it seems."

"She's been using the skills you taught her."

Julian stared at his wife through the window, watching as she helped an elderly maid navigate around water-damaged books. "I never meant for her to become involved in all of that."

A LADY'S LESSONS IN SIN

"Didn't you?" Rhys's voice carried a note of challenge. "You exposed her to the darker side of society. What did you expect?"

Before Julian could respond, Margaret's voice drifted through the window.

"No, Henderson, those documents require careful handling. Spread them in the morning room where they can dry properly, and ensure each page is weighted to prevent curling."

"Yes, Your Grace."

Julian felt his throat tighten at the natural authority in her voice. She had a way of fulfilling her role with a grace that both amazed and humbled him.

"She could have died," he said quietly, the words scraping against his throat. "If I hadn't made it to her..."

"But she didn't."

"I can't do this, cousin. I cannot continue to pretend our marriage is merely an arrangement born of scandal. Not when I nearly lost her. Not when the thought of existing without her makes me want to burn down what's left of London myself."

"Then stop pretending."

Julian laughed, though the sound held no humour. "How do I explain that I've been in love with her since she first burst into my office? How do I admit that every woman I claimed to help was merely a distraction from the one woman I couldn't have? That I hate myself for hurting her when my sole purpose was protecting her—"

"Julian."

Margaret's voice from the doorway cut through his words, and he turned to find her standing there in a borrowed gown marked with soot, hair escaping its pins, but eyes blazing with intensity.

"How long have you been standing there?" he asked, though he suspected he knew.

"Long enough." She stepped inside, closing the door. "Long enough to hear what I've been hoping to hear for months."

Rhys cleared his throat. "I'll inspect the east wing. Thoroughly."

He departed with tactical efficiency, leaving the married couple alone amongst the ruins.

"Margaret—" Julian began, but she held up a hand.

"Please let me speak first." She moved closer, her skirts rustling against the debris scattered at their feet.

Julian waited, scarcely breathing.

"When you exposed the duke's crimes, you didn't just save those ladies' reputations. You might have hurt me, but you saved me, too. I can see that now. And you taught them that they were deserving of justice, that their pain mattered, that they were worth fighting for. I want to be a part of that. I want to use everything you've taught me to help them and other women who have suffered at the hands of men they trusted."

"You are magnificent," Julian said softly. "Watching your confidence, seeing you become this fierce woman… It's been remarkable."

"Has it?" Margaret stepped closer. "Because most of the time, I feel as though I'm pretending to be someone worthy of this title, someone capable of being the duchess you need."

"Margaret, that's—"

"I've spent my entire life feeling like everyone's second choice," she said, her voice breaking slightly. "Father's least valuable daughter, trailing behind Catharine's brilliance and Eliza's wit. The sweet, cheerful sister who needed protecting rather than pursuing her own path. And then our marriage... it felt like more of the same. I didn't have any control. It was just the convenient solution to the scandal, an arrangement to save my reputation whilst elevating your status. Even when we were intimate, I... I couldn't help but secretly wonder if you were thinking of someone else. Someone better. Someone who deserved to be chosen rather than settled for."

Julian blinked at her. "You thought you were just an obligation to me?"

"What else was I to think? You married me because you had to, not because you wanted to. You never spoke of your feelings; you agreed so easily to my cold terms that I—"

"Margaret. You magnificent, impossible woman!" Julian crossed the space between them in two strides. "You were never my second choice. Never a convenience. Not an obligation or a scandal to be managed." He cupped her face, thumbs tracing her cheekbones. "Do you want the whole, terrifying truth of it, my darling?"

Margaret nodded.

"I've been in love with you since the first night you came to my office. From the moment you demanded I teach you how to seduce another man, I was lost. Every lesson, every touch, every kiss... it was torture knowing I was preparing you for someone else's arms when all I wanted was to keep you for myself."

Margaret's breath hitched. "Julian..."

"I didn't warn you about Strickland partly because of the investigation but mostly because I truly wanted to protect you from him. I accepted this dukedom for you. And I married you because I was selfish. I couldn't bear the thought of you belonging to anyone else. And once you were my wife... I was terrified your coldness would never end. That you truly despised me."

"Oh, you foolish man!" Margaret rose on her toes, pressing her forehead to his. "Don't you understand? I never wanted the duke, or his title, or any of it. I wanted you. I've always wanted you."

"Even now? Even knowing I'm the reason you almost burned to death?"

"Especially now. Because when faced with losing me, you literally ran through fire. Because you love me enough to blame yourself for things beyond your control. Because you were willing to love me without receiving my heart in return. Because you see me as someone worth fighting for."

Julian's control snapped. He kissed her then with desperate hunger, months of suppressed emotions pouring into the intimate contact. Margaret responded with equal fervour, her hands tangling in his dark hair.

When they broke apart, both breathing hard, Margaret smiled with radiant, wholehearted joy.

"I love you," she said simply. "I love your dramatic nature and protective instincts and the way you've taught me to see my own strength. I love that you make me feel as though I could conquer the world."

"And I love you," Julian replied, the words tumbling out like a prayer.

"Show me then," Margaret whispered against his lips.

Julian lifted her, carrying her towards the staircase as Margaret laughed softly.

"The servants and helpers will notice," she murmured.

"Let them. Let the entire city know that this duke is hopelessly in love with his duchess."

In their chamber with afternoon sunlight streaming in through windows and restoration efforts echoing below, Julian and Margaret moved towards each other with the desperate urgency of two souls finally free.

"I thought I'd lost you," Julian said roughly. "When I saw those flames... when I couldn't find you... I never want to feel like that again."

"I'm here, love..." she whispered. "I'm here. And I'm yours. All of me."

Their kiss tasted of tears and smoke and truths finally spoken, of walls torn down and hearts laid bare.

"I want to memorise every inch of you," Julian murmured as they undressed one another with trembling hands.

"Then do," Margaret said boldly. "Love me, Julian. You have my heart, my body, and my soul."

When they came together, it was with tenderness bordering on reverence. Julian's mouth trailed her throat, not with practiced technique but with the desperate devotion of a man granted a miracle. Margaret arched beneath him, her hands mapping the masculine lines of his back.

"My brave, beautiful wife," he whispered, his voice thick with emotion as he positioned himself between her thighs.

Margaret's breath caught as he entered her, not from surprise but from the overwhelming rightness of it. They moved together without urgency, savouring each caress, each whispered endearment.

"Look at me," Margaret whispered, her hands cupping his face as their rhythm deepened. "I want to see you. All of you. No more masks."

Julian's control wavered as he met her gaze. In her eyes, he saw not only desire but also complete acceptance. This woman knew his flaws, his shortcomings, his fears, his failures, and she loved him anyway.

"Margaret," he breathed, his voice raw with wonder. "*My Margaret.*"

"Always yours," she replied, her body tightening around him. "For as long as you'll have me."

"Until my last breath," Julian promised fiercely, his movements becoming slightly more urgent.

When Margaret's release claimed her, it was with Julian's name on her lips and love shining in her eyes. Julian followed moments later, a cry of completion muffled against her throat as he surrendered completely.

They lay tangled afterwards, hearts gradually slowing, skin cooling. But neither moved to separate the intimate contact. For the first time in their marriage, there was no need to flee, no walls left to hide behind.

"What happens now?" Margaret asked softly.

Julian pressed a kiss to her head, breathing in the familiar scent of her hair. "Now we rebuild. Though I would advise we stay in Yorkshire for some time. Together."

"Together," Margaret agreed, tilting up to smile at him. "I rather like the sound of that."

Outside their window, the sounds of hammering continued as staff worked to restore order in the aftermath of the fire.

But inside their chamber, wrapped in each other's arms and finally free to fully love one another, Julian and Margaret had already begun the most important reconstruction—building a marriage founded not on scandal, or convenience, or duty, but on the unshakeable bedrock of true love.

And for the first time since their wedding day, neither had any intention of leaving the other's side.

Chapter Twenty-Six

"Julian Ashcroft, please step forward."

The Lord Chancellor's voice boomed through the House of Lords like thunder, each syllable echoing off the ancient stone walls until it settled into the very marrow of Julian's bones. He stood straighter than he'd ever managed in his life, his tailored coat sharp enough to cut glass, his hessian boots polished to mirror brightness.

A duke. Him. The thought was still absurd, the irony so exquisite it belonged in one of his dramatic speeches.

The chamber was packed tighter than a penny theatre on opening night. Lords perched on crimson benches like well-dressed vultures, some wearing polite curiosity, others barely concealed scepticism. Julian caught more than one raised eyebrow—after all, earning a dukedom through exposing corruption rather than inheriting it through fortunate bloodlines was hardly traditional.

"Having demonstrated exceptional service to the Crown," the Lord Chancellor continued with ceremonial gravitas, "Mr. Ashcroft shall henceforth officially hold the title: Duke of Ashwick, with all rights and privileges appertaining thereto."

The weight of ermine-trimmed robes settled on Julian's shoulders like destiny wearing fancy-dress. Across the chamber, Rhys offered the smallest of nods—his version of wild celebration. Beside him, Alaric clapped once, firmly, a gesture so magnificently inappropriate that several peers turned to stare.

Julian nearly smiled. Trust Alaric to treat the House of Lords like his own parlour.

"The ceremony is complete," came the final pronouncement. "His Grace may take his seat."

His Grace. Even after weeks of living informally, the title hadn't made the adjustment any easier. Julian moved towards the ducal bench with measured steps, each footfall marking his transformation from untitled solicitor to peer of the realm. The entire affair felt rather like watching someone else's life unfold whilst he observed from the gallery.

The business of governing droned on—debates about corn laws and colonial disputes—but Julian's attention kept drifting. Strange how achieving everything he'd never dared want only made him think of the one thing that mattered most.

His duchess, in truth as well as in law, now.

"Congratulations, Your Grace."

Rhys appeared beside him as they filed out of the chamber hours later, his tone carrying the warmest approval Julian had heard from him in years.

"Feels rather like donning someone else's skin," Julian admitted, loosening his formal cravat slightly. "Magnificent skin, certainly, but decidedly peculiar, nonetheless."

"You'll grow into it," Alaric said, joining them with characteristic bluntness. "Took me months to stop expecting bailiffs to appear and repossess the title for fraud."

"At least you were born into such expectations. I'm rather improvising as I proceed."

"Aren't we all?" Rhys observed. "The only difference is centuries of practice at hiding our uncertainty."

The trio retired to Rhys's library, where his butler had thoughtfully prepared a modest celebration—nothing elaborate, for Julian's nature might have appreciated a grand gesture, but his practical side preferred intimate gatherings amongst those who had seen him at his worst and loved him anyway.

"To His Grace, the Duke of Ashwick." Alaric raised his glass with mock solemnity. "May he prove marginally more respectable than his previous incarnation."

"I wouldn't wager significant sums on that possibility," Julian replied with self-deprecating charm. "Respectability was never among my more refined accomplishments."

"Perhaps not, cousin," Rhys said quietly. "But justice was. And courage. Particularly when it meant protecting those who couldn't protect themselves."

Julian felt his throat tighten unexpectedly. These men had witnessed his failures, his fears, his spectacular mistakes, yet somehow still found him worthy of their friendship. And that was more precious to him than any parliamentary honour.

By the time Julian reached home, London had settled into evening's embrace, and his townhouse glowed like a beacon against the darkness. Every window blazed with welcoming candlelight—their home, truly theirs now, with the damage from the fire erased as though it had never existed.

Henderson barely managed to relieve him of his hat and gloves before soft footsteps sounded on the marble staircase.

"Your Grace."

Margaret's voice carried a teasing formality, but when Julian looked up, his breath caught like a fish hook in his chest. She stood at the stairs' crown, wearing lush violet silk that captured the candlelight like liquid moonbeams, golden hair flowing loose over her shoulders in waves that begged to be tangled in desperate fingers.

She'd waited. Despite the late hour, she'd waited for him.

"Your Grace," Julian managed, his voice husky.

Margaret descended with fluid grace, her bare feet silent on the floor as she smiled mischievously. "Such a formal ceremony between husband and wife?"

"Behind these doors," Julian said, reaching for her as she approached, "I rather think we might dispense with such tedious proprieties."

She flowed into his arms, warm and pliant against his chest. When she pressed her lips to his jaw, his temple, and then finally his mouth, Julian felt his composure shatter like poorly blown glass.

"Congratulations, love," Margaret whispered against his lips, her hands already attacking the buttons of his waistcoat. "I'm frightfully proud of you."

"Are you?" Julian stilled her eager fingers. "Even knowing what this means? The scrutiny, the expectations, the crushing weight of responsibility that accompanies such elevation?"

"Especially knowing that," Margaret replied with fierce certainty. "Because you'll use this power to defend people who have no one else standing for them. Because you, Julian Ashcroft, *earned* this through your own merit, not accidentally or through birth, or political scheming."

Her faith staggered him, leaving him speechless. Julian lifted her in his arms, carrying her towards their bedchamber as she laughed against his throat.

"Are we scandalising the household again?" she murmured.

"Thoroughly so," Julian growled against her throat.

Once in their chamber, Julian set Margaret down gently, his hands framing her face as he kissed her with all the reverence she deserved. This felt different from all their previous encounters—not desperate hunger, or raw need, or even tenderness, but a strange combination of all of them with the addition of love freely given. It was deeper. It was a celebration of everything they'd survived to reach this perfect moment.

"I love you," he said simply, the words carrying more weight from one minute to the next.

"And I love you," Margaret replied, reaching up to help him shed his formal coat. "My brilliant, impossibly noble husband."

When Julian slipped the silk from her shoulders, revealing skin of cream perfection in flickering candlelight, he whispered, "My duchess" with such feeling that Margaret stilled, her blue eyes filling with tears.

"Say it again," she breathed.

"My... duchess..." Julian repeated, voice hoarse with affection as he traced her collarbone's delicate curve with his knuckles. "My wife. My Margaret."

Her answering smile was radiant.

Their lovemaking was celebration incarnate—slow, intense, neither chasing dominance nor distraction, but fully present in each touch. Julian worshipped her with patient devotion, mouth and hands mapping her silky-soft skin until Margaret writhed beneath him, gasping his name in desperation.

"Please, Julian..." she whispered as his lips blazed down her throat. "I need you."

"Always so eager," Julian murmured, his hands skimming her curves with deliberate slowness. "But tonight, my darling, we shall celebrate properly."

His mouth found her breasts, his tongue circling each rosy peak until Margaret bucked desperately against him. When he finally moved lower, pressing kisses to her stomach, her hip bones, the sensitive skin of her inner thighs, she was trembling with desire and need.

"Julian... oh!" Margaret gasped when his breath ghosted over her most intimate flesh. "I can't bear it."

"You can," he said tenderly, pressing one gentle kiss to her core. "And you will," he stated before claiming her entirely with his mouth.

"Oh!" Margaret cried out at the first touch of his tongue, her hands flying to tangle in his dark hair as she spread her legs as wide as they could possibly go whilst he explored her with thorough dedication. Each stroke, each caress, each suckle was designed to tease her, to drive her higher and higher, to make her forget everything but the pleasure he gave her.

When he slipped two fingers inside her whilst his tongue continued its intimate dance, Margaret shattered completely, her body pulsing and quivering around him as she called his name to the heavens.

"Beautiful," Julian murmured against her thigh, pressing gentle kisses to her heated skin as she trembled through the aftershocks. "Absolutely breathtaking."

When he finally moved up to cover her body with his own, Margaret was ready for him, welcoming him home with a sigh of pure contentment. He entered her slowly, revelling in the feel of her, pushing forward carefully whilst his grey eyes held hers as they claimed one another completely.

"My duchess," he whispered as he began to move, each thrust deliberate and measured. "My heart, my home, my everything."

"My husband," Margaret replied breathlessly, matching his rhythm, her legs wrapping around his waist to draw him deeper. "My love, my forever."

They moved together in unison, in perfect synchrony, building towards a climax that felt less like physical pleasure and more like spiritual transformation. When Margaret's second orgasm claimed her, it was with love blazing in her eyes. Julian's own release followed hers precisely, and he buried his face in her hair as he surrendered everything he had to give to the woman who'd become his salvation.

Afterwards, Margaret curled against his side, her hand resting over his heart, and Julian stared at the ceiling, breathing slowly.

"What are you thinking?" she asked softly.

Julian considered the question carefully. "Six months ago, I was a man with no title, no prospects beyond my legal work, and no hope of ever deserving someone like you."

"And now?"

He looked at her, brushing golden strands from her face. "Now... I have you. I have us. And that makes everything else seem rather insignificant by comparison."

Margaret smiled, pressing a kiss directly over his heart. "Then it seems we're perfectly matched, Your Grace."

"Is that so?"

Margaret nodded. "All I ever wanted was you."

Tomorrow would no doubt bring fresh responsibilities, new challenges, and the ever-present weight of expectations that accompanied their elevated station. But tonight, wrapped in each other's arms with love finally spoken freely between them,

Julian felt richer than any man in England—even the head that wears the crown.

After all, they'd survived disaster, scandal, forced marriage, and an actual fire blazing through their home to get to this moment of perfect contentment.

Whatever came next, they'd face it together too—and that, Julian thought as sleep claimed him, was worth more than anything anyone could ever offer him.

Chapter Twenty-Seven

"Oh! Julian, love, just look at it all. Isn't it wonderful!"

The ballroom at Ashwick Manor in Yorkshire twinkled like something from a fairy tale, all golden light and swirling silks. Hundreds of candles flickered in crystal chandeliers, casting dancing shadows across the polished marble floors that reflected the brilliant colours of the ladies' evening gowns. Delicate music floated through the air with hints of perfume as guests moved in elegant patterns that reminded Margaret of a living tapestry.

This was their first ball. Her first as duchess.

Margaret stood proudly at the top of the grand staircase, one gloved hand resting on the marble banister, the other clutching her fan with almost enough force to snap the delicate ivory. The emerald silks of her gown pooled around her feet like liquified jewels, and the Ashwick diamonds at her throat caught the light with every nervous breath that she took.

"Steady, darling," Julian murmured beside her, looking devastatingly handsome in his perfectly tailored evening wear. "You look absolutely magnificent."

"Do I? Truly? You're not just saying that to ease my nerves?" Margaret's voice came out higher than usual, that telltale breathless quality that always betrayed her agitation. "Because I feel rather like I might throw up all over Lady Pemberton's skirts!"

Julian's grey eyes danced with amusement. "Now that would most certainly make an impression... though perhaps we might aim for something slightly more conventional for your ducal debut?"

"You're the one to talk about conventional," Margaret replied with a nervous giggle. "The untitled solicitor who became a duke through sheer brilliance and moral courage!"

Before Julian could respond, the butler's voice boomed across the assembly. "Ladies and gentlemen, if you please—may I present His Grace, the Duke of Ashwick, and Her Grace, the Duchess of Ashwick!"

The announcements rolled over the assembled crowd like thunder, and Margaret felt her knees go weak. Every head in the ballroom turned towards them, every pair of eyes fixed on the newest addition to England's nobility.

"Breathe, darling," Julian whispered against her ear as they began their descent. "We've earned this moment."

Margaret squeezed his arm gently. "You especially, my handsome, brilliant husband."

Margaret managed a brilliant smile as they moved through the receiving line, accepting congratulations and well-wishes from what felt like half the ton. Lord Pemberton pumped Julian's hand with genuine warmth, whilst Lady Pemberton kissed Margaret's cheek and declared, "Absolutely radiant, my dear!"

But it was the whispered conversations at the ballroom's edges that made Margaret's stomach clench with familiar dread.

"... such a romantic tale, though one does wonder about the rather hasty nature of their courtship..."

"... heard she was quite taken with that dreadful fellow before his public disgrace..."

"... rather convenient timing, wouldn't you say? Just when her reputation needed salvaging..."

The words stung like wasps, each comment a reminder that scandal had paved her path to her coronet. Margaret's smile began to feel painted on, her fan fluttering with increasing anxiety.

Near the refreshment table, two women in elaborately vibrant silks had tilted their heads together in the universal gesture of gossip being shared. Margaret recognised them as Lady Bramford and her daughter, both notorious for their sharp tongues and sharper memories.

"Such a fascinating transformation," Lady Bramford was saying, her voice pitched just loud enough to carry. "From pursuing one duke in scandal, only to marry another in haste... one might almost say she's made quite a career of ducal attachments."

Her daughter tittered behind her fan. "Mama, you're dreadful! Though I guess one must admire the efficiency of it all. Most ladies spend entire seasons angling for such elevation."

Heat flooded Margaret's cheeks, the familiar burn of humiliation rising in her throat. She opened her mouth to respond, to defend herself, but before she could speak, Julian appeared at her side like an avenging angel in immaculate evening wear.

He didn't look at Margaret. He kept his eyes fixed exactly on the two women, the grey orbs as cold as winter frost.

"Lady Bramford, Miss Bramford," he said, his voice carrying that stagey charm that could slice through pretention like a blade through silk. "What an absolute delight to encounter such... dedicated observers of society's finer dramas this evening."

Both women curtsied, suddenly looking rather less confident.

"I couldn't help but overhear your fascinating commentary regarding my wife's romantic history," Julian continued with elaborate courtesy, his smile sharp enough to cut crystal. "Such thorough attention to detail! One might almost mistake you for theatre critics reviewing a particularly complex play."

Lady Bramford's face had gone pale. "Your Grace, we certainly meant no—"

"Oh, but surely you did mean something," Julian interrupted with exaggerated solicitude, "for I cannot imagine ladies of your obvious refinement engaging in idle chatter without purpose. Perhaps you were composing material for the scandal sheets? Or conducting research for a novel? How wonderfully industrious!"

The silence stretched like a taut violin string, ready to snap.

"My duchess," Julian continued, his tone shifting to pure silk over steel, "chose to marry a man who began life as a mere second son with nothing but his wits and determination. She chose the untitled solicitor who earned his dukedom through service rather than inheritance. I find her judgement... impeccable."

Lady Bramford nodded frantically, her daughter practically cowering behind her fan under Julian's gaze. "Of course, Your Grace. We... that is... we're absolutely delighted for your happiness."

"How generous," Julian said. Then he turned to Margaret with a smile that transformed his entire countenance, offering her his arm. "Duchess, shall we join the dancing? I believe the musicians are just about to play a waltz."

Margaret placed her hand on his arm, feeling steadier than she had all evening. "I should adore that, Your Grace."

As they moved towards the dance floor, Julian leaned down to whisper in her ear, "How are you faring, my brave girl?"

"Much better now," Margaret replied, surprising herself with the truth of it. "Thank you for standing up for me."

"Always," Julian said simply. "You're mine to protect now, Margaret. And I don't protect you because you cannot do it yourself, but because I take care of what belongs to me."

The orchestra's opening notes filled the ballroom as Julian led her onto the polished floor. Around them, other couples began to take their positions, but Margaret barely noticed them. All her attention was focused on the man holding her hand, guiding her into the familiar steps of a waltz.

"Now then," Julian murmured as they began to move, "shall we give them something truly scandalous to whisper about?"

Margaret's eyes widened. "What do you mean?"

Julian's smile turned positively wicked. "Do you remember your lessons, my darling duchess? The art of seductive dancing?"

Understanding dawned on her, and Margaret felt a delicious shiver run down her spine. "Oh, Julian! We couldn't! Not here, in front of everyone!"

"We most certainly could," he replied, spinning her with perfect technique whilst drawing her closer than strict propriety allowed. "In fact, I rather think it's time you demonstrated to your instructor just how thoroughly you've mastered the curriculum."

Margaret bit her lower lip, fighting back a giggle. "You are absolutely incorrigible."

"I am absolutely right," Julian corrected, his hand sliding lower on her waist as they turned. "Besides, what's the point of having ducal standing if one can't occasionally scandalise the ton?"

With that, Margaret let her carefully maintained composure slip away like a discarded glove. As they moved through the dance, she employed every technique Julian had taught her—the subtle brush of her body against his, the way she let her fingers linger on his shoulder, the meaningful glances that promised wicked thoughts.

"Like this?" she whispered, allowing her chest to press against his during a particularly close turn.

Julian's eyes darkened. "Exactly like that, you little minx."

Margaret felt giddy with power and mischief. Here she was, the newest duchess in England, scandalising a ballroom full of nobility whilst dancing with her devastatingly handsome husband. It was rather like living inside one of her childhood fairy tales... except infinitely better because it was real.

"You realise," Julian murmured as he spun her again, "that half the men in this room are now desperately envious of my good fortune?"

"Are they?" Margaret asked, honestly curious.

"Oh yes. And the other half are wondering how a mere second son not only managed to capture a dukedom but also the heart of the most beautiful woman in London."

Margaret's cheeks flushed bright pink with pleasure. "You're being absurd!"

"I'm being honest," he replied. "Though I must say, watching you deploy those techniques on me in public rather than on some poor unsuspecting fool is infinitely more preferable."

The music began to wind towards its conclusion, and Margaret felt almost disappointed. Dancing with Julian like this—with love and laughter and complete understanding between them—was intoxicating.

As the final notes faded, Julian bowed over her hand with exaggerated gallantry whilst Margaret curtsied with perfect grace. Around them, the ballroom erupted in polite applause, though Margaret noticed more than a few fans being wielded rather vigorously by overheated ladies.

"Well," said a familiar voice behind them, "that was quite the performance."

Margaret turned to find her father approaching, his expression unreadable. Lord Fairbourne looked every inch the proud patriarch in his formal evening wear, his silver hair gleaming and posture ramrod straight.

"Father!" Margaret exclaimed, her words tumbling out in that breathless rush. "Oh, how wonderful that you're here! Isn't it all just absolutely magical? The lights, the music, the dancing—it's like something from a dream!"

Lord Fairbourne's stern expression softened slightly. "Indeed, my dear. Though I must say, watching my youngest daughter waltz as a duchess is rather surreal. It seems like just yesterday you were in the nursery, insisting that you would marry a prince."

"A duke is nearly as good as a prince, isn't it?" Margaret asked with sparkling eyes.

"Better," Julian interjected smoothly. "Princes are notoriously unreliable. Dukes, on the other hand, are paragons of stability and virtue."

Lord Fairbourne's mouth twitched with what might have been amusement. "Are they indeed, Your Grace?"

"Oh, absolutely," Julian replied. "We're practically saints. Ask anyone."

Before Lord Fairbourne could respond, Eliza appeared at Margaret's elbow, radiant in sapphire silk with Rhys trailing behind her like an elegant shadow.

"Margaret, dearest!" Eliza exclaimed, embracing her youngest sister warmly. "You look absolutely radiant! That gown is divine, and these diamonds..." She grazed the impressive necklace at Margaret's throat with one finger. "Goodness, Julian certainly doesn't do anything by halves, does he?"

"Nothing but the finest for my duchess," Julian agreed, pressing a kiss to Margaret's gloved hand that made several nearby ladies sigh wistfully.

"Speaking of duchesses," Rhys observed, his tone carrying that dry humour Margaret had grown to appreciate, "I believe this makes you something of a collector, Lord Fairbourne. Three daughters. Three duchesses. Quite an impressive achievement."

Lord Fairbourne straightened with unmistakable pride. "Indeed, it is. Though I cannot take all the credit for their choices—my girls selected their dukes entirely on their own merits."

Margaret felt a warm glow of satisfaction spread through her chest. Her father was proud of her, not just of the title she'd achieved but of the choice she'd made. After years of feeling like the least accomplished Fairbourne daughter, she was finally seeing approval in his eyes.

"Well then,"—Catharine's crisp voice announced her arrival—"shall we make this a proper family celebration?"

Margaret turned to see her eldest sister approaching with Alaric at her side. Catharine looked magnificent in deep burgundy silk, her dark hair swept into an elaborate arrangement that showcased the Vale family emeralds.

"Catharine! Oh, this is perfect!" Margaret practically bounced with excitement. "All of us together, all of us happy—it's exactly what I've always dreamed of!"

"Careful, Margaret dearest," Catharine warned with fond exasperation, "or you'll bounce right out of those diamonds!"

The family clustered together at the ballroom's edge, champagne appearing as if by magic whilst they caught up on the latest gossip and family news. Margaret felt surrounded by love and peace and acceptance in a way she'd never experienced before.

But it was Julian's quiet presence at her side, his steady hand on her back, that made it all tangible and real. This wasn't a dream or a wish or a fairy tale—this was her life now. *Their life.*

As the evening wore on and the dancing continued, Margaret found herself holding court with other young ladies, sharing advice about marriage and society with the easy confidence of someone who'd found her place in the world. Several asked about her transformation from youngest sister to confident duchess, and Margaret surprised herself by answering with poise and humour rather than stammering breathlessly.

"The secret," she told Beatrice Worthington, who was desperately angling for a marquess, "is to remember that you're not trying to become someone else. You're simply... becoming the best version of yourself."

It was, she realised with something like wonder, actually true.

Near midnight, as the ball began to wind down and guests started making their farewells, Julian appeared at her side with two glasses of champagne.

"A toast," he proposed quietly, "to my duchess—the most remarkable woman in all of England."

Margaret accepted the glass, her blue eyes sparkling with happiness and champagne bubbles. "And to my duke. The most wonderful, terrible, perfectly impossible man I've ever known."

They touched glasses gently, the crystal singing a pure note that hung in the air between them.

"No regrets?" Julian asked, his grey eyes searching her face.

Margaret considered the question seriously. Six months ago, she'd been the overlooked, bubbly youngest Fairbourne sister, dreaming of romance and desperately seeking attention from entirely the wrong sort of man. A desperation that led her to Julian. Tonight, she was his duchess, surrounded by family who loved her and married to a man who saw her exactly as she was—and accepted her.

"None whatsoever," she said firmly. "This is exactly where I belong."

"With me?"

"With you," Margaret confirmed, reaching up to touch his cheek gently. "Always with you. Dukedom or not."

Juian caught her hand and pressed a tender kiss to her palm, his eyes never leaving hers. "Then we've both achieved our heart's desire, have we not?"

Margaret smiled, feeling like sunshine had taken up permanent residence in her chest. "Even better than that, my love. We've achieved something neither of us dared to want."

"Which is?"

"A love that is pure and true and worthy of all the best fairy tales."

As the last of their guests departed and the servants began clearing away the debris of a successful evening, Margaret stood in the centre of the empty ballroom with her husband's arms locked around her. The candles were burning low, the music had faded, and the magical evening was drawing to a close.

But this, Margaret realised with deep contentment, was only the beginning of their real story—the best chapters were yet to come.

Chapter Twenty-Eight

"Oh, for heaven's sake, not again!"

Margaret pressed her palm against her mouth, willing her rebellious stomach to settle as she bent over the porcelain washbasin for the third time that morning. The very sight of their cook's perfectly innocent breakfast rolls had sent her rushing from the breakfast hall like a woman possessed, leaving her sisters no doubt wondering if she'd taken leave of her senses entirely.

Everything irritated her today. The sunlight streaming through the windows felt like tiny daggers aimed directly at her eyes. Her favourite morning dress pulled tightly across her chest in the most uncomfortable way. Even Julian's very existence seemed designed to vex her, though she could not determine why.

"Margaret, dearest, are you quite well?"

Eliza's concerned voice drifted through the door, followed by the soft rustle of silk as both her sisters entered her bedchamber without invitation. Margaret straightened slowly, dabbing her mouth with a linen cloth whilst trying her best to arrange her features into something resembling composure.

"I'm perfectly fine," she insisted, though her voice emerged rather more sharply than she intended. "Simply... I suppose the morning air doesn't agree with me."

Catharine settled herself on the window seat with typical precision, her sharp eyes missing nothing as she studied Margaret's pale countenance. Eliza perched on the edge of the bed, her expression a mixture of sisterly concern and something that looked suspiciously like amusement.

"Perhaps it was those lemon biscuits I brought from Cook," Eliza suggested with studied innocence. "Though I must say, Catharine and I found them perfectly delightful."

"The biscuits were perfectly acceptable," Margaret snapped, then immediately felt guilty for her harsh tone. "Forgive me. I'm simply... my stomach seems rather delicate of late."

"How curious," Catharine observed in that calm, measured way that had always made Margaret feel like a butterfly pinned to a board for closer inspection. "You have seemed rather... volatile in your temperament recently, sister. Yesterday you wept over a wilted rose, and the day before, you threw your embroidery hoop across the room simply because the thread had knotted."

"I did not throw it!" Margaret protested hotly. "It merely... slipped from my hands... with force."

Eliza's lips twitched with barely suppressed laughter. "Of course, dearest. Though you must admit, you have been rather more emotional than usual."

Margaret turned towards the mirror, ostensibly to tidy her hair but really to avoid her sisters' too-knowing gazes. "I'm simply... tired. The social season has been utterly exhausting, and married life requires... considerable adjustment."

The silence that followed felt loaded with unspoken communication. Margaret caught sight of Eliza and Catharine exchanging one of those maddeningly significant looks in the mirror's reflection, and something inside her chest ignited like a tinderbox.

"Will you please stop that!" she exclaimed, whirling around to face their questioning expressions. "Stop looking at each other as though you share some tremendous secret! If you have something to say, then say it!"

"My, my..." Catharine murmured, raising an elegant eyebrow. "Such fire from our usually gentle Margaret."

Before Margaret could formulate a suitably indignant response, the door opened and Julian swept in with his characteristic flair, a letter in one hand and his grey eyes bright with some entertaining gossip.

"My darling duchess, you simply must hear the latest scandal involving Lord Pemberton and his extremely unfortunate choice in..." He stopped mid-sentence as he took in the tableau before him: Margaret, dishevelled and clearly distressed, her sisters watching with barely concealed speculation and amusement, the entire atmosphere thick with feminine tension.

"Good heavens," he said slowly, his composed mask slipping somewhat. "What catastrophe has befallen our happy domestic scene?"

The gentle concern in his voice, so different from his usual dramatic flourishes, was Margaret's complete undoing. Without warning, tears began streaming down her cheeks—real, messy, unstoppable tears that seemed to spring forth from some bottomless well of emotion she hadn't even known existed.

"I don't know!" she wailed, pressing her hands to her face as her shoulders shook with sobs. "I don't know why I'm crying! I don't know why everything makes me so angry! I don't know why the mere sight of food makes me ill... I don't know anything anymore!"

Julian's expression morphed from amusement to alarm with startling rapidity. He crossed the room in three strides, gathering her into his arms with the sort of protective tenderness that made her cry even harder.

"Shhh..." he murmured against her hair, his voice rough with worry. "It's all right, my darling. Whatever it is... we'll sort it out, yes?"

"But that's just it!" Margaret sobbed into his waistcoat. "There's nothing to sort out! I'm simply... I'm simply falling apart spectacularly for no reason whatsoever!"

Catharine cleared her throat with characteristic directness. "Margaret, dearest... might I ask when you last experienced your monthly courses?"

The question fell into the room like a stone dropped into still water. Margaret lifted her head from Julian's chest, her eyes wide as she blinked through her tears, understanding dawning on her face with the full force of revelation.

"I..." She tried to think back through the weeks of wedded bliss, the days that had blurred together in a haze of happiness and passion. "I... I don't remember. I don't think... that is... It's been some time..."

Julian went very still against her, his arms tightening almost imperceptibly around her waist. She felt his sharp intake of breath, saw the way his grey eyes widened as the implications crashed over both of them like a tidal wave.

"You're not suggesting..." he began hoarsely.

"I am suggesting precisely that," Catharine replied with calm certainty, whilst Eliza's face broke into a brilliant smile.

Margaret felt as if she might shatter from the tension. Julian stared at her as though seeing her for the very first time, his countenance cycling through shock, wonder, and something that looked remarkably like terror.

"A child?" he whispered, the words barely audible. "We're going to have a child?"

Margaret nodded mutely, tears streaming down her face as the reality of it all settled around them like morning mist, enveloping them in a cocoon of emotion. She was carrying Julian's child... they were going to be parents. The thought was simultaneously thrilling and absolutely frightening.

Then Julian's face crumpled with emotion, and he pulled her against him with a strength that made her breath hitch audibly. He kissed her hair, her forehead, and her wet cheeks, repeating the motion over and over while his voice broke with pure joy. "It's all right, my darling. You're all right. This is... everything... an absolute blessing..."

"Are you pleased?" Margaret whispered against his throat, suddenly uncertain. "Truly pleased? I know it's rather soon, and we haven't even properly discussed children. I—"

"Pleased?" Julian pulled her back to cup her face in his hands, his grey eyes blazing with an intensity that made her knees feel weak. "My dear, extraordinary wife... pleased is far too pedestrian a word for what I'm feeling. I am positively euphoric! I am drunk with elation! I am so overwhelmed with joy that I may very well compose sonnets about your ankles and hire an orchestra to serenade your morning toast!"

Eliza clapped her hands together with delight. "Oh, how perfectly wonderful. Our children shall grow up together just as we did!"

"Indeed," Catharine added with one of her rare, genuine smiles. "Though I suspect this little one shall inherit quite the temperament from both parents."

Margaret laughed through her tears, feeling as though her heart might burst from sheer joy. "Do you really think so?"

"I think," Julian said, his voice deep and husky, "that this child shall be the most magnificent combination of your sweetness and my devastating charm. The ton won't know what's hit them."

Three days later, the physician's official confirmation made it real in a way that went beyond morning sickness and missed courses. Margaret was indeed with child, due to arrive some time in early spring. Dr. Whitfield departed with Julian's effusive thanks and a purse considerably heavier than his usual fee, leaving them alone to absorb the magnitude of their news.

That evening, as Margaret sat brushing her hair in front of the mirror, Julian appeared behind her like a man entranced. He said nothing at first, simply watched her reflection with an expression of such profound tenderness that it made her throat tighten with emotion.

"Come to bed," she said softly as she set down her brush and reached for his hand.

Julian helped her to her feet with exquisite care, as though she were made of spun glass rather than flesh and bone. "Are you certain you're up to it? The physician mentioned that expectant mothers require additional rest—"

"Julian," Margaret interrupted with a tender smile, "I'm with child, not dying of consumption. I'm perfectly well, love."

Still, when he drew her into their bed, it was so gentle that it made her pulse quicken. His hands shook slightly as he unlaced her chemise, his touch reverent as he revealed the body that was now carrying their child.

"You are awe-inspiring," he whispered, his voice thick with emotion. "So perfect."

Margaret felt tears prick her eyes at the wonder in his voice. "I love you so much it frightens me sometimes," she said simply.

"And I love you beyond reason, beyond sanity, beyond anything I ever imagined possible." Julian's mouth found hers in a kiss that tasted of tenderness and forever. "You're the best thing that's ever happened to me, Margaret. You and this child... you're my entire world."

Their lovemaking that night was slower, more deliberate, infused with a sort of tenderness that bordered on religion. Julian moved with unhurried care, as though he were memorising the feel of her beneath him, the way they responded to one another, both making soft sounds of pleasure as they loved one another with exquisite gentleness.

"My Margaret," he murmured against her throat as they moved in perfect harmony. "The mother of my child."

Margaret arched beneath him, her body singing with the sensation as he adored her with hands and mouth and the steady rhythm of his arousal. When release claimed them, it was with a tenderness that left them both shaking, clinging on to one another as though they were the only solid things in a world gone suddenly, beautifully mad.

Afterward, Julian traced lazy patterns on her bare shoulder whilst Margaret listened to the steady beat of his heart beneath her cheek. The future stretched before them like an unwritten book, filled with possibilities and promises and the prospect of little people who would be half him, half her, and entirely miraculous.

"What are you thinking?" Julian asked softly.

Margaret smiled against his skin, feeling more content than she'd ever believed possible. "I'm thinking... that six months ago, I was convinced I needed to marry a duke to be happy."

"And now?"

"Now I know I just needed the right man." She tilted her head to look at him, her heart overflowing with love for this complicated, dramatic, utterly wonderful person who'd become her everything. "Title or no title, you would have been enough for me. You've always been enough, Julian."

Julian's arms tightened around her, his voice rough with emotion when he spoke. "I used to think that love was for fools and romantics. I thought it was a weakness, a liability that could only bring suffering."

"And now?"

"Now I know that it's the only thing that makes life worthwhile." He pressed a kiss to the crown of her head, breathing in her familiar scent. "You taught me that, Margaret. You showed me how to love without fear."

Outside their window, the distant sounds of the English countryside trilled, all life settling into sleep beneath a blanket of stars, but inside their chamber, wrapped in each other's arms with new life growing between them, Margaret and Julian had found something far more precious than all the titles and treasures in the world.

They had found home. They had found love. They had found everything that mattered.

And for the first time in her life, Margaret Ashcroft, the Duchess of Ashwick, knew beyond a shadow of a doubt that she was exactly where she belonged.

Epilogue

Eight months later

"How much longer?" Julian's voice betrayed him, cracking slightly on the words as he turned to face the midwife for what felt like the hundredth time that evening while Margaret wailed in pain.

The woman, Mrs. Crawford, barely glanced up from her basin of steaming water. "Babes arrive in their own good time, Your Grace. Pacing a trench in the floor shan't hurry the matter along."

Julian resumed his restless circuit of the corridor, his usually immaculate appearance dishevelled beyond recognition. His cravat hung loose around his neck, his waistcoat was unbuttoned, and his dark hair stood in wild peaks where he'd repeatedly run his hand through it. Nine months of careful preparation had brought them to this moment—converting the nursery, interviewing wet nurses, reading every single medical text he could get his hands on— and all of it had done absolutely nothing to prepare him for this moment.

Another agonised cry echoed from behind the door of the chamber Margaret was situated in, and Julian's composure cracked entirely.

"To hell with propriety," he muttered, striding towards the door. "That's my wife in there."

Mrs. Crawford intercepted him with surprising speed for a woman of her considerable years. "Your Grace, the birthing chamber is no place for a gentleman. The sight of... such matters has been known to cause even the strongest of men to—"

"I don't care if it kills me," Julian snapped, his grey eyes blazing with intensity. "She needs me."

The midwife opened her mouth to protest, but before she could utter a single sound, another sound stopped them both—not Margaret's laboured breathing or painful screams, but her voice, calling his name with desperate urgency.

"Julian! Please, I need... Julian!"

Mrs. Crawford's stern expression softened marginally. "Well, I suppose... if Her Grace is requesting your presence..." She stepped aside with obvious reluctance. "But mind yourself, Your Grace. Birth is not a drawing room performance."

Julian's hand trembled slightly as he grasped the door handle. All his legal training, all his experience in managing the ton's most scandalous crises, had left him absolutely unprepared for the sight that greeted him.

Margaret lay propped against a mountain of pillows, her golden hair darkened with perspiration and clinging to her flushed cheeks. Her blue eyes, usually so bright with laughter, were wide with exhaustion and pain. The simple nightgown she wore was seeped with sweat, and her hands grabbed the damp bedsheets with white-knuckled intensity.

"Margaret," he whispered, crossing to her side in two swift strides. "My darling... I'm here."

Her eyes found his, and despite the strain on her body, she managed a tremulous smile. "I was afraid... afraid you'd listen to propriety for once."

"Never," he promised, settling carefully on the edge of the bed and taking her hand in both of his. "I'm exactly where I belong."

The next contraction seized her, and Margaret's grip on his hand tightened to the point where Julian silently wondered if she might actually snap his fingers off. But he found that he didn't care. If she needed to break every bone in his body to get through this, he would gladly offer them.

"That's it, my dear," he murmured, brushing damp strands of hair from her forehead. "You can do this. You're the strongest woman I know."

Mrs. Crawford bustled about with professional urgency, occasionally shooting disapproving glances at Julian's presence but no longer attempting to remove him. The second midwife, a younger woman named Minerva, whispered encouragement as she monitored Margaret's progress.

Hours passed with agonising slowness. Julian had faced down corrupt dukes, navigated treacherous political waters, and rebuilt their entire life from scandal's ashes, but nothing had tested him like watching the woman he loved endure such pain.

"I can see the babe's head!" Minerva announced suddenly, her voice bright with excitement. "She's nearly here!"

Julian felt his heart stop. "She?"

"Oh." Minerva's cheeks flushed bright red. "I shouldn't have... that is, it's not entirely certain..."

"A daughter," Margaret gasped between contractions, her eyes meeting Julian's with wonder. "Julian! We're having a little girl..."

The final moments passed in a blur of controlled chaos. Margaret's cries, the midwives' urgent instructions, Julian whispering every endearment he could think of into her ear, promising her anything—the moon, the stars, his very soul—if she would just hold on.

And then, cutting through the tension like sunlight through storm clouds, came the sound that tilted Julian's world off its axis entirely.

A baby's cry. High, indignant, and absolutely perfect.

"She's here!" Mrs. Crawford announced, her stern demeanour dissolving into professional joy. "A beautiful, healthy girl!"

Julian stared in stunned silence as the midwife held up a tiny, wrinkled creature who was making her displeasure at being evicted from her warm sanctuary abundantly clear. The baby's face was red and scrunched, her tiny little fists waving in protest, and she was absolutely the most beautiful thing he had ever laid his eyes upon.

"Is she..." he began, his voice failing him entirely.

"Perfect," Mrs. Crawford assured him, efficiently cleaning the baby and wrapping her in soft linen. "Ten fingers and toes, Your Grace. And a pair of lungs that would do a town crier proud."

Margaret collapsed back against the pillows, her face pale but radiant with joy and exhaustion. "Let me see her," she whispered. "Please, let me hold our daughter."

Julian watched in reverent silence as Mrs. Crawford placed the tiny bundle in Margaret's arms. The baby immediately quieted, as though recognising her mother's voice and warmth. Margaret looked down at her daughter with an expression of such pure love that Julian felt his chest constrict painfully.

"She's so small," Margaret sobbed, gently stroking one perfect pink cheek. "And so warm. Julian... look at her, love—she's absolutely perfect."

Julian leaned closer, his breath catching as he got his first proper look at their child. She had Margaret's delicate features but his dark hair, though it was impossible to tell what colour her eyes might be as they remained firmly shut. One tiny hand escaped the swaddling and lay curled against Margaret's chest, fingers smaller than pearl buttons.

"May I?" he asked quietly, scarcely daring to breathe.

Margaret smiled, the expression transforming her features from exhaustion into something luminous. "Yes. She's your daughter too, my love."

With a hand that trembled despite his best efforts, Julian reached out to touch one impossibly small finger. The baby's hand immediately curled around his finger with surprising strength, and Julian felt something fundamental shift in his chest—as though every cynical, guarded part of him had just cracked wide open to make room for a love so pure and overwhelming it threatened to destroy him completely.

"Good God above..." he whispered, his voice rough with emotion. "She's real. She's actually real."

Before Margaret could respond, the bedchamber door opened quietly, and familiar voices filled the space.

"How are they?" Eliza inquired, her voice tight with concern.

"The midwife said all was well," Rhys replied, though Julian could hear the relief in his cousin and brother-in-law's typically controlled tone.

"Oh." Catharine's voice carried genuine warmth—something that would have shocked Julian to his core not so long ago. "She's absolutely beautiful."

Julian looked up to find their family crowded in the doorway. Eliza stepped forward first, her face bright with joy and unshed tears. Behind her, Rhys looked unusually emotional for a man who typically treated sentiment like a dangerous weakness. Catharine stood with Alaric, both of them wearing gleeful expressions.

"Come in," Margaret said, her voice still weak but warm. "Come and meet your niece!"

The next few minutes passed in a blur of gentle introductions and quiet exclamations of wonder. Eliza wept openly as she held her newest family member, while Rhys stood with one hand on Julian's shoulder in a gesture of wordless support. Catharine, who had arrived with a practical basket of linens and baby clothes, cooed over the infant with a tenderness that reminded Julian why Margaret loved her eldest sister so deeply, despite years of authoritarian control.

"What shall we call her?" Alaric asked, his scarred face softened with genuine warmth.

Julian looked at Margaret, raising one eyebrow in silent question. They had discussed names, of course, but somehow, nothing had seemed quite right until this moment.

"Eleanor," Margaret said quietly, her eyes never leaving their daughter's face. "Eleanor Margaret Julianne Ashcroft."

"Eleanor," Julian repeated, tasting the name. "After your mother?"

Margaret nodded, tears slipping down her cheeks. "I thought... I hoped she might like her grandmother's name."

Julian pressed a gentle kiss to Margaret's temple, his own throat tight with emotion. "It's perfect, my darling. Absolutely, wonderfully perfect."

As their family settled around them—Eliza curled in a chair with her hands folded in her lap, Rhys standing with his characteristic quiet strength, Catharine fussing with baby clothes while Alaric watched her with fond amusement—Julian found himself overwhelmed by a sensation he had never experienced before in his life.

Completeness.

For thirty years, he had prided himself on his independence, his ability to remain emotionally detached, his skill at managing other people's crises while avoiding any meaningful entanglements of his own. He had simply been Julian Ashcroft, charming rake and untitled lawyer, a man who observed life rather than truly participating in it.

Now holding his daughter while his wife dozed against his shoulder and her family filled their home with gentle laughter, he understood what he had been missing. This wasn't just love—it was belonging. The kind of deep, unshakeable connection that transformed everything it touched.

"You know," Rhys said quietly, moving to stand beside the bed, "a year ago, if someone had told me you'd be holding your own child with that particular expression on your face, I'd have questioned their sanity and had them shipped off to the sanatorium."

Julian looked up at his cousin, his mouth curving in the first genuine smile he'd managed in hours. "A year ago, I'd have agreed with you entirely. I was quite convinced that domestic bliss was a myth perpetuated by romantics and poets."

"And now?" Eliza asked softly, her eyes twinkling with affection.

Julian looked down at Eleanor, who had begun to fuss slightly in her sleep, her tiny mouth moving in what looked suspiciously like preparation for another robust protest. Without conscious thought, he adjusted his hold slightly, rocking her with the natural rhythm that seemed to come from somewhere deep within him, more instinct than experience.

"Now I suspect I was the greatest of fools," he admitted, his voice thick with emotions that threatened to overwhelm him. "I'd spent so many years thinking that wanting nothing meant that I couldn't lose anything. I never realised that the true gamble was never having anything worth losing at all."

Margaret's hand found his free one, their fingers intertwining with the easy familiarity of marriage. "No regrets?" she asked quietly, though her eyes danced with teasing affection.

Julian considered the question with the thoroughness of a man trained in legal precision. Not too long ago, he had been an untitled lawyer with expensive tastes and a reputation for brilliant discretion. He had owned nothing but his wit and his wardrobe, owed allegiance to no one, and answered only to himself. He had been free in every way that mattered to society.

Now he was a duke with estates to manage and tenants depending on his decisions. He had a wife whose happiness had become more important than his own comfort and a newborn daughter who would no doubt require every ounce of protection and guidance he could provide. He now had multiple responsibilities that would shape every choice he made for the rest of his life.

"Not a single one," he said finally, his voice steady with conviction. "Though I reserve the right to panic appropriately when she's old enough to attract suitors."

The gentle laughter that filled the room seemed to wrap around them like a blessing. Julian closed his eyes for a moment, memorising everything—the weight of his daughter in his arms, the warmth of his wife's hand in his, and the sounds of family surrounding them with love and support.

When he opened his eyes again, Eleanor was peeking at him with dark blue eyes that held all the ancient wisdom of new life. For a heartbeat, father and daughter regarded one another with mutual fascination.

"Well, hello there, little one," he whispered, his voice catching slightly. "Welcome to this mad world. I promise you, whatever else happens, you will always—always—be loved beyond measure."

As if in response, Eleanor's tiny hand tightened around his finger, and Julian felt the very last remnants of his carefully constructed walls crumble into dust.

Julian Ashcroft, the Duke of Ashwick, husband and now father, was finally, completely, and irrevocably home.

THE END

VALENTINA LOVELACE

Also by Valentina Lovelace

Thank you for reading "**A Lady's Lessons in Sin**"!

I hope you savoured every moment! If you did, you're welcome to explore **my full Amazon Book Catalogue here:**

https://go.valentinalovelace.com/bc-authorpage

Thank you for helping me bring my dream to life! ♥

Made in the USA
Monee, IL
02 October 2025